MADE

OF

STARS

OTHER BOOKS BY KELLEY YORK

HUSHED

MADE

OF

STARS

Entangled Publishing, LLC
2614 South Timberline Road
Suite 109
Fort Collins, CO 80525
Visit our website at www.entangledpublishing.com.

Edited by Stacy Abrams and Alycia Tornetta
Cover design by Alexandra Shostak

Ebook ISBN   978-1-62266-021-6
Print ISBN   978-1-62266-020-9

Manufactured in the United States of America

First Edition October 2013

The author acknowledges the copyrighted or trademarked status and trademark owners of the following wordmarks mentioned in this work of fiction: Barbie, Jetta, Coca-Cola, Toyota, Sharpie, Cheerios, Olympics, The Godfather series, *Mission: Impossible, Rolling Stone*, Kmart.

For Wifey.
Nobody loves my broken boys as much as you.

HUNTER

When we first met Chance Harvey, he was playing with Barbies.

Not in the dressing-them-up sense. He had Malibu Barbie tied to the end of a fishing pole by her ankles and was reeling her in from the creek behind Dad's house. Even at eight years old, my half sister, Ashlin, and I both thought this was pretty bizarre.

Chance turned to stare at us with wide, round green eyes that didn't really fit his face. He was covered in grass and mud from crawling up and down the banks, camouflage paint smudged across his cheeks, and he stared at us like *we* were the weird ones.

"Who are you?" he demanded.

He was a runt, closer to Ash's size than mine, and I knew I could scare him off if he was there to cause trouble. My eyes narrowed. "That's my dad's house," I announced, pointing to the rooftop visible through the trees. "And this is *his* part of the creek. He's a cop, and you're gonna be in trouble if I tell him you're here."

In retrospect, I don't know why I felt the need to be so mean. I was a kid, and I guess being tough seemed like the thing to do, especially in front of my sister. But Chance, frustratingly unbothered by my threat, turned his back to us. "Well, let me finish this and I'll go away."

I crossed my arms to wait for him to get lost, but didn't it figure that Ashlin, in her mouse-sized voice, piped up with, "What are you doing?"

Chance regarded her with a crooked smile over his shoulder, like he'd been waiting for one of us to ask that very question. "I'm doing a rescue operation. Duh."

Ash's eyes widened and she took a step closer. "You're rescuing Barbie?"

Chance stood up, straightened his back, and placed a hand on his hip. I remember thinking that with that one simple gesture, he looked more grown-up than we did. "Yeah! But see, there are so many down there, I don't know where to start. You should help."

My sister didn't even wait for my opinion. She darted past me in her summer dress and grass-stained sneakers and crouched by Chance's side while he gave instructions on how, exactly, we were supposed to go about this rescue mission. He spoke to Ash, but his eyes were always on me.

That was how it all started. Fishing Barbies out of the creek.

November

HUNTER

We've spent our summers with Dad since I was five. Every year, when school let out, Ash flew to Otter's Rest, Maine, from her mom's on the West Coast, and I was put on a bus or train because my mom's place is only across the state.

And, when we showed up, Chance would be waiting. "It's about time," he'd say, hands on his hips where he stood on our back porch in his bare feet with his messy hair and big glasses. I'm not even sure he *needed* those glasses, seeing as half the time he took them off and propped them on his head or lost them altogether, and we'd spend hours searching for them while Chance wandered in circles, hands outstretched, claiming he was too blind to help.

I couldn't tell you where Chance lived, what school he went to, or what his parents' names were. But I could tell you his favorite type of ice cream and exactly how he ate it (rocky road, picking out the nuts and marshmallows to eat last), how he could recite every lyric from every Queen song in existence, and that he had a soft spot for animals and sad movies that made him tear up.

In my opinion, I knew all the things about Chance that mattered most. Chance was strangeness and whimsy in human form. Chance was our friend unlike any other friend Ashlin and I have ever had.

Chance *was* our summer.

We didn't see or talk to him through winter, but when we arrived for summer vacation, the three of us came together like we'd never been apart. For seven years, all I looked forward to as I plodded through school and my monotonous life with Mom and her boyfriend was the day I could pack my things and see Chance.

This is the first I've been at Dad's for more than a few days since I was fifteen, and I know a lot can change in two years. I had to fight with Mom just to get here now: she wanted me at college, and I wanted to take a year off. To spend with Dad. To spend with Ashlin. To think about my future and what I want out of it. Maybe, just maybe, to see Chance again.

It's weird showing up while there's slush on the ground and the air is damp and cold. Dad's house nestled off the side of the road looks different surrounded by skeleton trees instead of green, green, green.

There is no Chance waiting for me on the porch.

Not that I expected there to be; how would he know we were coming? We were here every summer without fail until

Dad took a bullet to the spine in the line of duty two years ago, and while he recovered, we were kept at our respective homes. Away from Dad, away from each other, and away from Chance, with no way of contacting him.

I have no clue where or how to find him. Don't know where he lives, don't have a phone number, don't know if he has any other friends in town... I called information once, but I didn't know his parents' names. Dad wasn't exactly in the physical state to be doing some detective work to find out, either.

Ashlin and I will have to put our heads together on how to find him when she shows up. Until then, I'll keep stepping outside, forgetting how cold it is even as the deck freezes my feet. I'll keep watching and waiting for the guy I haven't been able to get out of my head after all this time. That's the sort of person Chance is. He gets under your skin, and even when he's gone, you still feel him there like a dull ache. A warm memory you can never quite reclaim.

Ashlin arrives the next day. Dad and I pile into his old truck for the long drive to the airport. I haven't seen my half sister in six months—not since I flew out for her high school graduation. We only had the money for one of us to buy a ticket, and because I wanted to get the hell out of my house for a while, it was decided I'd be the one visiting her.

When I see her emerging from her gate, she still has the remains of a summer tan and a splash of freckles across her nose and cheeks. Once upon a time, she hated those freckles, until Chance told her they were cute and now she never tries to cover them with makeup. She goes to Dad first, careful in the way she hugs him. A rare smile pulls at his mouth as he puts an arm around her, the other not leaving his cane for support.

"My girl." He sighs. "I've missed you."

"Say that again after you've had us around for a few months." Ash pulls away and turns her attention to me.

"Hey, short stuff," I say with a grin.

Ash smiles a mile wide, throwing her arms around my neck. She smells like fruity body spray and shampoo and home. Being away from her and Dad all winter never felt right. *This* is how things were meant to be: me, my sister, and Dad.

All we're missing now is Chance.

• • •

Early on, Chance asked us about our parents. He knew that Dad was a cop, that we spent summers here with him. What he didn't understand was why, for the rest of the year, we lived with separate mothers. The idea seemed to baffle him. For us, it was as normal as night and day. (It wasn't until we got older and our friends at school *told* us our situation was weird that we realized how abnormal it really was.)

"Dad was dating my mom," I'd explained. "And they had a fight so they broke up for a while, and Dad was seeing someone else…"

And, somehow, that had all spiraled out of control. Dad ended up with neither of those women and had two kids instead. Maybe he didn't do right by our moms—as they so frequently remind us—but Dad has never failed to be a good parent. He says it's hard to view his bad relationship choices as a mistake because he got Ash and me out of the deal.

I think I resented him a lot at first. Him and Ashlin both. I saw them as the cause of my mom's unhappiness and, by extension, my own. It was hard to hang on to that resentment, though, when Dad tried so hard and Ash understood exactly how I was feeling because she was going through the same thing. Maybe our life was strange, but we loved each other. It worked for us.

Chance's life, on the other hand, was a puzzle of a thousand pieces that never fit together quite right. According to him, his parents traveled for work a lot and often left him home alone, and so he had the freedom to spend practically every day with us. But when we tried getting Chance's number or e-mail address to keep in touch, he insisted he wasn't allowed phone calls and his parents wouldn't get Internet connected at the house. Going to the library for computer access, he said, was too much of a hassle. It was one thing to walk to our place. It was another to walk all the way into town.

The more I think about it, the things that made little sense then make even less sense now.

That night, at dinner, Ash prods at her food and asks Dad, "Do you think maybe you could ask one of the guys at the station to pull up Chance's address? I mean, otherwise he's never going to know we're here."

"You know I'm not supposed to ask for information like that." Dad doesn't look up. And yet, after he takes another bite, he adds, "I'll see what I can do."

When we all retreat to bed for the night—Ash and me to our rooms upstairs, Dad to his converted room downstairs because navigating the steps is still impossible, even with as much progress as he's made—I take a few minutes to call my girlfriend, Rachael. It's the first time we've been apart for this long in the year we've been dating, and while I'm enjoying the space, I did promise I would touch base with her.

She sounds happy to hear from me, but this time of night, I know she'll be knee-deep in homework and studying and won't have time for me.

"I'm sorry, Hunter. You really need to call earlier in the day. Can we talk later?"

"Sure. Sorry for interrupting."

"It's okay. Why don't you call back in the morning? I miss you."

"Yep. Miss you." I do miss her, but I can't say that I would trade being here for seeing her. Rachael hadn't even wanted me to come to Dad's and argued with me on it for weeks. It's still a sore spot for me. This? Coming here? It was *important*, and Rachael, Mom, and her boyfriend…they all dug their heels in and thought of any reason why I shouldn't go. Why getting into college *right now* was more important.

After hanging up, I change clothes before collapsing into bed. My first order of business after getting here the other day was to tear down the old movie and band posters that were so outdated it hurt.

The only decorations I did leave up were the glow-in-the-dark stars on my ceiling. It was a summer-long project where Dad and I laid out a map of constellations and went to town, until an entire night sky stretched from corner to corner. I couldn't bear to take them down. Something about tracing their familiar patterns is still soothing as I lie alone, brain moving too fast and too loud to think properly.

They remind me of the times Ash, Chance, and I laid out on the back deck and watched the sky. Chance had a story for every constellation I pointed out. Ash used to love Orion, because the three stars that formed his belt were the only ones she could spot all on her own. Chance, though, went for the more elusive Draco.

He loved the stars, and he loved dragons. Draco was the perfect combination. He said his mom had taken him to a planetarium once when he was little. He'd fallen in love with the night sky right then and there.

I think about everything I've wanted to say to Chance over the last few years. The letters I wanted to write but had nowhere to send them. I wanted to ask him about school, about what he wanted to do after graduating, about maybe even coming to visit me at my place sometime. I wanted him to know how important he was. Not just to me, but to Ash and Dad. And about how there were a few years there where things got rough for me and what got me through was knowing, come summer, I would get to see him again.

I search out the Draco pattern on my ceiling. Chance would lay his head on my stomach while Ash laid on his, and he would twirl her long hair around his fingers as he told us the stories about Draco. Something with dragons and knights and princesses, maybe with witches and ghosts thrown in for good measure. I can't remember the exact story, but I fall asleep to the sound of his voice murmuring secrets and fairy tales in my head.

ASHLIN

This is the first time I've seen Dad since he's been able to walk on his own again.

It's kind of a miracle, if you ask me. After being shot, he was told by the doctors that he wouldn't get out of a wheelchair again. Last time I was here, Isobel—a nurse turned family friend who lives down the street—had to assist him with everything from getting dressed to going to the bathroom.

I think it killed him a little inside to need that kind of help.

He went from being an easygoing and smiley guy to withdrawn and mopey. Mom says it was natural for him to be depressed, and I still see the shadow of that depression hanging over him, but I'm sure he'll cheer up having Hunter and me around for the winter while the two of us decide what colleges we're going to apply to next fall. He wanted us to come out even while he was hurt. Swore up and down he could handle it. But both our moms jumped at the excuse to not let us visit; my mom because she never got over Dad and being *the other woman*, and Hunter's mom because, without Hunter there, she actually has to take care of the house on her own.

I can tell Dad is enjoying the freedom of being mobile again, even if he needs a cane. But there's plenty around the house that Dad can't do no matter how hard he tries. He can't scale a ladder anymore, can't haul boxes or move furniture. Isobel does a lot more than she ought to do, but she shouldn't have to. Not while we're here.

Hunter and I throw ourselves fully into cleaning, fixing, and organizing. Dad sits by anxiously as we go through the attic and drag down old boxes of clothes, photos, knickknacks, and paperwork. Eventually, he relaxes when he realizes we aren't going to throw away anything important.

We also take his truck a few miles up the road and food shop. Easier for Hunt and me to get the errands done in a quarter of the time it would take Dad to do it, and an hour later we're home with the truck bed full of grocery bags. When Hunt notices Dad staring at us as we put stuff away, he asks, "What?"

Dad shakes his head. "Nothing. Just not sure when the two of you got so grown-up, is all."

Hunter and I exchange looks and shrug. Back home, I never willingly did this kind of stuff, because Mom only made me do it out of her own laziness. Hunter was in charge of a lot around his house, so maybe he's more used to it. But I see him smile a little before he turns away. He's used to doing it but maybe not used to getting any appreciation for it.

When we're done, Dad has his face in the newspaper and a cup of coffee in hand. Before we can wander off, he slides a piece of paper across the table. On it is an address I don't recognize, and Dad says, "Drive safe."

We don't need to ask where and how he got it. Probably don't even need to say thank you. (Dad only grunts in response when we do.) We pull up directions on my phone, yank our shoes back on, and run out the door.

Hunter drives because I hate the truck. Too used to Mom's tiny Jetta back home. The snow has let up, but the roads are still slick and tricky. My phone navigation tells us the address isn't more than a ten-minute drive, but it's in the complete opposite direction of anywhere we've ever gone. Once we turn off Pearson Street, the trees become denser, darker, and the road is rocky and uncared for, and eventually dead-ends into a cul-de-sac. We almost miss the narrow entryway into a mobile home park, barely visible through the trees.

For a brief second, as Hunt parks the truck inside the unofficial entrance, I think this has to be a mistake. Chance used to talk about his house, about how big the windows were and how much he hated it, because anyone could come peeking inside while his parents were away. But his room was upstairs, so at least the peekers wouldn't see *his* stuff and think to break in. They had a big basement with a ping-pong table, and a pool in the backyard. He'd tell us it was too bad his parents wouldn't let him bring anyone over, because Hunter and I would *totally* love his house.

This place is nothing like what Chance described.

There aren't more than eight mobile homes and a handful of trailers near the back. They're spaced out, huddled against the line of trees like they're trying to get as far away from one another as possible. At first glance, the whole place seems abandoned. Except I spot a couple cars parked here and there, and someone is looking through her curtains at us before yanking them closed again. Not abandoned, then. Just…

Hunter and I exchange looks and get out of the truck.

"Address?" Hunt asks.

"6015 Stoneman Drive." I shove the phone into my coat pocket. I don't say anything about how wrong this feels, and neither does he. The questions lay between us, but we don't have the courage to ask. Would Chance really lie about something like this? Did he think we would care if he didn't live in some big fancy house? It's not like we live in a mansion. My and Mom's place in California is nice, but Hunter, Carol, and Boyfriend Bob live in a two-bedroom apartment. Maybe Chance moved. It's always a possibility. Maybe his parents lost their jobs and had to get rid of the house.

"You know," I mumble, "I think the creek runs up this way. I bet that's how Chance ended up at our place to begin with."

"Following the water." Hunter pockets his hands as we walk down the road.

Some of the homes are in better shape than others. Chance's is somewhere in the middle of the niceness scale; the roof isn't crumbling or caving in, and it doesn't have windows knocked out, but it's in dire need of a fresh coat of paint, and the porch steps creak dangerously. Off to the left is a rusted, crooked swing set that probably hasn't seen a butt on its seat in a decade. There's an old gray truck parked out front.

Hunter knocks on the flimsy screen door. I linger at his side, scanning the porch. They seriously need to spray down the collection of cobwebs they have going on. This place gives me the creeps. I'm not sure I would have had the nerve to get out of the truck without Hunter by my side.

A few minutes pass where no one answers, and my heart sinks.

"What if this isn't the right place?" I whisper. "What if Dad was wrong?"

"Stop worrying. I'm sure it's the right place." Hunt takes a deep breath and knocks again, louder. Finally, we hear footsteps inside, and the front door swings open.

The woman staring at us from behind the screen looks a lot older than my own mom but not old enough to be someone's grandmother. Her hair is short and choppy, like she cuts it herself, and her face is gaunt and tired. She's wearing a gray men's bathrobe over a nightgown and pink slippers that have seen better days.

She frowns. "Can I help you?"

Hunter hesitates. He's never been a talker, so I step forward. "Hi. Sorry to bother you. We're looking for Chance?"

The lady pushes open the screen door, causing us both to move back while she steps out onto the dirty welcome mat. This woman *has* to be related to Chance, a mother or maybe an aunt. There's no way anyone in the world unrelated to him has eyes that green. At one point in time, I think she must've been really pretty. Now, she looks kind of…worn.

"What do you want with Chance?" she asks, holding the

screen open with her hip, a cigarette dangling from her fingers.

"We're friends of his. I'm Ashlin Jackson. This is my brother, Hunter." Technically, I'm not a Jackson. Hunter got Dad's last name, but I'm Ashlin Carmichael. But if Chance told his family about us, he would have referred to us as *the Jacksons*. "We were in town and thought we'd stop by to see him." I offer out my gloved hand. The woman looks at it for a long moment before taking it, though there isn't an ounce of warmth in the gesture; she's just going through the motions.

From behind her, a gruff voice calls, "Who is it, Tabby?"

Possibly-Chance's-Mom takes a drag off her cigarette, casting a glance over her shoulder as someone—Chance's dad?—fills the doorway behind her. "Some of Chance's friends."

The man is broad-shouldered and stone-faced, with a jaw that hasn't seen a razor in a few days. The harsh downturn of his mouth makes it impossible for me to imagine him ever smiling the way Chance does. There are grease stains on his shirt. Overall, he is not the sort of guy I'd want to meet in a dark alley. "He isn't here."

I try not to let my expression fall. "Do you know when he'll be back?"

"How the fuck would I know? Kid takes off without any consideration for telling us what he's up to." With that, Mr. Harvey turns and retreats back into the house.

Mrs. Harvey seems to relax with his absence and takes a drag off her cigarette. Her expression is only mildly apologetic. "He goes off and does his own thing, you see. I'll let him know you stopped by, Ashley."

"Ashlin," Hunter corrects. Mrs. Harvey gives him a hollow smile.

"Right, yes. Bye now."

She steps back into the house and closes the door. The screen makes an obnoxious metallic sound when it clangs shut.

HUNTER

What kind of parent says, "I don't know" when you ask where her kid is? My mom would have a heart attack if I left without disclosing every detail of where I'd be, for how long, and who I'd be with. Maybe it's because Dad *doesn't* always drill us about where we're going that I make the effort to let him know anyway, just in case. Especially since it's his truck we're using most of the time.

The next two weeks, Ash and I mostly hang out near the house. We gut our bedrooms (and Dad's new one, for that matter) in order to redecorate, and both of us just...wait for Chance to come knocking at the door.

He doesn't.

We also head to the creek every couple of days to wander up and down the banks, Ash taking pictures of anything

and everything like she's done ever since Dad bought her a
camera when she was ten. We've been hit with a weird wave
of...not heat, but I guess "less cold"? It hasn't snowed in more
than a week, and it's not the right temperature for the creek
to be iced over. It bubbles and rumbles quietly, occasionally
dislodging some of the dirtied snow off the shore and carrying
it along for the ride.

Ash makes me nervous every time she creeps down the
bank and tries to get a picture of this. I've already caught her
by the back of her coat once to keep her from slipping. At one
point, I turn away, distracted by birds in the trees, and Ash lets
out a soft curse that startles me into whipping around, ready
to snatch her away from the edge if she's falling.

Instead, she gives me a frown and a pout, holding out
her camera. "My memory card is full. Can you run inside and
switch it out for me?"

My shoulders slump. I take the camera, give her a
withering look, and retreat to the house. It takes me no time
to find the memory card she wants; I was lying on her bed
last night, reading, while she had it in her computer to empty
it out. I switch the cards, pocket the camera, and head back
outside. Just as I'm hitting the back porch—

Ash screams.

I leap down the steps and tear into the woods. My heart is
in my throat. Ashlin isn't where I left her, which means she's
wandered one way or the other up the creek and I have no
idea where.

"Ash!"

"Over here!" Her voice is distant but not panicked. I

push through the pale trees just in time to spot both of them: Chance slogging through the water with Ash clinging to his neck. My breath catches as he looks up with those too-green eyes and smirks.

"Rescue operation," he says, breathless. "Saved Barbie from drowning."

I push a hand through my hair, trying not to laugh. The banks are muddy and steep; Chance helps Ash up high enough to grab my hand so I can haul her out. She looks like a drowned cat, blond hair plastered to her face and neck, clothes clinging to her body. Her boots squish when I get her up on solid ground with a shake of my head. "I really wish you'd stop and think things through before you get yourself into these situations." Chance waves off my extended hand and pulls himself out effortlessly using exposed roots and rocks jutting from the dirt.

I wonder if I look as different to him as he does to me. Gone are his Coke bottle glasses, which I'm glad for, because those eyes? You could lose yourself in them, but I try not to think about that because it's weird and totally not okay. He's dyed his hair black, cut it short, haphazardly spiked it. His black cargo pants have more pockets than I can count and drip steadily. Chance used to be half my size. He's still shorter than I am, but not by much. A couple of inches, maybe.

"Hello?" Ash says. "Earth to Hunt. I need the house key!"

I blink, breaking eye contact with Chance in order to fumble the keys from my pocket. She snatches them out of my hand and rushes off. It takes me a second to realize she must be heading inside to change.

And now it's just us. For some reason, the way Chance smiles so lazily at me results in a faint heat creeping into my face. I try to think of what to say and come up with nothing witty or charming. Instead I'm stuck with, "Hey. How's it going?"

"Wetly." Chance shrugs.

This time, my blush isn't nearly so subtle. "Oh, crap—sorry, let's get you inside." Were it summer, we could stand ten minutes in the sun and be bone-dry again, but not in this weather. Besides that, he's filthy from climbing up the embankment.

As Chance follows me back to the house, I keep stealing glances at him. We've spent all this time waiting for him to show up and now that he's here, it doesn't feel real. In the back of my brain, I stored up all these thoughts and questions to say to him, and now every one of them is lost to me. "We went to your house a few weeks ago."

Chance nods. "Yep. I was told."

"We were starting to worry you'd moved away or something."

His laugh is sharp. "Are you kidding? I've got a life sentence to this town. I was beginning to think *you* ditched *me*."

"Our moms didn't want to let us visit while Dad was recovering." We tromp up the back steps to the porch, careful not to slip on the icy wood. "You heard what happened to Dad, right?" No need to say we did come out to visit Dad a few times over school holidays but didn't know how to contact Chance. Besides, Dad might have been pretty hurt if I came for three days and ditched him to spend time with friends.

I feel kind of guilty knowing that I probably would have. Even if only for a few hours to spend with Chance. I could e-mail Dad or talk to him on the phone. But if I wasn't looking right at Chance, able to reach out and touch him if I wanted, then we had zero contact. And I missed him.

"Of course. How's he doing?"

"Better. A lot better." We let ourselves in through the back door. Chance lingers in the kitchen while I get him a towel. When I come back, he's staring up at some of the family photos on the wall, drip-drip-dripping on the floor but not seeming to notice. I chuck the towel in his direction. He catches it one-handed.

"We don't need a swimming pool in the kitchen," I say. Chance shrugs and steps aside into the laundry room, letting the door fall half closed. I can hear him shimmying out of his clothes. Shirt, pants, socks. I lean against the doorframe, staring at nothing in particular. "You can toss those in the washer." I hear him do just that before emerging with the towel draped around his shoulders, the only thing covering him from the waist up. He's managed to locate a pair of my sweatpants in the laundry, apparently, and I can't help but grin at how terribly they fit him. We're closer in height, but I still outweigh him by a fair amount.

"You've gotten taller," he observes. "And...muscle-y. What've you been doing, bench-pressing trucks?"

I give him a small smile, rubbing the back of my neck. "Swimming and track. Mom likes to keep me busy so I don't do something stupid with my free time, I guess."

Chance lounges with one shoulder to the wall, like it was built to support him. "Joining gangs, robbing banks, that sort of thing?"

"Pretty much."

"I can totally picture it, you criminal, you." He tips his head, looking behind me. Ash has decided to grace us with her presence and— Oh, cute. She's wearing a dress, and she took the time to put on lipstick and mascara. She's pulled her wet hair up into a twist with clips and pins. No wonder she was so quick to run inside.

She sidles up beside me, flashing Chance her brightest smile. "Guess I owe you for saving my life and all that."

"Any time." Chance doesn't even try to be discreet when he drops his gaze and lets it wander up the length of her legs. And Ash really is all legs. I can't figure out if the little knot in my stomach is because he's checking her out—even if he's only playing around—or because she's checking him out. Either way, I feel momentarily out of place. Doesn't help that Ash leans forward, touching a fingertip to his chest, and asks, "What's that on your back? Let me see."

Chance lifts his eyebrows, but he does as asked and twists around. I can't believe I didn't notice it. There, on Chance's back, is the constellation of Draco, each star done with intricate detail and a pale line traveling from one star to the next, forming the dragon he loves so much. With Chance's lean frame, every breath, every movement makes a muscle or bone somewhere in his back shift and ripple the little stars.

"Did it hurt?" Ash asks, fascinated, looking like she wants to trace the tattoo from top to bottom. I kind of do, too.

Always one to soak up attention, Chance smiles. "Not really. You like?"

"It's awesome." She grins. "Mom and Dad would flip if I asked for a tattoo before I'm, like, thirty."

Chance rolls his shoulders into a shrug. "If you're asking your parents for permission for *any*thing at thirty, you've got bigger problems than them saying *no*."

She smacks him on the arm and he laughs, catching hold of her wrist and taking care in the way he twists her arm around her back and holds her there. Ash giggles, calling for me to rescue her, and I snake an arm around Chance to get him in a loose headlock.

And I think how incredible this is, that we've been together less than twenty minutes but things are already slipping into how they've always been. How they should always be. We've fallen into this easy pattern of teasing and laughing, and I like it.

I've missed this familiarity. I've missed being *home*.

ASHLIN

I go to sleep afraid I'll wake up in the morning and find myself back in California. Away from Dad and Hunter and Chance. But Chance is there again the next day, and the day after that, and the day after that. Waiting for Hunter and me just like he used to when we were kids. Sometimes we find him at the creek, sometimes on the back steps staring up at the sky. Sometimes Dad spots him and invites him in, and he's eating breakfast at our kitchen table when we come downstairs, still in our pajamas.

Today, Chance is at the creek, which is trying to ice itself over again. It's freezing outside, but he still isn't wearing a jacket. He isn't trying to skip stones so much as throw them at the water, and I wonder what the creek ever did to him.

"How are you not getting hypothermia?" I ask. Chance

graces me with a smile.

"I'm not a wimp like you Californians who've never seen snow."

"Hey, we *get* snow. Just not where I live."

He shrugs. "Whatever. Where's your brother? We have places to go."

I can't help but grin, eager to see where Chance is leading us. Even the most mundane of places is made exciting with him along. After day in and day out of dealing with Mom trying to control every aspect of my life, being out here and going on adventures with Chance and Hunter is a breath of fresh air. "Probably talking to Rachael. He'll be here soon."

Chance arches an eyebrow. "Rachael?"

"Yeah. Girlfriend." We turn to wander back to the porch. "He didn't tell you?" It seems weird Rachael wouldn't have come up once in conversation, when we've spent the last several days catching up.

"Nope." He looks away, expression unreadable. "Must not be anything serious."

"No, it is." I frown, feeling oddly defensive on Rachael's behalf, since she isn't here to defend herself. "They've been together for, like, a year now."

"Uh huh."

"Carol adores her." Not that Hunt has ever cared what his mom, Carol, thinks about his relationships, but whatever. "So does Dad."

I have this image in my head of what Rachael and Hunt's relationship must be like. What it *should* be like. This perfect high school romance that stretches out into college and leads to marriage and kids. Like I've always wanted for myself and never managed to find. I mean, I haven't met Rachael, but I've never heard a bad word spoken about her. *She's sweet and very smart,* Carol told me once on the phone. *She's the perfect kind of girl for Hunter. She'll keep his head out of the clouds.*

Chance smiles, but it doesn't reach his eyes. "The *parents* love her. But does he?"

My face flushes. I shouldn't have said anything, but then again—why shouldn't I? Rachael isn't some fling. They're serious, and Chance shouldn't brush it off. For that matter, neither should Hunter. He should have mentioned her. Rachael's feelings would be hurt. I know mine would be, if I were her.

Just as we reach the bottom of the steps and before I have time to respond, Hunter shuffles outside, dressed and messy-haired.

"Sorry," he says, voice still a little rough from sleep. "What's going on?"

All the life seems to rush back into Chance's face, and his eyes light up. "We can use Mr. J's truck, right?"

Hunt runs a hand through his hair. "Uh…yeah."

"Super. What about shovels?"

Hunter and I exchange looks. There's really no point in questioning Chance. He'll tell us what we're doing when he feels like it. That's part of the fun, isn't it? Going along for the ride.

We bundle into the Toyota, and Chance navigates. At first, I think we're heading in the direction of Chance's house, but he instructs us to drive right on by. We're still following the creek; I think I can spot it here and there when the trees are at their thinnest. Eventually, he has Hunt pull over to the side of the road, and we get out.

"Middle of nowhere." I zip up my coat. "What are we doing, burying bodies?" Admittedly, this would be a place to do it. Isolated, off any main roads.

"Nope. We're going to war." Chance grabs the shovels from the back of the truck, one for each of us.

There's no real discernible path leading through the trees, but Chance seems to know where he's going, and the truck shouldn't be hard to spot when we find our way out again. A half a mile into the woods, we come to a clearing. Not just a patch, but a wide stretch of land, maybe forty feet from one side to the other.

What's more, the snow has fallen perfectly here with no one to disrupt it. Just a white blanket over the earth. I have to resist the urge to throw myself into it and roll around. We stop on the outskirts of the clearing, each with our shovels in hand. Chance puffs out a breath, exhales on his bare hands, and rubs them together. His face is flushed, but he's smiling.

"So, Hunter takes that edge. Ash, you're here. I'll be right over there."

That's all the explanation he gives us before circling around the perimeter. Hunter hesitates but eventually makes his way to his assigned spot while I stay put. We watch Chance, curious as to what we're supposed to be doing. He thrusts the shovel into the snow, starting a pile beside him. It takes a few minutes before we realize he's constructing some kind of wall. Occasionally taking a handful of snow, packing it neatly, and setting it aside. Snowballs.

Hunt leans on his shovel, arching an eyebrow. "Really? Aren't we a little old for this?"

Chance lifts his head, lips drawn thin. "Says who?"

"Says…us. And most of the population?" Yet I'm getting started on shoveling some snow into a pile to make my own wall. There's no point in arguing. We can participate in his game, or we might as well go home and leave him here. He'll do it with or without us.

"That's stupid." Chance crunches another snowball together, turns, and pitches it at Hunter. It smacks Hunt's arm, shattering into a mess of white slush and making him yelp in surprise. Chance dusts off his hands. "Get a move on, 'cause there's more where that came from."

Hunter opens his mouth, closes it again, scowls, and starts shoveling.

Even through the gloves, my fingers are starting to go numb. When we're done, I've built the tallest wall out of the three of us. It circles halfway around me, keeping me safe from the front and both sides if I crouch down a bit. Hunter is fighting with his—I've seen it topple over more than once. Chance finishes before we do, and I see him building his collection of snowballs while we struggle to raise our defenses.

He isn't nice enough to wait, either. The first snowball zings past my head, startling me into stillness. Chance throws his head back and laughs. Hunter makes a valiant attempt to toss one at Chance, but he doesn't pack it right and the snow crumbles to pieces halfway through the air. My attempt is a little better; the snowball stays together, but it flies too low and hits Chance's wall instead.

Eventually, we get the hang of it. Our aim improves, and we start hitting our marks. Which means Hunter and I turn our sights on each other, too. I have the upper hand. Every time he hits me, all it takes is a whimper and a look and Hunter stops, eyes wide, worried he *really* hurt me. Just enough time for me to chuck a snowball right at his face.

My and Hunter's walls are soon nothing more than mounds of snow around our legs. Only Chance's remains. He's an expert wall-builder...which means Hunt and I bring the war right to him so he can't hide.

Chance crows in delight, darting from behind his cover and managing to dump an armful of snow over my head. I shriek only because I can feel the cold sliding down the back of my jacket. While I'm dancing around, trying to shake it out, Hunt catches Chance around the waist and hauls him away from me. He loses his footing and they both go down, Chance's barking laughter filling the clearing.

My opportunity! I crouch to gather up an armful of snow. They're too busy wrestling around to notice me. By the time I stand up again, Hunt has Chance pinned to the ground, snow in their hair, in their eyelashes, faces flushed.

Chance grins in that way of his, breathless. "Is it really okay for you to be panting on top of someone who isn't your girlfriend?"

Hunter goes perfectly, deathly still.

Melted snow trickles down my spine.

Chance's expression is tight, conflicted. Like he wants to be smug but is frustrated that his moment of triumph doesn't feel so great after all. Tension floods the clearing, chasing away every ounce of excitement and fun we'd been building. His jab shouldn't make me feel guilty for having said anything to him in the first place. If anything, it should make me angry that he'd throw something like that in Hunter's face. I don't know why he would care. I don't know why Hunter having a girlfriend would matter.

This isn't how today was supposed to go. We were having fun. I'd dressed nice, did my hair, tried to make myself look nice for Chance. Instead, he's spent all morning thinking about Hunter and his girlfriend?

There's only one thing I can think to do: I dump the armful of snow on them.

Hunter sucks in a breath. Chance sputters, squirming until Hunt releases his arms so he can wipe the slush from his face. They sit up and stare wordlessly as I shove at Chance's wall, angry with it for being there. Him and his stupid walls. Some force and it caves and crumbles, nowhere near as well constructed as I thought it was.

When I'm done I turn back to them, hands on my hips, out of breath, a strained smile in place.

"I think this means I win. You two can buy me lunch."

HUNTER

"Why didn't you tell him about Rachael?"

I've waited all day for Ash to ask me that question. From the second the mention of my girlfriend spilled from Chance's lips, I knew she would corner me when we were alone later that night, when she knew I'd be in my room checking e-mails on my laptop. I pretend to be so interested in what I'm reading for an excuse not to look at her. "What?"

"Don't *what* me." She's wearing one of her silky tank tops and shorts-that-are-too-short, something Dad would probably have a hernia to see her wandering around in. Being upstairs, though, she's safe; he won't venture up here unless he absolutely has to.

Not that it exactly makes me comfortable, either. The idea that my sister isn't a little kid anymore doesn't sit right with me. All the more reason to focus on my computer screen. "I don't know, Ash. Does it really matter? Obviously, he knows now."

"Yeah, and I felt like a jerk for saying anything about it because I thought he knew."

From my peripheral, I see her shifting her weight from one foot to the other—seriously, her mom buys her those kinds of clothes?—before wandering over to take a seat beside me. Sighing, I shut the laptop and set it aside, head dropping back against the pillows. "It slipped my mind, okay?"

"He specifically asked what we'd been up to. About school and friends and all that."

God, I hate that accusing tone.

"He asked *me* if I had a boyfriend. Didn't he ask you if you had a girlfriend?"

"No," I say honestly. He didn't. I may have kept this nugget of information away from Chance, but only because he hadn't *specifically* asked. "I wouldn't lie to him."

"You *did* lie. Omission of information is lying." Ash jabs me in the arm. "She's coming out for Christmas. Were you planning on surprising him with it then?"

Girls. They have to turn everything into the end of the world. Chance called me out on it, and by lunch he was back to laughing and joking around and stealing my food. Done and over with. "Okay, I'm sorry. What the hell do you want from me? What's the big deal?"

"It's not a big deal *to me*. But Chance looked really hurt you kept something from him. You and Rachael are a serious thing, aren't you?"

I finally look at her. Not because I want to—the way she's frowning at me, trying to figure me out, leaves me feeling guilty all over again—but because I have nothing to say. I'm not capable of outright lying to my sister any more than I can outright lie to Chance. Ash knows what my relationship with Rachael was like in the beginning. That I loved that she was smart and grounded, and I liked how she had everything in her life figured out. Rachael was safe. Rachael promised security, and that was what I felt confident I needed.

Coming back here is shaking that confidence.

From the dresser, my phone rings. There are only three people who would be calling me. One is downstairs, and I'm looking at the other. Which means it's Rachael. I make no move to get up and answer it.

Ash's mouth forms a thin, tight line. "Are you going to get that?"

I debate whether I'd rather continue this conversation with her or talk to Rachael. I vote for the latter. Ash watches me swing myself off the mattress to grab my phone. I give her a long look until she gets the hint and leaves.

Oh, she's not satisfied by my answers. Or lack thereof. And I guess she shouldn't be. *I'm* not. I wish I had something more solid to offer, something beyond *I didn't tell Chance because I didn't want him to know I'm seeing someone.* Because that would lead to *Why didn't you want him to know you were seeing someone?* and what the hell would I answer to that?

That it feels wrong?

That I'm not in love with Rachael and I'm not even sure I want her coming out for Christmas? Because this life and the life I led back home are entirely different and I don't have a clue how to make those differences mesh.

"Rach. Hey."

"I was starting to think you weren't going to answer."

Every word out of my mouth feels thick. How are you grateful to hear from someone, but dreading it at the same time? "Sure. Why wouldn't I?"

Rachael sighs. "Well, you haven't exactly been responsive since you got to your dad's. Too busy running around with your friends. If I didn't know any better, I'd think you didn't miss me at all."

To be fair, she called this morning. I stared at the phone. Circled it on my bed. And, eventually, it stopped ringing. If it had been important, she would've called back, right? That was the line of thought that ran through my head until halfway through the day, when I started to feel bad about it.

A pang of guilt buries itself between my ribs. I slump back down into bed, arm draped across my eyes. Because there's a difference between not caring about someone and not being in love with her. I *care* about Rachael. I know the things I say, and the things I don't say, can hurt her as quickly as they can make her smile.

"I'm sorry. I've been…distracted. Sort of a big transition and all that. How are you?"

This seems to placate her. There's a softer, pleasant tone to her voice. "Don't worry about it. I miss you, you know. I see Madison and her boyfriend together all the time and it's just…"

I'm listening intently, at least at first. But she talks for nearly an hour—with minimal input on my part—about school and her parents and what Florida is like...and someone has started throwing rocks at my window.

When I get up to look, Chance is on the back porch. In the snow blanketing the deck, he's traced with his shoe:

CAN'T SLEEP CLOWNS WILL EAT ME SLEEPOVER ?

I laugh.

Rachael pauses. "What're you laughing at?"

"Nothing, sorry." I press a hand over my mouth. Rachael takes a breath, holds it a few seconds, and decides to keep talking rather than comment on my slip-up. She's going on about classes again, giving me enough detail that I could probably do the homework assignment right along with her. (See? I'm paying attention.) Cradling the phone between shoulder and cheek, I grab a sheet of paper, scribble as large as I can with a Sharpie, and press the page to my window:

ONE SEC

Chance squints, tosses his arms in the air, and scuffs out his current message to instead write:

COOOOOOLD

The *O*s are more random squiggles than actual letters. The way he hugs himself and twirls in circles gets me grinning ear to ear. Given that he's not wearing gloves or a coat, I need to drag him out of the snow before he catches pneumonia or something.

"Uh huh." I tiptoe out of my room and downstairs. "Rach, it's pretty late. I should probably get some sleep. Talk to you tomorrow?" Or later today, I guess, given it has to be around midnight by now.

Rachael *hmms*. We've been talking for a while, so at least there's no frustrated sigh like I'm purposely trying to shuffle her off the phone in favor of doing other things. "Okay. Get some rest; tell Louis and Ashlin I said hello."

It sort of weirds me out that Rachael has only talked to Dad on the phone a handful of times and she's already on a first-name basis with him. Chance has known him for years and still refers to him as Mr. J, even when Dad insists he shouldn't.

"Will do. I'll talk to you tomorrow; sleep well."

"Hunter?"

I stop at the back door, flipping the lock. "Yeah?"

"I love you."

I'm watching Chance through the glass with his snow-flecked hair, his red cheeks, and long lashes. "Love you, too."

I open the door. Chance slips inside.

It isn't until I've hung up and he's there grinning and shivering that I realize what I've said.

A year and I've managed to avoid saying it because I knew I wouldn't mean it. A year. And now I've screwed it all up.

Chance hugs himself tightly, teeth clenched to keep them from chattering. "Damn, it's cold. What's your problem? You look like someone spit in your Cheerios."

Feels that way. I shake my head and turn to head back upstairs. Chance follows, not pressing the subject. I wonder what he would say if I told him. Would he be annoyed after what happened earlier today, because I kept her a secret? Would he say I was a moron for letting the words slip out like that? It seemed like reflex. Someone says "I love you" on the phone and you just...say it back. Like every time I talk to Dad or Ash. *Sure, love you, talk to you later.*

Rachael's going to take it in all the wrong ways.

Do I let it be and hope she'll forget about it? Be careful not to repeat it again? Do I call her back and verify—*hey, I didn't mean it like* that.

We creep upstairs. I don't think to wake up Ash. If Chance had come to see her, he would've gone to the front of the house and pelted rocks at her window. He's done it before. Besides, the idea of him seeing her in that sad excuse for a nightgown she's wearing makes my insides twist all up.

No sooner is the bedroom door shut than I toss the phone onto my dresser like it's burning my fingers to hold it. Way to go, self. Way to make things awkward. Chance latches onto me from behind. His icy arms come around my neck and he hangs there, burrowing his face against my back.

"Ohhh my God. It's so cold outside. And you let me *sit* out there. What the hell is wrong with you?"

My skin prickles all over from the nearness of the human icicle that is Chance. I manage to twist around to face him while he hangs off me like an overgrown rag doll. Even after all this time, Chance's tendency to be overly physical doesn't faze me. If it were any other boy, it would be different, but this is Chance. There are no rules when it comes to him. "Let me get you something to change into. You're not sleeping in my bed like that."

This should be weird, letting some guy sleep in my bed.
With me in it. We did it for years as kids because when you're
eight you aren't thinking anything other than that it's cool to
have the comfort of a friend nearby.

Then you hit fourteen, fifteen, and you start to realize
you're watching that friend and marveling at how peaceful he
is when he sleeps. You're fascinated by the shape of his mouth
and how soft his lips look. You're wondering what it might be
like to play with his hair, or how you could be so in love with
the shadows of someone's cheekbones.

Suddenly, it isn't so cool anymore.

Once he lets go and starts undressing, I get him a flannel
button-up shirt and some sweats. Both of which will be too big
on him, but it's better than nothing. I flip on the television, a
random channel, for nothing other than the white noise.

Chance is shirtless, and his dragon tattoo is beautiful. I
have the urge to reach out and touch it, to trail my fingers
from one star to the next, and the next…creating the image of
Draco mapped out on his skin. Without entirely meaning to,
my gaze dips lower and catches on his hipbone, a splotch of
dark. Mottled black and blue.

I sit up a little straighter, expecting it to be a trick of the
light.

Chance must feel my eyes on him, because he snatches
the flannel from my hand and quickly turns his back to me
while slipping it on. "Take a picture, why don't you."

"Did you hurt yourself?" I ask. "Your—uh. The bruises."

"What?" He slips into the sweatpants and turns back

around. The shirt buttons are done up wrong but he clearly doesn't care. He pushes a hand back through his damp hair and falls carelessly into bed beside me, stretching out. I have the urge to pull up the shirt and point to exactly what I'm talking about. Let him worm his way out of that.

But I don't. I just stare down at him, wondering if I imagined it. Wondering if I'm over-thinking, because there are a million ways a person can get a bruise on his hip, and Chance is not exactly the most graceful of creatures. Besides, he'd probably think I was a freak for having been staring to begin with. Maybe something *is* wrong with me, seeing as all that staring and visually tracing that tattoo with my eyes has left me a little uncomfortable. His close proximity in the bed isn't doing a thing to help how warm my face has gotten, either.

We aren't kids anymore, so I wonder if this isn't okay like it used to be. Maybe I should tell him, but I can't think of a way to word it that wouldn't hurt his feelings. Chance doesn't see things like most people do. We used to share a bed, he would say, so what changed?

He stretches out on his back and stares up at the stars on the ceiling. Lifting a hand, he points. "It's glowing bright tonight." Without taking my eyes off him, I know he's talking about Draco.

"They're plastic stars, Chance," I say. "They all glow about the same."

A crease forms between his brows. "Nuh uh. Look at it. The dragon is brightest."

His cold fingers grab my face, turning it to look up. Bizarre. I could swear that he's right. As though by saying it, the stars forming his favorite constellation are brighter than the others. I smile a little, made difficult by his fingers pressing into my cheeks, but he doesn't let go.

"Nah. Looks the same."

"Don't be difficult. You're still in trouble for lying to me."

Oh. So much for the hope he'd let that slide. The stars give me something to focus on. "I'm sorry. I didn't think it would be that big of a deal."

"If it weren't a big deal, you would've mentioned it." His gaze burns into me. "Rachael's feelings would probably be hurt."

No *probably* about it. Rachael has always been insecure about how invested I am in our relationship. No matter what I've tried to do to change that over the year we've been together, nothing seems to help. Over the last few months, my resolve for trying has weakened.

Except what I said on the phone to her... How much is that going to change things? It has the potential to make them a lot better, but knowing my luck, it'll make everything a hundred times worse. Because what am I going to do the next time she calls and says *I love you*? Say it back even when I don't mean it? Skirt around it, which will inevitably lead to questions or an argument?

Chance rolls onto his side to face me. "What's she like?"

I really don't want to be talking to him about her. I'm not ready to take these two polar opposites and try to crush them together. His scrutinizing gaze makes me shift restlessly, itching to get out of bed. "She's kind of intense, a little critical, but hard-working. She's smart." Rachael's intelligence is the first thing I think of when someone asks me about her. There's *nothing* she can't learn. She used to tutor me in subjects I had a hard time with. She's the kind of girl who would read up on history before visiting a museum and probably know more than the tour guide once she got there.

"Is she hot?"

"She's beautiful, yeah."

"Blond hair?"

"Black. About Ash's height, I guess." I finally look over. "What's with the twenty questions?"

He shrugs, dropping his gaze, plucking some lint from the borrowed shirt. "Trying to imagine it."

"Imagine…?"

"She's this phantom person in my head. I'm trying to picture you with her."

Might as well give him warning. "You can meet her. She's coming out for Christmas."

Chance rolls away from me, yanking the covers up to his chin. "That ought to be…interesting."

I feel like I've missed some vital part of this conversation. But that's Chance—always more aware of what's being said and not being said. I almost apologize to him again and bite my tongue. Better to let it go. Give him some time to get over whatever it is that's bothering him. So I settle beside him, the TV flickering quietly, the stars shining from the ceiling, and nothing but an inch of space separating Chance's body from mine.

December

ASHLIN

Mom hardly believes me when I tell her I got a job.

"Why would you do that?" she asks on the phone, completely bewildered. "I've been putting money in your account. Your father isn't blowing it on booze, is he? I swear to God, if he is…"

I roll my eyes, contemplating the merits of hanging up on her. It's like this every time we talk. She hates that I'm out here. Can't seem to accept that Dad does the best he can with us. He always has. I think she's waiting for Dad to mess up with me because he did with her and Hunter's mom.

"Dad doesn't drink, Mom. And I doubt he realizes you give me money."

"Oh, great! So he thinks I'm some deadbeat parent not taking care of my girl—"

"Breakfast is ready, and Hunt is waiting for me. Love you. Bye." She's still going on when I hang up the phone.

I'm offended she doesn't think I'm capable of holding down work. It isn't like I've never *tried* before—just never needed to. Hunter has had a bunch of part-time jobs over the years, but he and his mom aren't as well off as me and mine. Dad always sent child-support, but if anyone has spent anyone's money on booze, it's probably Carol's boyfriend, Bob.

Hunter is waiting for me downstairs. I started at the bookstore the first week of December, and Hunt landed a job a few blocks away stocking shelves at a grocery store, so it's convenient for us to ride together.

Chance wasn't happy about this. He made a lot of faces at the idea of us having so much of our free time monopolized, even though we pointed out the extra cash would let us take more trips farther from town, which we've already explored from top to bottom. He wasn't at all pacified—not until he realized he could hang around the bookstore all day and read while I worked the counter.

Sometimes, he comes up to ask me and the other girls questions—"Where can I find self-help books on male pregnancy?" "Where do you keep the dirty magazines?" "I'm looking for a copy of the bible. Where's your nonfiction area?"—just to see how far he can push my coworkers. Thank God they got used to him quickly.

Dad, on the other hand, was absolutely thrilled we took the initiative and are doing something productive with our time. Even if this year was meant to be our "time off" before settling on colleges, I know he thinks it's wasted lying around the house all day. Which is why he beams at me when I come downstairs, already done with his own breakfast.

Hunter is halfway through devouring his food, and mine sits on the table, untouched. Isobel must have been by early this morning to check on Dad and cook breakfast. Really, a nurse isn't needed for Dad anymore. A fact he glosses over when I've asked him why he and Isobel still spend so much time together.

Not that it's a bad thing. At all. I adore Isobel, and it made me feel less worried being away from Dad so much for two years knowing someone was at his side, taking good care of him.

"They keeping you busy at that shop?" Dad asks.

I sink into my chair. "Sure. It's getting close to Christmas, so there's plenty to do." Not that our town has a crapload of business, but we're never left idle.

The back door creaks open. I hear Chance stomping his feet on the welcome mat before venturing inside, greeting us with a smile. "*Hola*, neighbors. Morning, Mr. J."

Dad gives a nod of his head. "More food on the stove. Help yourself."

As though Chance needs to be told twice. He snatches the remaining strips of bacon and at least tries to display some semblance of manners as he wolfs them down. You would think his parents never feed him.

Though after seeing his house that day and meeting his mom, one has to wonder. Mrs. Harvey didn't exactly strike me as the always-traveling-with-a-well-paying-job sort of mom like Chance told us she was.

"Have you thought about getting yourself a job, too, Chance?" Dad asks. "Maybe one of these two could get you a position at their places."

Hunter snorts and nearly chokes on his milk. I bite back a grin as Chance shoots him an offended scowl. "I don't think Lotsa Books or Pappy's Groceries are really the kind of jobs Chance would enjoy," I say.

Chance shoves another piece of bacon into his mouth. "Why not? I could do it. I can lift stuff."

"And talk to customers?" Hunter asks.

"And talk to customers. Sure. I love people!"

Liar, liar. Chance thinks most people in this town are dull and idiotic. Can't say I blame him, especially after having interacted with so many of them at work. But he can be perfectly charming when he wants to be.

"He wouldn't always have a way to get there," Hunt points out. "We're already struggling with one car between Ash and me."

Chance slouches into the seat beside me, munching away. "I don't know. Maybe that car out front is for me."

Hunter lowers his fork. He and I exchange glances before looking to Dad. In unison: "Car?"

Dad heaves a dramatic sigh. "Guess the cat's out of the bag." He pulls a set of keys from his pocket and slides them across the table. They come to a halt after clinking against my plate. I stare down at them, fascinated.

"Car?" Hunter repeats, equally in awe.

"Figured you two needed something of your own to get

around in. And cramming all three of you into the Toyota's a bit of a tight fit, isn't it?"

It is, though we've never complained. Sometimes, Chance likes to ride in back, standing up at red lights and pounding on the roof in (what he insists is) Morse code. We won't mention that to Dad.

"Nothing special or pretty." Dad shoves his chair back, grabs his cane, and rises to his feet with a grunt. "You gonna go have a look or what?"

Hunter and I scramble out of our seats to dash outside. Chance does, too, but only after snatching the bacon off my plate.

Dad's right about the car not being pretty. It's probably as old as we are, and the blue paint is chipping in spots. But the tires look brand-new and, as we peer inside, I can tell the interior has been recently redone. It's big enough to hold all of us, but it isn't a monster like the truck. I might actually be able to drive it without wanting to close my eyes every time I make a turn.

While Hunt starts it up, I throw my arms around Dad— delicately, of course—and hug him. "You really didn't have to do this, but thank you."

He actually *smiles*. A big smile, too. I can't remember the last time I saw Dad look so pleased, but it's been a really long time. "Yuh huh." That's all he says. No explanation for why he did it or where he got it. Just *yuh huh* and that's that. Along with, "Thank Isobel when you see her next, too. She's the one who found it and has been keeping it at her place while I paid to get it fixed up. Now get going or you'll be late for work."

I run back inside long enough to get my and Hunter's things. When I return, Chance has made himself comfortable sprawled across the backseat, and Hunt is messing with the dials. Radio, cassette player ("We'll have to get a new stereo," he says), heater. Definitely the heater. Dad waves to us as we pull out of the driveway. And crunch, crunch, crunch, Chance is still eating his bacon, savoring the last piece. I swear, he could eat a whole pig's worth of the stuff.

"So," he says. "I think I'll give this work thing a try."

Hunter glances at him in the rearview mirror. Despite being ancient, our little car runs surprisingly quiet and smooth. "I can talk to my boss, I guess."

"Like hell! Not yours. I don't want to lift crap all day." He slips a hand between my seat and the door to pinch my arm. "I'll go work with Ash."

I giggle and swat at his hand, trying not to sound as pleased as I feel at the idea he'd rather come work with me. "The problem being everybody at my work knows you. You're the lazy brat who occupies the sofa all day and never puts his books up when he's done. And you never buy anything, for that matter."

A lazy smile creeps across Chance's face. "I'll get a job, just watch."

In town, Hunter drops us off first outside the bookstore. Lotsa Books isn't really a hole-in-the-wall place, compared to some of the other shops in town. I mean, it takes four of us each shift to keep things running smoothly between assisting customers, ringing people out, taking orders, cataloguing the used books, and handling any online purchases we get. I don't tell Chance that one of the shift leaders, Debbie, has been looking for a fifth person for the holiday season now that things are picking up. No point in getting his hopes up before they shoot him down.

I slip in back to put away my purse and lunch while Chance, I assume, wanders off to troll the aisles and stock up on books to keep him busy. Except when I step out onto the floor with a "Love Books?" apron tied around my waist, I spot him leaning gracelessly across the counter, chatting away to Debbie.

And my only thought is: *oh my God, they're going to kick him out. Or fire me. Or kick him out and* then *fire me.*

Scuttling over, I grab hold of his arm. "Morning, Deb! Um, sorry, Chance was just—"

Debbie waves me off with a roll of her eyes. "He's talking, Ashlin. Let him finish trying to tell me why in the world I should consider giving him a job."

Chance throws me a triumphant smile. "As I was saying… There isn't a book in this store I don't know how to find by this point. I can sell anything. With Christmas around the corner, isn't that what you really need? Someone to upsell?" He tips his head, brandishing one of those beautiful and sincere Chance smiles. The smile that Hunter and I are immune to now, and that Deb probably doesn't believe for a second, but it drives his point home that his pretty face could sell a surround sound system to a deaf man.

Debbie purses her lips, tapping a ballpoint pen against the counter like she always does when she's thinking. Finally, she looks at me. "Opinions?"

Rock and a hard place. I can't tell her she shouldn't hire
Chance because he's too…Chance-like. I can't imagine him
showing up on time every day. Can't imagine him not snapping
at customers when one of them says something he doesn't like.
Sure as hell can't imagine him taking orders from someone as
snippy and temperamental as Debbie can be.

"Don't ask her," Chance cuts in. "Let me prove it. Let me
work today and I guarantee, by the time the shop closes, you'll
be begging me to stay."

Deb looks at me, looks at him. And, because there isn't a
lot to lose—except maybe customers, I want to point out—she
sighs and shrugs. "Whatever. Ashlin, get him an apron." She
wanders off for her morning coffee.

Chance grins.

HUNTER

After work, I head straight to the pizzeria around the block to meet up with Chance and Ash. My phone is going off. It has been through most of work. I ignore it, because I told Rachael I had to work today, and I know she thinks part-time at a grocery store doesn't count as *real work* and therefore I can be disturbed or…something.

I'm making a point by not answering. Because that's only fair, right?

Ever since I told her I loved her, things have been changing. Subtle changes, but changes nonetheless. She calls more often. She sounds more cheerful—which, I mean, is a good thing—but it's been…

Smothering. Yeah, that's the word.

And considering I was feeling a little claustrophobic to

begin with, that is really not sitting well with me.

I've already ordered a large pizza, breadsticks, and drinks, and I'm on my second slice by the time Chance and Ash show up. Chance is grinning from ear to ear as he sinks into the booth beside me, his hip to my hip, and slowly any thoughts of Rachael seep to the back of my brain. Ash sits across from us, looking bewildered.

"Chance got the job," she says.

I arch an eyebrow, glancing between them. "Really? Well, that's great. I thought you said your shift manager was kind of a tight-ass?"

"Oh, she is." Chance leans across me to grab a slice of pizza. "But she also thinks I'm cute."

Ash rolls her eyes and helps herself to pizza, too. "No. She really doesn't. Chance bullied her into letting him work for a day to prove he could do it. He ended up taking, like, eight special orders, and the customers adore him."

"Because I'm cute," Chance says again around a mouthful of food. "I filled out all my paperwork. I'll be on the same shift as Ash, so I can hitch a ride with you guys."

I shrug. The fact that Chance has a job is great, so I should probably be feeling happier than I do. If I'd known he was serious about it, I could have gotten him work at the grocery store. "Fine, but let us pick you up at your place. It's too cold for you to be walking to our house every day."

Just like that, the smile vanishes from his face. He's silent for the length of time it takes him to bite, chew, swallow, before he says, "No. I like walking."

"It's fine for now," Ash says. "But seriously? Dad said the

temperatures here get ridiculous in winter. Your house isn't that far out of the way."

"I said *no*," Chance snaps. He takes one look at Ashlin's stricken expression and turns away, yanking pepperoni off his pizza. "It's just easier. I'd rather walk."

Ash opens her mouth like she might say something further. I give her leg a nudge under the table, and she stops, frowns, and turns her attention to her food. We struck a nerve, obviously. Pushing Chance to talk about it will backfire. He isn't even looking at us anymore. As far as he's concerned, the subject is closed. His eyes are glued to the old television mounted in the corner; it's too low for us to hear, but the subtitles scroll along the bottom, disjointed and not entirely coherent.

Ash and I twist in our seats to watch, too. Better than staring down at the table while we eat in awkward silence. The newscaster is talking about a family in New Jersey, murdered by their daughter in cold blood. Her parents and two younger siblings were all poisoned at dinner.

"How could any kid do that?" Ash mutters. "I mean, I kind of want to punch my mom in the mouth sometimes, but—"

"Drastic measures." Chance sets the crust aside. He never eats it. "Maybe she and her parents didn't get along."

"She was seventeen." Ash straightens and focuses her frown on Chance. "Even if she were that miserable, it's not like she had long to go before she could leave."

"Sometimes that isn't the point." Chance licks the grease from his fingers, slowly because he's still focused on the television. "People killing their spouses, their children, their parents... Obviously, there's something wrong in their heads.

They needed help. No one knew to give it to them."

"Doesn't make it right," Ash insists.

"No, it doesn't. I'm just saying…to that particular person, maybe she didn't realize there are other options. Maybe, for some of them, there *aren't* other options. When you feel that trapped, that smothered, like they're breaking you… When you feel like you're going down anyway, you might as well take them along." Chance finally looks at us again. Whatever irritation was there moments ago is gone, replaced by a subdued, vacant shine to his eyes that makes me uncomfortable.

"Sometimes," he says, "people get desperate, and no one is listening."

Ashlin says nothing. I have the strongest urge to reach out and put my hand on Chance's cheek, to try to make him smile again because I can't stand that look on his face. Everything about it is wrong and un-Chance-like. I don't, because I wouldn't know how to explain it without it coming across in all the wrong ways. I already told my girlfriend I loved her when I don't; that sort of fills my yearly quota for messing up my relationships.

We finish our late lunch, pile into the car, and head home. Rather than stop by the house, though, I follow the road until we hit the dirt of Stoneman Drive. Chance straightens up in the backseat.

"What the hell are you doing?"

At the end of his street I stop, out of view of the mobile home park. I peer at Chance in the rearview mirror. "Compromising. You know how to do that, right?"

Chance's mouth is drawn tight, but his shoulders relax as

he pushes open his door. "Yeah. See you guys tomorrow?"

"Tomorrow," Ash says. We don't work tomorrow, which means we might be off on some other adventure that Chance has come up with for us. He slides out of the car, hands shoved in his pockets as he heads down the road.

"Maybe he's embarrassed by his house," Ash murmurs. "Or his parents. They obviously aren't who he said they were."

"Maybe." It's the first time we've admitted this to each other out loud: Chance lied. About a lot. He told us about the big house and how his parents were always gone because of work. It has me rethinking everything Chance has ever told me — because the lies we've caught him on aren't little things. It isn't *I didn't take the last of the cookies.* It's *My entire life isn't what I said it was.*

I think about the bruises on Chance the night he stayed over. Ash says he's embarrassed; I hope that's all it is. Too bad things with him are never that simple. I remember the year he broke his arm. The times he refused to go swimming because he didn't want to take off his shirt. All the times Dad did something nice for him, and Chance would look up with the biggest eyes and say, "You're way better than any other dad, Mr. J." Like doing something as simple as buying him a shirt or an ice cream cone made him Super-dad.

I'm questioning everything now, searching for the hidden meanings behind it all. Wondering which parts were true and which parts weren't.

As I pull forward to turn the car around, I catch one last glimpse of Chance stepping off the road. Moving away from his house and into the trees.

...

We went to the beach all the time growing up, but never directly to Harper's Beach. To be fair, it isn't a swimming-friendly sort of beach—more rocks than sand, and the tide can be a little vicious at times. But besides that, Dad probably didn't want us asking questions about Hollow Island, which is perfectly visible from Harper's Beach, and not so much from the one we went to on the other side of Hollow Point. He was probably worried we'd get ideas about visiting the island.

Which is true. We would have gotten all sorts of ideas.

Which is why we snuck out there once with Chance instead.

As we stood on Harper's shore with the ocean lapping at our feet, Chance, at thirteen, told us the history of the island while we stared, transfixed.

"They had plans to build a bridge to connect the island to the mainland," he said. "There are buildings over there. Kinda hard to see, huh? But they're out there. Some houses and stuff. Weird, creepy problems and accidents kept happening while they were plotting the construction of the bridge, though, so they finally gave up and abandoned the island all together. Some say it's haunted."

I didn't think to ask who *they* were. City officials, I guess. I never researched it online then, and I don't plan to, because it would take away some of the magic Chance has built around it. The island really did look like a piece of land humanity forgot.

"I swam there once," Chance announced.

Ash marveled at him, as she always did at his stories, but I frowned. "You did not."

"Did, too!"

"It's, like, miles out there. No one could swim that unless you're in the Olympics or something."

"Not *miles*." Chance sniffed indignantly, chucking a rock as far into the water as he could. "I could do it again, too, if I wanted."

I crossed my arms. "Do it, then."

The two of us were always like that. Daring each other. More often than not, I was the one who backed down because the things Chance dared me to do were way too out there. Like stealing the huge cardboard cutout of the donut on the roof of Happy Donut, or going to the mall wearing Ash's clothes— which never would have fit me anyway. Chance, though, was up for anything. There wasn't much he'd skip out on.

That was one of the rare times he did. Of course, it wasn't backing down to Chance. He wrinkled his nose, eyes unreadable behind the huge sunglasses perched on his freckled face. He turned away.

"That's stupid. Why would I swim all that way while you cowards stay here?"

• • •

Chance knows all the best vantage points to see Hollow Island and where we can more or less safely scale down the cliffs to little coves below. Trees lining the cliffs are half bare, their bony arms stretching to the moody gray sky. The waves crashing against the shore seem angrier than I remember, more urgent, and the wind whips at my hair and pulls at my coat. Chance stands right at the ledge, overlooking Hollow Island and the beach, so close the tips of his shoes peek over the rocks. I grab his arm out of reflex, and he looks at me and laughs.

It isn't that I'm afraid of heights. I'm afraid of Chance-and-heights.

Climbing isn't much fun. Chance goes down first, careful to watch his footholds and handholds but moving with such ease it's obvious how often he does this. I follow, slower, making sure not to risk looking down. I don't understand why we don't drive the mile and a half up the road to Harper's where we can reach the water not twenty feet off the side of the road, but there's no talking sense into Chance. This is the place he likes.

Ashlin doesn't budge from the cliff above. Not until Chance and I are safely at the bottom, staring up and beckoning her to follow. I cup my hands around my mouth. "Stop worrying. It's fine!"

"We'll catch you!" Chance calls. Our voices are dulled by the waves.

Ash looks like she has half a mind to flip us off and go back to the car, but she finally starts her descent down the jagged cliff-face for the beach below. When she has about six feet left, she drops the rest of the way, wincing on impact and falling on her ass. I help her up, but I can't stop laughing.

"See?" Chance says. "Not so bad."

We cross the rocks to where the water rushes in to meet our feet. It's too cold to take off my shoes, so instead the ocean soaks through the canvas of my sneakers and the socks beneath, instantly numbing my toes.

From here, we have—what Chance would say is, and I'm inclined to agree—the best view of Hollow Island.

I take a breath and spread my arms wide. The salty winter air here is delicious. Revitalizing. "So...we're here. Now what?"

Chance crouches, unbothered by the tide licking at his jeans. "I've decided."

"Decided what?" Ash asks.

"We're going to get onto that island."

My arms fall limp at my sides. We're both staring at Chance in a way that suggests we think he's lost his mind. Chance glances at us, nose wrinkling.

"What? Jesus, I didn't say we were going to *swim*, did I? We'll buy a raft."

"A raft," Ash and I say together.

"One of those big inflatable ones, yeah? Doesn't have to be fancy. Can get one for a hundred bucks with our next paychecks. It can be my Christmas present."

"We'd also need oars," Ash points out. "Rafts don't steer themselves."

Chance shrugs. "Well, whatever."

I ask, "What are we supposed to do on the island?"

"Look around. Take pictures. We can play hide-and-go-seek for all I care; the island is great for stuff like that."

Ash frowns. "How do you know?"

Chance scowls. "I told you before that I've been there."

Yeah, he did. He said he swam, which is a fact I'm having

a hard time wrapping my head around. "Nuh uh. No way in hell."

"Seriously?" Chance heaves a heavy sigh. "There's a big brick building in the middle of the island where you can see all around you. Just wait. Now, are you guys going to do this with me or what? I can go by myself."

I stare out at the island. The breeze whips the hair back from my face, and my cheeks have begun to sting from the cold. Rachael will be out in a few days to visit for Christmas and New Year's, and she would not approve of this idea. In fact, she would disapprove so much she'd probably burst a blood vessel while lecturing me. It's going to make things really interesting when she visits—and by *interesting*, I mean I might want to throw myself out of a moving vehicle by the time she leaves.

But I've wanted to see the island for myself since Chance brought us here years ago. How many more adventures like this will I be granted before I have to apply for college and leave this behind? Rachael says that's what it means to *grow up*.

"Yeah... Yeah. All right. But we're going to get a decent raft. If we get stranded out there, we're screwed. Ash?"

She doesn't miss a beat. "I'm totally in."

Chance hops to his feet, draping an arm around Ash with a grin. "That's my girl! This is going to be awesome."

Ashlin

he way Hunter tells it, he and Rachael met in calculus at school when she took on the task of tutoring him to bring his C up to an A because it was the only subject he struggled in. She was the one to ask him out, in fact. Then they graduated, and Rachael picked a school all the way down in Florida with a good biochemistry program. Naturally, she begged Hunter to go with her.

He could've gotten in; his grades were good enough, and the college had a track program he would've qualified for in order to get at least a partial scholarship.

Hunter, though, wants to stay in Maine. Or at least not move so far away as Florida. He wanted to be here for Dad this year, and he wanted to spend time with Chance and me. The bullet that almost took our dad also stole a lot of my time with my brother. Even if we communicated almost daily through e-mail and text and phone, it wasn't the same. I wanted to be able to see Hunter's face. I wanted to come home and fight with him over stupid stuff, like chores and who was cooking dinner and what movie we were watching. Our lives could've been way different if we'd grown up living together. Maybe this bond we have wouldn't be as strong and we would hate each other. I have no idea.

All I know is that Hunter doesn't have his future figured out in the least. "I asked her to give me some time to think about it," is all he would tell me. "She wants me to come down there and get a place together near campus." But the way he says it suggests that those are *Rachael's* plans, and not necessarily his.

I like to think Rachael understood about Hunter taking a year off to spend in Maine, but then I remember she's only human and any girl whose boyfriend is states away isn't going to be happy with the arrangement. I'll bet she's ecstatic to visit over the holidays.

I don't understand why Hunter isn't as excited.

He was when he first announced Rachael's visit the week we got to Dad's. Then that excitement slowly ebbed away. In fact, if I didn't know any better, I'd say now he is *dreading* it. He dragged his feet when setting up the extra bedroom— Dad's old room—for her to use. (Why Dad thinks they're actually going to sleep in separate rooms, I have no clue. His own peace of mind, I guess.) And at the airport, his shoulders are a little tense, his arms folded, mouth curved down, like he's *bracing* himself for this.

It bothers me. I have this image in my head of what their relationship is like, but Hunter's lack of enthusiasm about his long-time girlfriend and his willingness to live so far away from her indefinitely is starting to dash my hopes and dreams. Hunter has always spoken fondly of Rachael, but I'm the first to admit he isn't the sort of person to gush about anyone or anything. Still, I got the impression they were happy. Why would you date someone for a year if you weren't?

Rachael's plane is right on time. She comes through the gate in boots, leggings, and a white sweater, with her dark, wavy hair pulled into a ponytail—she doesn't even look like she's spent the last several hours on a plane. Jeez, when I got here, my hair had been a mess, my makeup gone, and I was carting enough baggage under my eyes they could have charged me an extra carry-on fee.

This is the Rachael I pictured, though. Put-together and pretty. She smiles wide when she spots Hunter, but there is no grand reunion like I imagined. She approaches, sets her bags on the ground, and kisses him on the cheek. The *cheek*. No big hug, no passionate kiss. It throws me a little, but maybe she's being polite. Reserved. Because she's in a public place and I'm standing right here.

I think Hunter's expression has smoothed out, though, a small smile slipping across his face. "How was the flight?"

"Fine, just fine." Rachael turns her pretty smile to me. "You must be Ashlin. It's great to finally meet you." She gives *me* a hug, which startles me, but I awkwardly return her squeeze.

"Yeah—it's great. Here, let me get your stuff."

The long drive home, Rachael and I fall into easy

conversation. She tells me about school and her classes, and I tell her how Dad's been feeling. I mention Chance, of course. It's impossible not to when he spends nearly every waking moment at our place.

And yet, when we arrive home, and Chance is seated on the couch watching TV, Rachael looks surprised. I don't think Chance being here is anything less than intentional. He waited because he wanted to meet Rachael.

Chance rises to his feet. The shirt and sweats he's wearing are Hunter's, so they don't fit quite right, and his hair is wet from a shower. Making himself at home, like he always has, like we've always wanted him to. Before, the situation never seemed strange to me. But now, seeing the perplexed expression on Rachael's face, I wonder how it looks through the eyes of an outsider.

"There you are. I told Mr. J I would wait up to make sure you didn't crash and die on the way home or anything." He grins, all easy words, but there's a sharpness to his eyes that makes me nervous for Hunter's sake. I know it's going to be important to him that his girlfriend and his best friend get along.

Recovering from her surprise, Rachael smiles. "You're Chance."

"The one and only." He looks pleased she knows who he is. Which, I guess, makes sense given he might not have known who *she* was had I not spilled the beans weeks ago. "And you are the mysterious and lovely Rachael Li."

His compliment seems to soothe Rachael's unease, and she tips her head, expression warming. "Oh, I don't know about that. It was nice of you to stick around to see us home."

Hunter catches my eye from beside Rachael, and I wouldn't be surprised if he sank right into the floor and vanished. We both know Chance won't go home this late. We wouldn't want him to. Not with how cold it is outside and on an unlit road.

"Uh, Hunt, you should get Rachael to her room. I'm sure she's exhausted," I say, and he looks grateful for the opportunity to slip away.

"See you crazy kids in the morning," Chance chirps, earning him a quizzical look from Rachael as she follows Hunter upstairs. The moment they're gone, the smile slips from his face, and I'm left cringing at the uncomfortable silence settling over the room like a cold blanket. He doesn't look at me. I flick off the TV and tableside lamp, leaving us in darkness, and then give Chance a push toward the stairs. He's never spent a night on our couch, and I'm not going to make him start now. He grunts but goes without complaint.

Chance hasn't shared a bed with me since the summer we met him. After that, the closest we got was all three of us crashing on the living room floor or the back porch beneath the stars. A huge difference from actually lying beside Chance. Alone. In a bed. I get changed into shorts and a sweatshirt in the bathroom, and when I come back Chance has already made himself comfortable in my bed. Dad loves Chance, but I'm not sure he'd be as pleased as I am at the idea of him and me sharing such close quarters.

What he doesn't know won't hurt him.

As I sink down alongside Chance, he asks, "So, was that well-behaved enough?"

I give him a sidelong look and pull the blankets up around me. Even with the distance between us, I can feel the warmth Chance gives off. I wonder what he'd say if I curled into him, fit myself against his side. "Was it that much effort to behave?"

He stares at the ceiling, not meeting my gaze. "It didn't show? I'm a better actor than I thought."

"Why should you have to try, though? What's wrong with Rachael? She seems nice."

Chance looks at me only after I've flicked off the lamp next to the bed. In the darkness, it's hard to make him out, but I'm not sure I'd understand his expression even if I could properly see it.

"Nothing is *wrong* with her." The way he says it makes it seem like that, in and of itself, is a flaw. "But she's not going to like me."

I roll onto my side to face him. "Of course she'll like you. Why wouldn't she?"

Chance mirrors my movements and reaches out to toy with a strand of my hair. The gesture is so absent that I think it's because he can't stand to stay idle. A restless habit, but I'm enjoying the attention all the same. "Pretty, smart, got her shit together, going places in life. She'll hate my guts."

"That's kind of judgmental, don't you think?" I sniff indignantly. "I'm smart, pretty, and have my shit together." Sort of. I have no clue what I'm doing after my year of free time is up. I mean, I had thoughts of going to community college here, maybe taking some photography classes or journalism, and I had hopes of getting a little apartment all my own that Chance could come visit whenever he wanted, but…

His eyebrows shoot up, but at least he smiles, even if only a little. "Not the point."

"Isn't it?"

"Just watch, Ash."

"She's not that different, you know. She's smart, but *you're* smart." I tap his forehead with one finger. "You know a freakish amount about the most random subjects. She's pretty, you're handsome."

"I don't have my life together."

"Sure you do. I mean, you're getting there. You've got a job and a family—us—who love you." I clarify, because whatever is going on with the family he avoids talking to us about, he has Hunter and Dad and me. We'll be his family. We always have been.

"So," I continue, "all that said, name one thing Rachael has that you don't."

I half expect him to jokingly say *breasts* or any number of other things. Typical Chance things, because serious subjects aren't ones he broaches and certainly doesn't stay on once touched. Chance snakes an arm out beneath the blankets and winds it around my waist, draws me closer until my head is on his shoulder and my heart is in my throat, and he's so warm and comfortable, and I completely forget what we were talking about until he says—

"She has Hunter."

HUNTER

Rachael puts her bags in the spare room while I linger in the doorway, wanting to inch out, say good night, and flee before anything else can happen. She looks around appraisingly.

"I get the master suite, huh?"

"It used to be Dad's room." I scuff my socks against the carpet, staring down at them. "Bathroom's right across the hall. You know where I am if you need anything."

She nods, sinking onto the edge of the mattress. But she's watching me. Waiting.

When did being around my own girlfriend get to be so weird? Things were fine the last time we saw each other. She'd cried a little and kissed me as her parents were preparing to drive her and her things down to Florida. Not that we've ever been *normal* by most people's standards. We aren't overly affectionate. We haven't slept together yet, and neither of us is big on public displays of affection beyond holding hands when we go out. And I'm aware it isn't because I'm not an affectionate guy. I like it when Chance clings to me, whether we're in public or not. Hell, I don't mind when my own sister takes my hand or latches her arms around my neck. I don't care what people think there, but with Rachael... I don't know what it is.

Now she's watching me like she expects me to stay. Or to ask her to come back to my room. I like my space, and I've already crossed one line with her I didn't mean to cross.

I give her a smile. "So...good night. Sweet dreams."

"Hunter?"

Crap.

She rises off the bed, wringing her hands together. The one thing everyone can tell you about Rachael—she's fucking gorgeous. All that sleek dark hair and big brown eyes. I should consider myself the luckiest guy in the world to have her slipping her arms around my neck and rising up to kiss me. Properly this time. Not like she did in the airport.

It isn't that difficult to relax, and I've missed kissing her. It only takes me a minute to get into it, into the taste of her mouth and the feel of her pressing up against me, inviting in a way she's never been before. Is it because she missed me, or because of what I said on the phone? If "I love you" was the magic phrase for getting into Rachael Li's pants, I know a lot of guys who would've screamed it from the rooftops.

But something isn't quite the same as it was a few months ago. It's a niggling in the back of my mind that is keeping me from completely immersing myself in her. Maybe it's the insistence with which she kisses me, or maybe it's the idea that she might want to do this because I said something to her I'm not sure I meant. Or maybe it's that my sister and best friend are only a few doors down.

Something is clearly wrong with my head. Here I am, making out with a gorgeous girl, possibly being invited to stay the night with her—whatever that might entail—and my brain will. Not. Stop. What is wrong with me?

After a few minutes, she pulls back. Not much, but a little. Just enough to smile against my lips. "I've really missed you."

"I can see that." My voice comes out hoarser than I mean it to. I could stay here. I could try to shut up my thoughts, but…what happens after? When I wake up in the morning and realize I'm still not in love with her, but I care enough about her to feel insanely guilty about what I've done.

Yeah. Not going to happen.

I pull away, looking down to avoid the bewildered crinkle of her brow. "You've had a really long day, what with… traveling…and stuff." *So articulate, Hunter, guh.* "Get some sleep."

Rachael smiles, but it's a smile that clearly says she doesn't understand. Thankfully, it also means she lets me go without further protest. So I can shuffle back to my own room, head down, contemplating a cold shower and reminding myself I'll survive this visit.

• • •

After last night, I'm leery about being left alone with Rachael. Which is stupid, really, when I stop to think about it. It's not like she's going to drive me to an abandoned parking lot and jump me the second she has the opportunity, but I just…

It's easier, I guess. Having other people around. Breakfast isn't bad, because Dad and Isobel—who came by with donuts for breakfast, and to meet Rachael—keep Rach occupied the entire time. While Ash continually nudges my foot with a tilt of her head, mouthing, *Are you okay?*

Even though I nod in response while shoving food into my mouth, Ash knows me better than that. I don't know what I would do without her. Her suggestion of going to the mall has nothing to do with wanting to shop and everything to do with making things easier on me. Rachael hesitates, but I swallow a bite of chocolate-and-sprinkle goodness to say, "Yeah, sure," before she can figure out a way to politely decline. We wolf down the rest of our breakfast, thank Isobel, promise Dad we'll behave (ha), and head out.

I could hug Ash. Here, in a public setting, there won't be as many awkward pauses and uncomfortable silences. Here, it's more neutral ground. Plus I can lead Rachael away from Chance if things start to take a wrong turn between the two of them.

I don't know why I'm still nervous. I don't know why the looks Chance keeps giving me make my chest tighten. This guilt is drowning me, and I don't know what the hell I have to be guilty *for*. He's my best friend, and Rachael is my girlfriend. A little anxiety about them getting along is normal, but what I'm feeling? Not so much.

As we climb out of the car, Ash catches me by the arm and leans in. "What's going on?"

"Nothing. Why would something be going on?" I smile, draping an arm around her shoulders. She jabs a finger into my ribs, which, thankfully, I barely feel through the padding of my jacket.

"Don't start, mister. You were giving these pathetic *save me* looks all through breakfast. Shouldn't you be devoting what little time your girlfriend is here to…I don't know, spending time with her?"

Guilt nibbles at my insides, and I shove it back. "Things are a little weird right now, Ash." I sigh. "Just…give me some time to get my head right. Please?"

There's no time for protesting. Rachael and Chance are already footing it for the front door to get out of the snow, and Rachael keeps casting furtive looks over her shoulder. Like she knows I'm talking about her. Ash is the same way. How do girls always know when you're trying to have a conversation that involves them?

We're here early enough that most of the people inside are those who come in for a daily walking club. Mostly old people in tacky track suits who do a few laps around the perimeter, where it's not too hot or too cold and there are plenty of places to stop for a rest. Shops are still in the process of opening. The food court has barely cracked its shutters and turned on its stoves.

I like this time of day. No crowds, no lines, fewer noisy kids squealing or shoving past.

God, that makes me sound old.

After browsing the stores—correction: after the *girls* browse a few stores while Chance and I trail around patiently after them—Chance buys himself a hot pretzel that he shares with Ash, while Rachael gets a smoothie for her and me to split. I'd rather have some of the pretzel. Chance is licking salt off his fingers when he says, "Hey, Hunt."

Rachael's all-natural smoothie tastes like pureed grass. Guess it's a good thing we ate right before coming here, so I'm not starving yet. "What?"

"Didn't we tie last time we were here?" He hands the remainder of the pretzel over to Ash, who gladly shoves it into her mouth. Rachael glances at me, questioning, and I can't help the silly grin pulling at my mouth.

"No. I won. You just wouldn't admit it."

It's a challenge, and Chance never backs down when I say I can do something better than he can. Probably a stupid idea. The last time he and I raced through the mall, we were fifteen years old and people kind of expected that sort of stupidity from boys our age. We could've hurt someone, or ourselves. Besides that, security tossed us out after we crossed our imaginary finish line. We're lucky they didn't call Dad.

When did I get old enough that I started worrying about stuff like this?

It was years ago, but the memory of how it felt is still so vivid. That's how it is with my summer memories; they're all about *sensation* rather than details of who said or did what. But that was then, this is now, and I can only imagine how Rachael will feel if she sees me acting like a kid in the middle of a public place. She doesn't like to be embarrassed.

"Did not," Chance counters.

"Did too."

Rachael looks between us, confused, and Ash says warningly, "Guys…"

Chance isn't listening. He's watching me with a glint in his eyes, coming to a halt and bouncing on the balls of his feet like he's limbering up. "Come on, then. Rematch."

I make a valiant effort to stop grinning, and fail. "We're not kids anymore. We'll make a scene."

"Then admit I won."

"You didn't," I say. "But I'm not running."

"Come *on*."

"No."

Chance spins, and with a squeak of his sneaker on linoleum, he's off.

Rachael emphasizes this with a startled *"Oh,"* and then "Hunter!" because without another thought, I take off after him.

We sprint through the mall, the thumping of my pulse and Chance's breathless laughter a duet in my ears. We weave in and out of the occasional mall-walker. Chance rounds a bench, and I hop right over it to gain the lead, just by a few feet.

Suddenly, it's summer and we're fifteen again. Chance is all ungainly limbs and freckles with a shirt too big on him and sneakers that are falling apart. It's one of those moments where everything else in the world fades to a dull hum in the background because all that exists is Chance and me, and I want to take his bright-eyed, exhilarated face and bottle it up for safe keeping.

At the end of the mall, a play area has been installed since the last time I was here. Little tunnels, a slide for toddlers, and a ball pit that can't be any more than two feet deep. I slow down out of fear I'm going to trample some poor kid or his unsuspecting parent, but Chance plows right into the ball pit headfirst, laughing, but so out of breath not much sound is coming out.

My chest burns. My legs are jelly. But, God, what a fantastic feeling, and I'm laughing, too, as I stumble over to the edge of the pit and brace my hands on my knees while I try to reintroduce air into my lungs. I can't remember the last time I felt like this.

"Did I win?" Chance pants, squirming onto his back in the array of red, blue, and yellow plastic balls.

I grin around my labored breathing and extend my hand, which Chance takes. "Yeah. You won that one."

Instead of crawling out, he yanks, and I find myself sprawled out half on him, half sinking into the pit, with Chance laughing in my ear.

We lay there for a minute or two, relearning how to breathe. Or maybe waiting to see if security is going to boot us out. Rachael and Ash find us first. My sister looks amused, but Rachael's pretty face is offset by a deep frown, and her arms are crossed. Chance and I get to our feet, only the vague residual burn in my lungs a reminder of our fun. Too bad Rachael's disapproval is kind of a buzzkill.

I haul myself out of the pit. Chance snags the belt loops of my jeans to drag himself out along with me, nearly sending us both right back where we started.

"I won," Chance announces proudly.

Rachael's gaze never leaves my face. "What was *that*?"

"What?" I push a hand through my hair, feigning innocence. "We were just playing around. No big deal."

"You could've run right into someone," she says. "What if you'd tripped over a poor little kid?"

"There are never kids here this early," Chance cuts in. "We wouldn't have done it if I'd seen any the entire time we've been here."

Rachael casts him a sour look, clearly displeased at having our conversation interrupted. She's not used to that. When she's unhappy with me, it's usually just her and me. No one else to interject his opinion.

I hate Rachael's lectures. They never fail to make me feel like I'm five years old. I cram my hands into my pockets and hunch my shoulders, torn between wanting to apologize just to appease her and not wanting Ash and Chance to see that this is how our relationship works. Rachael gets upset, I do what she wants to smooth things over.

"I'm sorry," I find myself saying.

It's all she's getting out of me, but it seems to be enough. Rachael sighs, shoulders slumping, but at least her irritation is short-lived. Her tone is mild as she says, "Let's just get out of here."

I will myself to relax, grateful that's—hopefully—over and done with. And I try to ignore the way Chance rolls his eyes before putting his arm around Ash and walking away.

• • •

We have lunch at a diner across the street. The girls sit on one side, and Chance crowds in beside me, squishing me effectively against the wall when I try to put some distance between us. His elbow is digging into my side. He had asked the waitress for a kid's menu so he could draw on it with the crayons they provide while simultaneously sipping at his drink.

I busy myself by picking at my chicken and fries. Ash and Rachael delve into their own conversation. School and boys. Go figure.

"I don't have a boyfriend," Ash is saying, swirling her soda with her straw. "I mean, I've had a few. Off and on. But they're kind of— How many guys have you dated through high school?"

"Two others," Rachael says. "Not sure if the first one counts. We only dated for a few weeks."

"Please. That's how long most of my relationships last! Why didn't they work out?"

"Oh, I don't know. The first guy was someone I had been friends with for years. I guess we got it into our brains it was a great idea to start dating when we got to high school. Bad idea, let me tell you, dating a friend."

At this, her gaze flicks to Chance and lingers. What the hell was that for?

"The other one I really liked, but he dumped me for someone else. Which crushed me at the time; he was a great kisser."

I don't know if Rachael is doing this on purpose to bother

me or to make me jealous, but it doesn't matter because it *doesn't*. At least, not for the same reasons it probably should. It only bugs me because it's one of those situations where I don't know if she's *trying* to get a reaction when I don't feel like giving one.

"That makes you lucky." Ash sighs, jabbing her salad with a fork, skewering a tomato and popping it into her mouth. "Anyone I've dated has been severely lacking in the kissing department."

My spine stiffens. Note to self: get a list of the boys my sister has been making out with and break their legs.

Chance, who I didn't think was even paying attention, doesn't look up when he says, "That's because I set the bar too high, being your first kiss and all."

Ash throws her head back and laughs. "I don't know. Hunt, how would you rate Chance's kissing on a scale of one to ten?"

My stomach flip-flops and I can feel my face burning. I'm going to crawl under the table. Maybe stab a fork into my jugular. Rachael can't stare at me with such intense horror if I'm bleeding all over the place, right?

The last summer we spent here—in fact, right around the time we raced at the mall—Dad dropped the three of us off at the lake for a few hours, armed with water guns, a raft, and some hot cinnamon buns from a snack bar up the road. At some point, the subject of Ashlin and a boy she liked at school came up, which led to talk of dates, then kissing…and Ash said, "I wouldn't know how to kiss a boy anyway."

"It's not like rocket science. Watch." Chance scooted over,

cinnamon bun in hand, and leaned in close. I tried to pretend I was more interested in blowing up the raft, but I watched them from the corner of my eye. Ash couldn't stop giggling nervously even as Chance pressed his mouth to hers.

It was only a moment later that Chance pulled away with a pleasant laugh. "See? Just like that."

Ash caught me looking, and my expression must've been less than impressed, because she blushed and pointed accusingly. "What're you staring at? It's not like you've ever kissed anyone."

"Yes, I have," I lied. In truth, I could have…if I'd wanted to. There was a girl in my English class who cornered me in the halls one day, told me she liked me, and leaned in for a kiss. She never got one. I panicked and ran away. So, by all technicalities, I *could have* and chose not to. That still counts.

"No, you haven't," Ash insisted. Chance took a slow bite of his cinnamon bun, polishing it off. I plugged the stopper on the raft, turning away, determined not to get into that argument because it would end with me either having to admit she was right or making up some lie that I would undoubtedly be found out on later.

I didn't see Chance coming. One second, I was preparing to head into the water, and the next—he was on me.

His body was wet from swimming, slick and cool against me, his chest to my chest. And his mouth caught mine, every inch insistent and eager. I couldn't think. Couldn't react. Couldn't form a coherent thought beyond the fact that his fingers were sticky where he grabbed my waist to hold me still, and he smelled like cinnamon. When his tongue slipped into my mouth, he tasted like it, too.

It was only when Ashlin squealed and clapped like we were putting on some kind of show that I thought to jerk back and did so, gasping. Chance grinned.

"There. Now you don't have to lie about it."

If there were ever a moment in my life I wish Ash hadn't witnessed, it was that.

And it dawns on me, as Chance is reaching over to steal one of my fries, that I wish Ash hadn't seen it. Not that it hadn't happened.

God. What is wrong with me?

"Wait a second." Rachael lowers her fork. She doesn't for a moment take her eyes off me. "You and Chance—"

"It was just a peck on the cheek," Chance interrupts with a curt laugh. "I was goofing around. Trying to embarrass him. Granted, it's not that hard to do."

Ash is looking between Chance and me around bites of her food, and her flat expression seems forced. Rachael is trying to smile, but her frown is overpowering it, and that means she isn't happy but she realizes she has no reason to blow this up into a bigger deal than it needs to be. I could kiss Chance for saving me.

No—no, I could hug him. That's safer. Yeah.

ASHLIN

Rachael's pissed off. Hunter is either oblivious or ignoring it.

Okay, maybe *pissed* isn't the right word. Maybe she's just…put off. Confused. Uncomfortable. I have no idea. But ever since Chance and Hunt made a scene at the mall and she and I had to walk through people who were muttering about the two idiots running like their pants were on fire, she's been awful quiet. The whole kissing conversation at lunch didn't help matters much.

"They always do stuff like this," I told Rachael, but I think my attempt to make it better made it worse. Hunter has always been the sort to goof around a little, especially when Chance is involved. Judging by Rachael's reaction, maybe he isn't entirely like that with her. Maybe the Hunter I'm used to isn't the same as the Hunter she knows. Hell, I'm sort of confused about how well I know Hunter anymore, too.

Because the Hunter I talked to through e-mail and phone and text from California may not have been the sort to gush about his relationship, but I know he cared about Rachael. I know they went on dates to eat sushi, usually with Rachael's parents, and they went to the movies or a museum a few times a month. It's definitely different than the things he, Chance, and I always did together, now that I think about it.

Chance is a big kid. Hunt and I know this. I'm not sure about my brother, but *I* like it. I'm not ready to grow up and be one of the so-called adults who stop doing all the fun things in life. Like having snowball wars or impromptu races in the most inappropriate locations. Or plotting adventures to secluded islands.

An adventure Chance hasn't forgotten about. When we swing by the only department store our town has to offer, a Kmart, it's to pick up snacks and sodas in preparation for a movie night. But Chance catches me by the hand and makes a beeline across the store to the sports section. More specifically, to their selection of rafts.

Standing there staring at the inflatable boats leaves my mouth a little dry from equal parts excitement and nervousness. We're *really* going to do this. We're going to paddle out to Hollow Island where, as far as we know, no one has set foot in years.

I've always sat back and watched Chance and Hunter challenging each other. They were the goofballs causing trouble and daring each other to do stupid things, while I acted as the referee on the sidelines. This will be one of the first times I've gotten to participate. I'll be a part of the real action.

A sudden thought dawns on me. "When are we doing this?"

Chance is crouched, peering at the product details on the side of a box. I hope he knows what he's looking for, because I sure don't. "Mm. I was thinking New Year's Eve. Wouldn't that be a cool way to celebrate at midnight?"

That's what I was afraid of. "Rachael goes home New Year's Day."

His expression doesn't change. He won't even look at me. "Then we'll take her with us."

I have a feeling Rachael will not be as gung ho about this idea. If mall races horrified her, then a midnight rafting trip to an abandoned island is sure to burst a blood vessel in her brain. Before I have a chance to say as much, Rachael and Hunt, pushing a cart of snacks and drinks, round the corner in search of us.

"You're looking at rafts?" Rachael asks. I wonder if she's still giving Hunt the ice-queen treatment. Judging from the tired set of his mouth, I'd wager yes.

"Uh huh."

"Why?"

"To go rafting," Chance answers with a vague undercurrent to his voice that sounds a lot like, *Duh.*

"Oh. All of us?"

Chance finally taps a box, communicates to Hunter with nothing more than a look, a tilt of his chin, and Hunt moves to help him lift the box into the cart. Two hundred bucks for a raft and oars. I would ask how Chance is affording this, but I don't think I've seen him spend much of his paychecks since he started working with me. He's likely been saving up.

"Of course we are," he says once the box is settled. It now takes both the boys to steer the cart to avoid crashing into anything. "New Year's Eve. We have to show you the best place in town before you leave, don't we?"

Rachael folds her arms loosely but says nothing. At least she isn't openly adverse to the idea, but then again, she doesn't know all the details. I really don't want to be the one to tell her. Which is why I try to keep at Chance's side, but my plan fails and Rachael manages to accost me somewhere near cosmetics when the guys get distracted looking for a line that isn't a mile long.

"Rafting?" she asks. "Hunter's never been rafting. Has he?"

"Don't think so." I bite my lip. Really, *really* don't want to have this conversation. But I guess if I tell her, I can try to make her see it's not as terrible of an idea as it sounds. "There's this island off the beach with a bunch of abandoned buildings and stuff. So we thought we'd raft out there and explore."

Rachael squints, mouth forming a small *O* as realization sets in. Her back stiffens, shoulders squaring. "We're…"

I catch her arm before she can march over to Hunter and say anything. "Look, Rachael, I know you're feeling a little out of place. But we just *do* stuff like this, and we've never gotten hurt. We've been hiking in the woods past dark, jumping from trees into lakes, and scaling cliff faces since we were kids.

We're still in one piece, aren't we? This is only a short rafting trip there and back, and there'll be four of us, so it's not like we're wandering into the wilderness alone, right?"

Her already thin mouth thins out farther. She isn't convinced, but she isn't saying anything, so I grapple blindly for some way to explain. "This is just...how it is. These have been our summers as far as I can remember. I know it's probably weird to someone who hasn't been around it, but Chance isn't just a friend. He's *family*, and we love him. But..." Deep breath. Take one for the team. "If you *really* aren't comfortable going rafting, I'll stay home with you. We can have a girls' night." The thought leaves me so unhappy I could cry. I've been looking forward to this trip, and the idea of being third wheel, the one left out, yet again...

Rachael turns back to the guys, who are almost to the checkout and are arguing over a pack of gum like five-year-olds. No, I guess Rachael wouldn't understand this. How comforting it is, how much fun we have, how much Chance means to us.

And I also know I've crammed her between a rock and a hard place. After calling Hunter out earlier on being kissed by Chance when we were younger, and seeing Rachael's reaction, I'm willing to bet she doesn't particularly want Hunter and Chance alone together. On an abandoned island, of all places. After my conversation with Chance last night, I'm not sure what I think about it, either. There isn't something going on between them, I know that much. At least...not physically. There's no way in hell either of them could keep something like that from me. Is it possible for Chance to have feelings for my brother? I can't rule it out. If he does, what about Hunter? I'm feeling so helpless, not knowing the answers and being too afraid to ask.

Where would that leave me?

Finally, Rachael sighs. "Maybe I'm jumping to conclusions."

"About what?"

"I don't know. I'm just being unfair and...jealous." She lets her arms drop to her sides. "I can give rafting a try. It'll be my last night with Hunter before I go home; I don't want to waste that."

I grin as the boys, impatient with our slacking behind, wave us over. When we catch up, Rachael links her arm with Hunter's and smiles.

· · ·

There's no way to explain the raft to Dad, so we keep it stashed in the trunk. Dad spent his free time growing up with unlimited access to creeks and beaches and hills with his friends, too, so he's pretty lenient as far as us running around and doing what we want. But even he would not be ecstatic at the idea of us paddling across a freezing ocean to get to an abandoned island where any number of injuries could occur.

It's easy to dull the excitement of our rafting trip when Christmas is around the corner. Rachael and I get our shopping done together and let the boys do their own thing. Rachael seemed reluctant at the idea, and I'm not sure if my feelings should be hurt or not. Logically speaking, I know it isn't that she doesn't like me, but that she wants the time with Hunter. Preferably without Chance around.

We hit the mall bright and early Tuesday morning after dropping Hunter off at work. Chance never came by, and he isn't scheduled to work today, so maybe it's one of the rare times he decided to stay home. Funny how it's stranger for him to be home than it is for him to be at our house every day.

For Chance, Hunter and I are pitching in together on a cell phone. It drives us nuts that we can't find him when we need to, so it seems logical. I plan on buying some new shirts for Dad. Maybe a few books. He's the only person I know in existence who reads Westerns, and I have a rocking employee discount.

For Hunter, I pick out a fancy box set of The Godfather series, which are his favorite movies. You'd think, being a guy, he'd be easy to shop for. Yet he isn't big on clothes, video games, or sports—unless his mom forces him to be—so that leaves a narrow selection of stuff he wants. Rachael eyes my purchase with a funny look on her face, mouth downturned, and I've honestly had about enough of her moping today. If she has something to say, she should say it.

Sighing, I hand over money to the cashier. "What's wrong?"

Rachael's gaze roams from the box set to my face and then off to nothing in particular. "I'm kind of envious."

Okay. Not the answer I was expecting. "Of what?"

She shrugs. "Even though you only see Hunter now and again, you seemed to know exactly what to get for him. I spent two months before his birthday looking for a present, and even then I don't think he liked it much."

I can't honestly remember Hunt telling me what he got

for his birthday. Which means, while he didn't *dislike* it, it certainly wasn't memorable or else he would've been excited to share. I'm not about to tell Rachael that, though; Hunter would never have wanted her to think he hated her present.

"I'm sure he loved it. He's a simple guy, you know? There aren't a lot of material things he wants." I pocket my change and take the bag, and we head out of the store. As much as it makes me inwardly groan and her sullenness gets on my nerves, I do feel bad Rachael is having a hard time here, and that she seems to genuinely care about Hunter and wants to do something nice for him, so— "Here." I hold out the bag.

Rachael stops, stares at it, frowns. "What?"

"Pay me back for this and give it to Hunt. I can find him something else."

"I couldn't do that, Ashlin." But she bites her lip, and I know she's considering it. I stand there with my hand outstretched, silent, until she reluctantly takes the bag from me with an embarrassed smile. "Only if you're sure…"

I'm a little disappointed, but she is right. I see Hunter pretty rarely, and yet when I find something he'd like, I know it immediately. I'm not going to admit to myself I'm feeling guilty. Even with her sulking and the tension between her and Chance, I know she's *trying*. I know she cares about Hunter, and sometimes I need to remind myself this is just as strange for her as it is for him. So I smile and shrug, nudging her with my elbow. "No worries. Come on; we still need to find a present for Dad."

HUNTER

Chance tears into his present with the fervor of a hungry lion ripping into a zebra. He has the bow stuck to the top of his head, a ribbon cascading down his forehead. You would think he'd have stayed at home last night to wake up and have Christmas with his parents. I mean, no matter how bad it is there, he's got to at least have a Christmas with them, right? He told me it didn't matter. He gets to spend every other Christmas at home, so he might as well enjoy this one with us. When he saw the Christmas tree this morning with the presents underneath, his eyes got so wide and his smile so big it broke my heart.

After pitching in for the raft and blowing a good chunk of money on movies, gas for driving around, and eating out, Ash and I couldn't afford the most amazing phone, but it'll serve its purpose. Chance gets the box free and stares at it, expression twisted up in confusion.

"It's a…?"

"A phone, genius. What's it look like?" I say.

"I get that." Chance's gaze flicks to me, then to Ash. Rachael's eyes are downcast, focused on the earrings she got from Ash. Should I have asked her if she wanted to go in on the phone with us? Chance begins prying open the box. "But…it's like, you know, I can't…"

"It's a pre-paid phone," Ash explains, abandoning her lapful of wrapping paper and crawling from the floor up to the couch beside him. "You pay for minutes as you need them. Way easier than a phone bill, 'cause you don't have to pay for minutes you don't use."

Chance hesitates then smiles. I let out a relieved breath.

"Can I use it to text you guys?" He unwraps the phone, handling it with care like he's never held something so delicate before.

"Sure can," I say.

"And since you won't get far without some minutes," Isobel pipes up, while Dad holds out an envelope. Chance takes it and flips open the tab. Inside are a handful of 100-minute cards. Not cheap, but given that Dad bought Ash a new camera and me a new laptop, I'd say he's been preparing for this.

Chance's smile widens. He loops an arm around Ash and crushes her against his side, planting a wet kiss on her forehead while she squeals and laughs. I can't tell if the affection bothers me or not. There's something so playful and innocent in the way he handles Ash that I'm not sure I have reason to get worked up about it. Chance then gets up and gives Dad and Isobel a hug, before setting his sights on me. And what can I do but grin when he throws himself at me, arms squeezing me tight, mouth against my cheek.

Except less my cheek and more my jaw.

An inch of difference that multiplies the intimacy of it tenfold.

A pleasant shiver jets straight down my spine. When he pulls back to sit down again, I can tell by the tense set of Rachael's shoulders that she saw, and it did not go unnoticed. I pretend not to see the way she's staring at me. It's Christmas. It's supposed to be a good day, and fighting with her over things she thinks she knows isn't how I want to spend it.

Things I think I'm starting to know, too. Things I haven't given a name and I don't want to. What's wrong with how everything is right now? Why does anything need to change?

• • •

Christmas dinner consists of cranberry sauce, honey-glazed ham, mashed potatoes, and salad, all compliments of Rachael. It might be the first time today that she looks happy. Even when she unwrapped the necklace I bought her—complete with her birthstone and name engraved—there was an absence of sincere joy on her face that made me think I completely screwed up in picking the gift. Chance warned me buying jewelry for a girl was a bad idea.

But Rachael is smiling now. Maybe because, for as long as we're sitting at the dining table, everyone's comments are focused on how delicious her meal is, and Rachael has always enjoyed being the center of a conversation. She blossoms under the attention. Got to hand it to the girl—she's a good cook. I'm not too bad a chef myself, but her stuff blows mine right out of the water.

Chance devours his food with hardly a word, and it isn't until after we're done and have cleaned up any stray pieces of ribbon and wrapping paper around the house that he announces it's about time for him to get home.

Immediately, I reach for my keys on the counter. "I'll drive you."

"I can walk," Chance insists, pulling on his coat. "Got this new jacket from Mr. J, and the phone you gave me, so I'm good and safe."

"Don't be ridiculous." Rachael dries her hands on a dishrag. "Have you looked out the window? The snow is coming down like crazy."

Chance opens his mouth to protest again, but Dad sets his coffee mug in the sink and gives him a reprimanding look. "You're not walking home, kid. I got y'all a car to avoid anyone being out in this weather."

That's all it takes. Dad might be the only person in existence Chance at least tries to listen to. His mouth snaps shut, and he gives a strained smile as he zips up his jacket. "Sure thing, Mr. J."

Ash stays behind to help Dad and Isobel with the remaining cleanup while Chance, Rachael, and I pile into the car and crank the heat up. Still haven't gotten around to buying a new stereo, so we listen to static-y radio stations along the way. Chance is silent in the backseat, staring out the window. It's times like these I wish I knew what was going on in that head of his. What flurry of thoughts is rattling around in his skull? Chance talks so much, but I always feel like for every word that comes out of his mouth, there are twenty more being kept hidden away under lock and key.

"Stop here," he says when we reach the edge of the trailer park. I ignore him, because it's still a bit of a walk to his doorstep and it's pitch black outside. I park just beside his house, taking note of the face peering out at us from the window. Not Mrs. Harvey, but Chance's dad. I see just the hard set of his jaw, his steely gaze zeroed right in our direction. The skin along the back of my neck prickles. Then the curtain swings shut, and Mr. Harvey disappears.

A moment later, as Chance is unbuckling, Rachael turns down the volume on the radio with a frown. "Do I hear someone yelling?"

Chance tucks his phone not into a pocket but into the waistband of his jeans. "Thanks for having me over. Great dinner, Rach." He shoves open his door and there is, most assuredly, yelling emanating from his house. "See you guys later."

He leaves us in silence, trekking through the snow up to his door where I see him square his shoulders and take a deep breath as though bracing himself before going inside.

I feel sick to my stomach leaving him behind. What if I went to the door and knocked? Asked him to come back with us? To come *stay* with us? Whatever is happening behind those walls, I have the most urgent sensation that I need to get Chance away from it.

But I don't know how.

You push Chance, Chance pushes back, and then he runs away.

"Hunter? Are we going?" Rachael asks.

My fingers flex against the steering wheel. Wordless, because I don't trust my voice, I turn the car around and head home.

ASHLIN

Hunter doesn't so much as say good night when he gets back. In fact, he's slipped upstairs before I even realize they're home. Rachael popping into the kitchen to see if I need help with anything is my only clue. I incline my head toward the sound of a door shutting upstairs. "What's his problem?"

Rachael shrugs. "I don't know. Something with Chance."

I set down my new camera instruction manual, frowning. "Did Chance say something?"

"No. We heard Chance's parents yelling when we dropped him off. Hunter hardly said anything the whole way home."

Oh. Well, yeah, that'd do it.

I smile wryly and look back down at the camera. "You're lucky he didn't jump out of the car and run in there. I'm actually surprised he didn't."

Rachael leans against the doorway, crossing her arms, lips pursed. "Why?"

What kind of question is that? "Because it's the sort of guy Hunter is. He's protective and…well." Shrug. "If it were me, Hunter would've stormed in there, grabbed me up, and stolen me away."

"Would he have done that with Chance if I hadn't been there?"

This is going somewhere, and I really don't want it to. These questions about Hunter and Chance… I lower the camera and raise my gaze. "If you're getting at something, then get to it."

Her jaw tenses. "Okay. I think Chance has a thing for Hunter."

"All right."

"And I'm not so sure it's unrequited."

A nervous laugh bubbles in my chest, and I fight it back. This isn't a conversation we should be having. I don't want to think about it. If Chance has feelings for Hunter, then he doesn't have feelings for me, and— "Hunter isn't gay."

"You don't have to be gay to like someone of the same sex, Ashlin."

"Point." I lace my fingers behind my neck. "Look…Hunter cares about you. He had you come out here for Christmas, to see his house, to meet his family, even though he was really nervous about it. That says a lot. If you don't trust him…"

Rachael pushes away from the door, shaking her head. Her voice is tight. "It isn't Hunter I don't trust."

I can't really defend Chance on that one. If there are some sort of feelings there, I don't trust him not to try something to win Hunter, either. Especially after how sad he looked and sounded that night in my bed. So…defeated. Chance never lets anything keep him down long. It's only a matter of time before he decides to do something about it—which likely means confronting Hunter.

"Are you two sleeping together?" I ask.

Rachael startles, pulling herself to standing up straight. "What?"

"You've been together for months. So I just assumed…" What would I know? I haven't had the opportunity to ask Hunter, and I'd sort of classified it under the topic of *Really Not My Business*. But for the sake of this conversation here and now—

"No," says Rachael.

That was unexpected. "Really?" I raise an eyebrow.

She shifts uncomfortably, voice a touch defensive. "I haven't exactly…approached him about it. Yet."

In some weird way, I'm glad for that. I don't think Hunter knows what the hell he wants with much of anything, and I don't pretend to fully understand what's going through his mind, since he won't talk about it, but I'm glad—at least—he hasn't done something stupid like sleep with a girl he isn't 100 percent about.

Which means I have no advice for Rachael. I can't encourage her to go for it, only to either pressure Hunt into something he doesn't want or to be rejected by him. So my only reply is another reassurance: "Hunter cares about you." Because he does. He never would have brought her out here otherwise.

Rachael nods. She tells me good night, then turns to leave.

I hear her steps retreating upstairs, and I think maybe I should have said something more to comfort her. Something along the lines of, *Hunter isn't interested in Chance, no way. They're just friends.* But there's a fine line between being encouraging to Rachael and not wanting to lie to her about things I'm unsure of.

Growing up, Chance and Hunter were closer than I was with either of them. They turned to me for some things, and they never excluded me, but I'm not blind. I've always been aware there was *something* there that brought the two of them together again and again while I was just along for the ride. I used to think it was a guy thing.

And, meanwhile, I was the girl who tagged along and thought that just maybe, one day, Chance would look at me like I was an actual girl. Like I was pretty, like I was interesting and maybe we could have something, just the two of us. He and Hunter shared something special. I wanted that with him, too. Something no one else had.

Now and again, I thought maybe we did. Like how he was my first kiss, or the way he looked at me the day he fished me out of the creek. It never occurred to me to pay attention to the way Chance looked at Hunter to see if their special something was precisely what I was wanting for myself.

I turn my camera back on, flipping through the images I took this morning. I have a single snapshot of Hunt and Chance, grins plastered on their faces, the stupid bow on Chance's head and another stuck to Hunter's cheek. They look so happy. Natural. Like this is the proper order of the universe and nothing else should matter.

So where do Rachael and I fit into all this?

Hunter

By the time we got back home, Isobel's car was gone from the driveway. The kitchen light was still on. I wasn't much in the mood to stay up and have a conversation with Ash or Dad, so I hung our coats and slinked upstairs without a word. Rachael didn't follow immediately, and I can only hope tonight will be a night we can both go straight to sleep without any of the awkward cuddling she's been using to hint that she wants something more.

I have a few minutes of quiet before she shows up, knocking lightly on my door. I had just enough time to get changed and convince myself I'm not driving back over to Chance's to kidnap him. It takes everything I have not to snap at Rachael to leave me alone. *Don't be a jerk, Hunter.* It's Christmas, and here I am trying to shrug off my girlfriend because—

I run my hands over my face and sit on the bed. "Come in."

Rachael cracks the door and slips inside. "Sorry. I was saying good night to your sister." She sinks down beside me. "Are you all right?"

"Yeah." My hands drop to my lap. I fall back onto the mattress, casting my gaze to the ceiling of stars. "I'm good. Just…you know."

"I'm sure Chance is fine. Sounded like his parents were having an argument, is all." She stretches out on her side next to me, propped up on an elbow. Her fingers brush the hair from my forehead, trace down the side of my face. My jaw has gone tense. She doesn't know a thing about Chance and his family; how could she make an assumption like that?

Precisely, I tell myself. She doesn't know because I haven't told her. I can't blame her for something she doesn't know.

"Christmas shouldn't end on a sour note." Rachael's hand continues downward, tickling my throat, collarbone, to my chest. "I was thinking…you know, since it's Christmas, maybe we could…"

I drop my gaze to Rachael. Given the hints she's been dropping, the fact that she's been sleeping in my bed without any invitation from me, I knew this was coming. But what do I do about it? I've run in circles inside my own head thinking of ways to say no without upsetting her. None of them have led anywhere.

"We could…?" Play dumb. Brilliant, Hunter. Way to grow a fucking spine.

Rachael narrows her eyes like she suspects I'm being

purposely difficult. She sits up a bit straighter, leaning over me. Her dark curtain of hair cascades over her shoulder and, God, she's so pretty.

"You know what I'm talking about. I know it was my idea to wait in the first place, and I just thought…maybe now is a good time."

I fold my hands behind my head. "What changed?"

She blinks slowly. "What?"

"What changed between now and the last time when you said you weren't ready?" Which was…jeez, had to be seven months ago. I tried once, and only once, and Rachael saying it wasn't the right time for her was all it took for me to back off. I wasn't about to be one of those guys who make it out to be some big deal. Besides that, a part of me had been almost relieved.

Sighing, Rachael sits up, running her hands through her long hair. "That was ages ago. We'd only been dating a few months. It's been a year now and… I've already told you, Hunter. I love you. I want this thing with us to last for a really long time."

"And in order for that to happen, we need to have sex?" An amused twitch pulls my lips up into a smile. Wrong move, if the way Rachael's eyes narrow is any indication.

"If this is *funny* to you, I can leave."

"No, no. It's…" I shove myself back up to sitting with a groan so I can take Rachael's hands in mine. I'm trying to imagine what Ashlin would coach me to say, because I have no clue. "Babe, I'm really touched. But if you aren't one hundred percent into it—"

Rachael squeezes my hands. "I *am* ready, Hunter! I *have* been. Being away from you all this time made me realize that." Then her grip loosens. I don't know what it is she sees in my expression—whether it's fear or nervousness or the uncertainty I'm battling to keep in check—but whatever it is, it isn't good, and I have the gut feeling this is a conversation that isn't going to end well.

Her hands leave mine. "But you aren't ready at all, are you?"

I'm at a loss. My mouth is open but words aren't coming out, because there's nothing I can say. There is no appeasing her this time. Instead, I'm left staring at her like a moron, with no excuses left.

Rachael shakes her head. She stands. "Is there someone else? If there is—"

"There's no one else. What other girls have you seen me talk to, Rach?"

She levels a narrow glare in my direction but says nothing.

I owe her an explanation, don't I? Even if it's hard, I have to figure out the best way to explain to my girlfriend what's going on in my head. Had she done this four, five months ago, I could have—would have—gone through with it. So…what's the problem now?

You know what the problem is. Chance, Chance, Chance.

"Okay. You know…you're right." I spread my hands, palms up, helpless. "I'm not ready for this. Things have been strained since you got here, and I feel like this is your way of trying to…"

"Trying to *what*?"

"Trying to…reconnect, I guess." Sigh. This talking thing is not my strong point. Rachael is good at taking things the wrong way. That's something that makes Ash and Chance special to me: I can tell them anything, and they can figure me out even if I articulate things about as well as a goldfish.

Rachael uncrosses her arms. Good sign? But then she puts her hands on her hips. Bad sign. "I told you, I was thinking about this before I even came out here. And the only reason things have been strained is because I've had to fight just to get a few hours alone with you. Everywhere we go, Chance and Ashlin are right there with us."

"Because that's so different from us going out with all your friends or family tagging along back home?" I reply hotly. "In the three months before I left, I can count on one hand the number of times you and I did something alone."

"You told me you *liked* my friends and family!"

"What, and you don't like Ash and Chance?"

She rolls her eyes to the ceiling. "You know I like Ashlin just fine…"

Ah ha. "But you don't like Chance."

"It's not that I don't like him, he's just…" Her hands flutter about, a sign she's getting flustered because now she's having trouble finding the right words. "He's so… He's like a kid, Hunter. Like the kind of boy who wants to pretend to be sixteen forever. He'll be happy living with his parents, working at Lotsa Books for minimum wage, and running around town getting into trouble."

The more she talks, the less I want to look at her. I stare down at my hands in my lap, tension coiling under my skin and making my neck and shoulders ache. "Don't talk about Chance like you know him."

"He's unpredictable and, frankly, sometimes he makes me nervous. He's the kind of guy you hear about in the news shooting up his school. Am I wrong?"

My mouth slips into an unpleasant smile. She isn't wrong, no. Chance is impulsive and childlike, and after realizing his home life was nothing like what he told us, it's hard to know when what he's saying to me is true or not. Yet none of that matters. Chance is Chance, and he's important, and I won't sit back while Rachael pretends like she knows the inner workings of his mind when even *I* don't. "Yeah. You really, really are. Because you don't have a clue what he's going through at home right now, or how his father probably beats the hell out of him, or how Dad had to buy him a jacket for Christmas because his own parents didn't bother. And you have no idea how guilty I've been feeling that, all these years, Chance has been going through this completely alone because I was too stupid to see the signs.

"So, sure, maybe he acts like a big kid and he could stand to grow up some, but he has a reason for it. Maybe *you* could stand to not act like such an uptight old lady once in a while."

She presses her mouth together thinly. "I thought that's what I was trying to do just now."

"And I'm saying it's not a good time for me, Rachael, okay?" There. That's what it comes down to, isn't it? That I don't want to, and— "When you told me no, I backed off. I said it was cool and didn't push it. Why is it all right for you to make *me* feel like crap for saying no? Because that's a pretty shitty double standard. Girl should only have sex when she's ready; guy should have sex when girl says so."

Rachael opens her mouth, but I can see I've gotten her. "Hunter, I'm—"

"Don't apologize." I shrug, willing myself to look at her even though I don't want to. "I'm sorry I've been...distant or whatever. We'll spend tomorrow alone if you want. I'll take you out to lunch and a movie."

"Like a good old-fashioned date?" She lifts her gaze to me, lips tilted in a faint smile.

The pain in my back slowly seeps away as the tension does. What is going on with us? Back home, things weren't this bad. When Rachael and I started out, we had fun. We laughed. We talked about nothing important. I miss that friendship. More than that, I miss when everything between us didn't feel like such an effort, when every conversation wasn't about our future while we were never living in the here and now.

Could this be my fault? Am I not trying hard enough? Has my attention really been so focused on Chance and Ashlin that I haven't been giving us a fair shot? I can't be happy with myself until I try. She's only here for a bit longer, and during that time...I should—no, I *need*—to give her more of my attention.

I reach for her hands, brushing my thumbs across her knuckles. "Sure. It's a date."

ASHLIN

Chance makes good use of his phone. He texts me bright and early every morning, which might annoy me because I like my sleep-in time, but he's saved me from being late to work more than once.

I want to ask him about Hunter. After talking to Rachael and thinking about it incessantly, I can't get it out of my head that there might be something between Chance and my brother. Hunter would undoubtedly get defensive and awkward. Not that Chance is a pro at being open and honest, but I feel like…maybe talking to him about it would make him feel better. Maybe it would make *me* feel better, too.

Maybe I really am imagining all of this. And then I think it's just my way of trying to avoid being heartbroken that the boy I want to be with might never have wanted me to begin with.

Instead of asking about Hunter, I try to bring up the subject of Christmas night and his parents' yelling that Rach and Hunt witnessed, but he brushes me off easily and avoids me the rest of our shift. How do you talk to someone who always runs away?

Otherwise, we manage to truck through the week with minimal drama. I try to keep Chance occupied so Rachael gets her time with Hunter. Which would work great, except Hunter himself seems put off by the idea of Chance and me always hanging out on our own. He doesn't complain, and he takes Rachael out several times just the two of them, but I can see the protest in his eyes, which means Rachael can surely see it, too. There's a sort of underlying tension in Hunter's demeanor toward Rachael now that wasn't there before. It isn't the same as his nervousness when she first arrived. Now, I think he's genuinely unhappy and something must have happened. When I try to ask him about it, he only shrugs me off.

There is so much being unsaid among everyone, and it's driving me crazy.

Come New Year's Eve, I'm almost unsure about this whole rafting trip. We're going to be stuck on a flimsy piece of inflatable plastic, needing to work together to get to Hollow Island, and then we'll be secluded and with no distractions but one another for who knows how long.

Almost unsure. But not enough to call the whole thing off.

The cold is biting. We bundle up and promise Dad we'll be safe—just going to a party with some friends in town. A lie I'm not sure he totally buys, but we're eighteen. He can't do much other than give us worried looks as we leave. He has Isobel for company tonight, and she loops her arm with his and gives us a wave as our car pulls out of the driveway. He'll be just fine.

Hunt drives us to the beach. It's a farther row from here than it would be from our cliff-side location, but the water is calmer, and getting the raft (not to mention Rachael) up and down the cliffs would be impossible. The wind yanks at my coat. Snowflakes skip and dance across the rocky beach while we struggle to get the raft out of its box and blown up. It doesn't look nearly as secure as I thought it did in the store, but you get what you pay for.

Chance pulls from the car a cooler where we packed drinks and snacks, and where my camera is tucked alongside a couple of flashlights into a plastic bag to keep it from getting wet. Rachael huddles in her baby-blue coat and mittens, worrying at her bottom lip.

"Are you sure that thing's safe?"

"We'll find out," Chance says, and with a grunt he begins hauling it to the water with Hunter's help.

"Is it *big* enough?"

"Box says it holds up to four people. We'll make it work. If you don't wanna go…"

Rachael shoots Chance a hard look, brushes the hair from her face, and stalks after them. It would seem her last few days of having Hunter to herself have boosted her confidence, because she hasn't been tolerating his sass today, and she hasn't been shy about keeping at Hunter's side every moment she gets.

Getting the raft afloat and all of us into it requires rolling up pants, yanking off shoes, and wading into the freezing cold water. After a few minutes of flailing and splashing and shrieking, we manage to pile into the raft. The waves threaten to shove us back onto the rocks, but with some careful maneuvering and lots of shouting, Hunter and Chance get us going in the right direction.

The farther from shore we get, the easier it is to row. But it's cold. Unbearably cold. The wind stings my face and my hands, even through my gloves. I keep my arms wrapped around the cooler, not wanting a wave to roll beneath us and knock it right out of the raft.

I have no idea how long it takes, only that by the time we bump against the craggy shore of Hollow Island, our teeth are chattering and the boys are out of breath. We drag the raft up shore, tucking it and the ores behind part of a crumbling brick wall where the water doesn't have a chance of sweeping up and stealing it away. Then we stand there and stare at the dark island before us, breathing hard. Shivering but triumphant.

"Look the same as when you swam here last?" Hunter asks Chance, elbowing him with a grin.

"What?" Chance blinks, rolls his eyes, gives him a shove, and ventures forward. "Shut up and come on. Get the flashlights!"

I haul the cooler while the others get the flashlights, the only three we could find because no one thought about actually needing them until an hour before we left home. Kudos to us.

The island smells of salt and dirt. All around us are buildings barely standing, torn down in a relatively short time thanks to the onslaught of harsh wind and the waves eating at the shores. They're all condemned, meaning the island itself is legally off-limits. The threat of fines, I'm sure, is only a small deterrent for anyone who really wants to come out here, but I didn't see any other boats on the shore. It's safe to assume we're alone.

Chance veers into one old building that is missing a wall but is otherwise in relatively decent shape, and I set the cooler down before following. A set of wooden steps once led up to the porch but is gone now. Hunter grabs my upper arms and lifts me over the steps to the porch, which creaks in protest beneath my weight, before turning to do the same to Rachael.

She tucks her hands under her arms, shaking her head. "I'll wait here."

Hunter frowns. I see his mouth working like he might argue, but he only says, "Okay," hops onto the porch, and moves past the door hanging on one lonely hinge.

"Maybe we should've saved this for next weekend," I whisper to Hunter. Chance is picking his way across the floor, checking for holes, easing his weight when he steps so the rotting wood doesn't give way under him. Hunter's eyes follow his every movement, almost worriedly.

"No. I offered last night to stay home with her if she didn't want to go. She insisted we should do it. If she wants to mope all night, then whatever. I'm not going to let it ruin our time."

Fair enough. Hunter and I both gave her an out, and she chose not to take either. I shake my head and roll my shoulders back, just as Chance is calling us over to look at the remnants of some old machinery across the room.

We explore the place top to bottom. Well, maybe not *top*, because the stairs to the second floor are ruined, and Hunter refuses to give Chance a boost. Nothing here feels sturdy. Nothing feels safe. That's part of what makes it exciting.

And, man, is it awesome. I fish out my camera and take pictures of everything. Chance poses in the corner, back to the lens, head down, like something out of a horror movie. I get shots of caved-in ceilings, missing walls, the places where nature has encroached in on the man-made structures to take them back where they belong. Grass and weeds poke through the floorboards. Cobwebs floating from the eaves catch my hair and shoulders, tugging at me like ghostly fingers.

We move from one building to the next, getting bolder with the weak architecture and braving the stairs in some to look out through second-story windows, shuffling through broken glass and the occasional reminder that, yes, people used to live and work here. A scrap of material that might've been a sock. Some papers pinned beneath a rock that have long since yellowed and lost their ink.

Through it all, Rachael stays out in the open, sitting atop the cooler and watching us. When we move farther into the island, she picks up the cooler and drags it along, sets it back down, and sits again. I don't know whether or not to feel bad for her. Maybe annoyed she's being such a drag. Maybe bad that it must be so boring to be her.

After losing my camera to Chance and letting him snap a shot of Hunt and me outside a lopsided structure, Chance announces we've got thirty minutes until midnight. Toward the center of the island, we locate the most intact building. A tall, red brick structure, just like Chance told us there would be. He only could have known about it if he had, in fact, been here before. I stop just outside, turning to glance at Hunter, who looks from the building to me with an expression as surprised as I feel.

The surrounding buildings have likely shielded it, so it's stayed upright a little better, enough that we can actually head upstairs, watching for any broken steps. This time, Hunter manages to prod Rachael into tagging along. She cringes the whole way up, clinging to Hunter's arm, and I'm worried they're both going to drop right through the floor because she won't let him go.

On the roof, we have a picture-perfect view of the island around us. Granted, it's dark, so we only have the vague outline of trees and buildings here and there, lined with snow, and the glistening of the ocean. Maybe we'll be able to see one of the New Year's fireworks shows on the mainland in the distance.

We're miles away from existence, and it's so beautiful.

HUNTER

There aren't words to describe it. The island is desolate, lonely, eerie, but it has an ethereal charm to it. Hauntingly beautiful in its solitude.

Chance and Ash agree, but Rachael obviously does not. All night, she's given me strained smiles when she catches me looking. Tired sighs and weary scowls when she thinks I'm not. But what can I do? Since our argument on Christmas, I've really tried spending time with Rachael and Rachael alone. We've gone to a few movies, shopping, sightseeing.

It's been the most *boring* couple of days since I returned to Dad's.

Even last night, I grudgingly gave her the option to stay home with me, and she insisted she wanted to give it a try. *Brave the crazy adventures of the Jacksons and their fearless leader, Chance.* Her exact words, even. But the tone of her voice when she said Chance's name was enough to tell me things aren't as okay as we're both trying to pretend they are.

Now that we're here, I can tell she's not enjoying it. She greets everything on the island with a look of wary disdain, as though she's better than this place, like touching anything or taking a risk for once in her life might result in her untimely demise. I only manage to talk her into coming into the red building (Chance told the truth about coming here before; color me surprised) because: "We're going to eat on the roof if it's steady enough." In other words, she can come along, or she can ring in the New Year all by herself.

Rachael takes a step back, eyes the structure with her mouth drawn tight, but reluctantly allows me to pull her inside. How can she not love this? The view is stunning. The smell of the ocean and the feel of the salt-tinged air every time a breeze happens by. It's the perfect way to spend New Year's, and Rachael seems determined to not enjoy a second of it.

"This is our castle," Chance says as he stands at the edge of the rooftop, too close to the ledge for comfort. "This is our kingdom. How fucking amazing is it?"

"Pretty fucking amazing," Ash and I say together.

Rachael stares down at her shoes. "I thought we were going to eat? It's almost midnight."

I glance at my phone. It's 11:50, yep. "Where's the cooler?"

"I thought Rachael had it," Ash says.

"I left it downstairs. It was too heavy for me to drag up here by myself."

I give Chance's jacket sleeve a tug to draw him away from his self-induced trance as he gazes out over the island. "Come on, your highness. Your loyal subjects are hungry."

Chance swivels around and latches onto my arm, grinning like this is the best thing he's heard all evening. We leave the girls behind and pick our way back down the rickety staircase. When I spot the cooler just outside the door, I heave a sigh of relief. "Still there."

"Where the hell would it have gone? The island spirits sleep on holidays, you know." He hefts up one handle while I grab the other. It isn't heavy, really—more awkward and ungainly to maneuver. We didn't pack anything in ice; it's cold enough outside, so why would we need to? It was more a precaution to keep everything dry rather than cold.

"Five minutes to midnight," I announce as we head up to the second floor. "Let's get a move on or we'll never hear the end of it."

"Oh!" Chance stumbles, his side of the cooler going down. "My legs. My poor, poor legs. I don't think I can walk another step. All that rowing has crippled me." He sinks to the floor, the back of a hand pressed to his forehead.

I laugh and set my end down, too. "Come on. Seriously. We only have a few minutes."

Chance's expression sobers. "Until what?"

"Until midnight, genius."

"And at midnight, what's the ritual? You're supposed to kiss the person you want to be with the next year or something?" He studies me, and I can't make my voice cooperate, so I only stare back. Chance *hmm*s. "In that case...I'm right where I want to be."

I'm not laughing anymore. In fact, every one of my gut instincts is telling me I ought to be dashing up those stairs right now, cooler be damned. I should be there with Rachael.

So why am I still standing here, staring at him dumbly like I have no idea what he's talking about? Like we haven't been dancing around something neither of us has named ever since we came back into each other's lives?

No, longer than that. Even back when we were kids. When he kissed me. When he slept in my bed and I'd wake up to his hand on my chest, his head on my shoulder. On Christmas, when his lips brushed my jaw in that little intimate way, like it was a secret just for us.

My throat is dry. This big, empty, decaying room feels too small for the two of us and everything we have not said or done.

"We should go…"

Chance gets to his feet and steps not over the cooler, but onto it, putting him several inches taller than me. My eyes are level with his chest. His hands brace against my shoulders. This is something I need to run from. And I can't. I can't, I can't.

Chance asks, "What time is it?"

It takes everything for me to pull out my phone so we can both see the screen. It's 11:59. Chance nods.

"Acceptable," he says, prodding my face to look up at him. Then he kisses me.

I saw it coming. I knew it would happen. Yet I'm stunned into silence, into stillness, with any capability I ever had of rational thought right out the door. His mouth is soft and his lips are salty from the ocean air, and even if they're cold, his tongue is warm, and a hundred thousand memories of summers long past come rushing back all at once.

Chance, with a broken arm, trying to wade around in the creek while keeping his cast above water, until I scooped him up and let him ride on my shoulders.

The three of us dressing up, makeup and all, to perform plays for Dad.

Lying out beneath the stars while Chance recites stories we've heard a hundred times and still love.

Chance, going on about how his parents are rich, how they love him, how he has plans to attend a fancy college in Greece—or London, or Rome, or Japan—after high school.

Chance, pointing out the constellation of Draco and telling me, *Dragons don't kidnap princesses or set fire to villages. They're noble. Honorable. Worshipped, in many countries. Dragons protect.*

I think of the constellation on his back while my hand touches it through his shirt, and I wonder if he had that in mind when he got it. Dragons protect. Something secret and hidden to protect him when he needed it most, because nothing else could.

Then I hear something overhead. A laugh. A shout. Whooping and hollering and *Happy New Year* and I remember the world isn't about Chance and me. There's a girl upstairs I should be kissing at midnight. Not this boy, who keeps his secrets locked away so carefully, who lies about stupid, little things just because he can, and who breaks my heart every time he does.

I jerk away, not knowing if I'm more horrified with him for kissing me, or me for kissing back, even if only for a moment.

"You shouldn't have done that," I manage, taking two, three, four steps away. "Why did you... I have a *girlfriend*."

Chance's expression darkens. "Oh, please."

"I *do*." My voice cracks.

"You aren't in love with her."

"You don't know that!"

He crosses his arms and hops off the cooler. "Are you?"

I open my mouth. Close it again. Rachael is someone I care about. Someone I'd never want to hurt. On Christmas, it dawned on me just how badly my lack of *trying* had been hurting her, so I was putting forth the effort. Trying to reconnect. Trying to rediscover what it was that made me decide I wanted to date Rachael to begin with.

Or did I never want to, and I've gotten tired of pretending?

"It's none of your business, Chance. Either way, I'm still her boyfriend, and I'm not going to—"

He cuts me off with a sharp, bitter laugh. "You're a shitty boyfriend, is what you are. Pretending to care more than you do when you're secretly pining after someone else."

God, I want to hit him. "I've worked really, *really* hard for this relationship. I'm not going to screw it up now."

"Why, though?" He drops his arms to his sides, gesturing around us. "That's what I want to know. Is it because she's pretty? Good in bed? *Why* are you so eager to keep this going?"

"Because it's *normal*," I snap. "Okay? It's fucking *normal* because everything else in my life has been so *not* normal. Do you have any idea how weird it is to explain half the things that have gone on in my life? The fact I've got a half sister my exact age because my dad cheated on my mom and had a one-night stand? How that little family arrangement has worked out all these years? Why I act like the head of the household at home, because Mom and Boyfriend Bob are too busy drinking and being wrapped up in themselves?"

I've hated it. I hate being at home with Mom. It isn't that she doesn't love me; it's that she feels she's paid her dues to the world and shouldn't have to *do* anything anymore. On the rare occasions I made friends, I never had them over to the house because Mom always found it appropriate to share with them our family history. She would introduce Boyfriend Bob and make sure to confirm, *Oh, he's not Hunter's real dad… His real dad is a lying cheat.*

And just because she and Boyfriend Bob aren't *angry* drunks doesn't mean a goddamn thing. They're still drunks. Mom still wakes me up at all hours of the night to chat my ear off, then kicks me out of bed early because she's too hungover to make breakfast or go to the store.

"Or how about when people ask me why I've never had a girlfriend before I started seeing Rachael?" I continue. "Up until I met her, Mom and Bob would hound me about never having an interest in girls. Because I kept thinking—"

No. That's where I stop myself. Before I say something I'll regret. Something I can't take back. Rachael and Ash are going to come looking for us, and I don't want to be found standing here like this, in the heat of an argument.

Chance is watching me with a subdued sort of expression,

as though none of this surprises him. Which pisses me off further. Don't I get to keep any secrets from him? He has a million, so why can't I have a few? Yet he looks at me as though he can see under my skin, see every muscle and bone and exposed nerve that makes me tick, and it's not fair. "Hunter, I—"

I hold up a hand. "Don't. Whatever you're going to say, just...don't."

Chance draws in a deep breath. He picks up the handle for the cooler. I almost tell him to stop standing there and *say something*, except I just told him to stop talking, so that isn't going to work. Instead, I snatch the other handle, and we carry the cooler up the stairs in silence while I try to lick away the taste of him on my mouth.

Back on the roof, Chance drops the cooler immediately, leaving me to cart it the rest of the way over to the girls. Ash spins around to face us, smiling. The brief, questioning flicker across her features tells me she knows something is wrong, but when she mouths, *You okay?* I only nod and flip open the cooler lid to dig out a soda.

"Thought you two got lost," Rachael says. She startles me by looping her arms around my neck and planting a firm, warm kiss against my mouth. She's never kissed me in public before. Though I would have thought she'd be annoyed I wasn't here when the clock struck twelve.

I wish she'd waited, at least until Chance and Ash weren't looking. Because Chance has the most wounded, bitter glint to his eyes, and when I awkwardly kiss Rachael back, all I can picture is Chance stepping onto that cooler and me realizing what he was about to do.

But I don't pull away from Rachael. Maybe because I know it took her a lot to be able to do this in front of others. Or because I'm trying to prove a point to Chance—and myself. *This* is normal. *This* is where I belong. I may not be in love with Rachael, but I trust her to be honest. Isn't that what matters most?

Once the excitement of the New Year has ebbed, we dig into our food then stretch out on our backs to stare at the sky. I've never had as clear a view of the stars as we do here. There are no trees in the way like at Dad's house. No smog and pollution. Just us, the ocean, and billions upon billions of stars. When Chance begins telling us his stories about the constellations, when he looks in my direction, I swear every one of those stars is reflected in his eyes.

"It's so lonely," Rachael murmurs from beside me.

This statement breaks Chance out of his trancelike storytelling state, his gaze sharpening as it snaps to Rachael. "What does that mean?"

She sits up. "It's just, I mean, they're so beautiful, but they're so far away. Isn't it lonely to think how big the universe is and how displaced we are from it?"

Chance's stare could burn a hole through metal. I should say something about the look he's giving her—as if she's ruining everything—but I haven't spoken a word to him since we got back up here, and I don't intend to change that.

He says, "If that's how you think, then you're looking at it all wrong."

Of course she's wrong. Everyone who doesn't agree with

Chance is wrong, aren't they?

"Okay, then," Rachael says. "Enlighten me on how I should be looking at it."

Chance turns, pulling the hood of his jacket over his messy hair. He steps up to the edge of the rooftop. I have that natural instinct to reach out and grab his sleeve to drag him back, worried he'll slip and fall.

"It's true," he begins, "that the universe is this big, vast thing, and humans will probably never explore even a tiny fraction of it. But that doesn't mean we're alone or we're displaced from it. All these elements, everything around us, the building blocks of the Earth and life—even the very air you're breathing—originated from those stars. We're a part of them. Orion, Draco, Sirius…they're a part of us, too."

Just like that, I can't keep my eyes off Chance. Even Rachael is momentarily entranced, looking bewildered and amazed all at once.

I can't help thinking about it, how we could've all come from different stars, light-years away. Wondering, maybe, if Chance and I came from the same star. If that's what they mean when two people feel they've known each other in a past life.

No, not in a past life—but that the building blocks of one person's existence could have originated right alongside that of another's.

I wonder if that's why I can't seem to shake him. Why so much of my life has been focused on someone like him.

"So we're all made of stars," I murmur. So much for not opening my mouth.

Chance twists around, a sad smile on his face as his eyes meet mine. "We're all made of stars," he agrees. "We burn bright, then we flicker away."

ASHLIN

We stay on the rooftop for another three hours, until the food is gone and we've made ourselves hoarse trying to hold conversations in the cold. Maybe we should've thought ahead and brought blankets or something, because it didn't dawn on us that being as freezing as we are would make the rafting trip back to shore all the more difficult. But we manage it. We're on solid ground again, fighting to deflate the raft enough that it can be crammed into the trunk along with the oars and cooler.

It's nearly four in the morning when we return home, and I've convinced Chance to stay at our place rather than try getting back to his place.

He's being quiet.

No, more than that, he and Hunter are ignoring each other. They played it off normally and talked on the rooftop, but thinking back, they didn't really talk to *each other*. Just to Rachael and me. What happened in those minutes they were gone? I can't ask until I get Chance alone.

Inside, Chance watches Rachael and Hunt retreat down the hall and into Hunter's room as though he'll never see them again. He doesn't say good night. I catch him by the arm and drag him into my room.

"Okay," I say, balancing on one leg while peeling off my damp socks. "Spill it."

Chance casts one last forlorn look at the door before giving me his attention. "What?"

I grab some pajamas and toss them to the bed. I need to change. My clothes smell like seawater and salt. Frankly, I want a shower, but that can wait until morning. "You two vanished."

"We were getting the cooler." He starts undressing. He still has a pair of sweats and a T-shirt in my closet from the last time he stayed over. In fact, I think they're Hunter's. Hunter has lost a good chunk of his clothing to Chance over the years. I don't think Hunter minds, though, and Dad's never said anything about it.

"And when you came back, you would hardly look at each other. Not to mention the death-glares you kept giving Rachael all night."

Chance pauses. Which is pretty funny-looking, given he's halfway through pulling off his shirt and it's still stuck on his head. His shoulders rise and then fall with a deep breath. He balls up his shirt and tosses it to the foot of the bed, not turning around.

"Why are you so worried about it? What do you want to know, Ash? Maybe you should talk to him about this. He's the one not right in the head."

"I want to know what's going on between you two," I say.

Chance groans, pushing a hand through his hair. "I kissed him. All right? I kissed him, and he wasn't happy, and that was that."

"You…" Deep breath, while I give myself a second to wrap my head around that. Chance and Hunter. And kissing. I shouldn't be surprised, and yet…my heart hurts. "He has a girlfriend. Why would you put him in that position?"

"How funny, he said the same thing." Chance casts me a wry smile over his shoulder. "But you know what he didn't say in all of his 'No, Chance, bad dog' lecture?"

"What?"

"He never said he didn't feel the same way."

I'll be the first to admit, there is a lot in what Hunter says. There is even more in what he *doesn't* say.

"Okay," I murmur, unsure what to make of that. Unsure what to make of any of this, frankly. Just because I'd pieced it together doesn't mean I've made sense of my feelings on it. Chance has a thing for Hunter. It's a safe bet to say Hunter has a thing for Chance, too. How humiliated would I have been if I'd told Chance how I felt about him, not realizing the truth of things?

When I look at it from a distance, the idea completely baffles me. But when I look at it closer up, at all the little details, the stars that form the constellation, as Chance would say, suddenly…it all makes sense.

How could I not have noticed it years ago?

Sure, I was always included, but Chance and Hunter were the inseparable ones. Chance, who always wanted to go everywhere Hunter did. Chance, who always showed off the most when he knew Hunter was watching. Chance, who kissed Hunter that day at the beach as a joke, then spent the rest of the day staring at him like nothing else existed in the world. Chance orbits Hunter like the planets orbit the sun, aching to be closer but never daring.

Until now, I suppose.

Chance braces his hands on the wall on either side of the window and stares outside. My gaze is drawn to a dark, purpled bruise on the back of his arm. "He doesn't trust me."

I step up behind him. When I wrap my fingers around his bicep, my thumb covers the finger-shaped bruise almost perfectly. The mark of someone grabbing him, and grabbing hard. Maybe to yank him around. A bruise slightly larger than my thumb, so a hand bigger than mine. Beneath my touch, Chance's muscles tense, a reaction so quick it can only be reflex.

I ask, "Why don't you ever talk about your parents?"

"I have talked about them." He lets his arms drop to his sides, sounding perplexed by the change of subject. Except it's not *really* a subject-change if we're talking about trust, is it?

"You told us your mom was a researcher and your dad played a minor role in politics, and they traveled all the time."

"So?"

"So, I've seen your mom, Chance. She's no researcher." I'm not even sure she was sober when we saw her, but I won't point that out. I can already tell by the detached tone of his voice, the distant gaze, that I'm about to lose him in this conversation completely. "If there's something going on at home, you have to know Hunt and I are here for you. So is Dad, for that matter. Nothing is going to change that. But how can we trust you when you never tell us the truth?"

"I do tell the truth."

"Like what? Like about your house? Or how your parents were sending you out of the country for college? Their jobs? How you weren't allowed to keep in touch with us?"

"We did live in a bigger house," he says defensively, all but ignoring everything else I pointed out. "We lost it two years ago."

I want to believe him, but why has he lied about anything? Just because he doesn't have a *reason* to lie doesn't mean he's telling the truth. "Okay. What about the rest?"

Chance walks away then sinks onto the edge of my bed. He picks up my camera—the old one—from the nightstand and turns it over in his hands with the utmost delicacy.

"Can I borrow this?"

I have half a mind to rip the camera out of his hands and throw it. At him, maybe. *"Chance."*

"Just for a few days? It'll come back in one piece. Promise. You have the new one now." He nods at my Christmas camera on the desk.

Frustrated, I turn his face back to look at me in an attempt to get his full attention again. "The point I was trying to make is that the only person who can cause Hunter not to trust you is *you*. But a few less secrets couldn't hurt. Maybe if you opened up to him some, tried being honest for a change, it'd make things a lot easier all around."

Chance lifts his chin, narrows his eyes in a most thoughtful manner that makes me think that maybe he's back on the same track as I am. Except he says, "So, can I borrow it?"

I've lost him. Completely and utterly. We're having entirely separate conversations, and he isn't even listening to mine. I sigh, shoulders slumping. "Yeah, Chance. Do whatever you want."

January

HUNTER

My morning is spent trying to help Rachael pack, until she tells me I'm making a mess of her attempt at organizing and shoos me away. I sit on the bed and watch instead, trying to make heads or tails of how I feel about her leaving. I think I'll miss her, and yet I'm relieved at the same time. It's been stressful trying to take one life and mash it together with another. I can't help but wonder if Rachael is at all glad to be going back to school.

I want to tell her Chance kissed me, but I don't know how to get the words to leave my throat. Maybe I don't have to tell her. Maybe it's better that I never say anything because it isn't going to happen again, and it would only hurt her in the long run. In this case, would ignorance be bliss? We're having enough problems as it is.

When her suitcase is zipped up, Rachael lets out a big breath and turns to me, smiling. "Well. There we go. All packed." She slides into my lap. "I'm going to miss you."

"You sure about that?" I wind an arm around her waist reflexively. "You haven't been enjoying yourself much."

She sighs. "It's not that I haven't enjoyed myself, it's just… You know. This is a lot different than how we spent time back home."

Back home. Yeah. Back home, the big difference between here and there is that *there*, our lives revolved around her. What she wanted to do. Who she wanted to hang out with. It's no wonder she was unhappy up until the days she and I spent alone—doing what she wanted to do.

I stare at her without saying a word. Rachael's dark eyes narrow thoughtfully. "You haven't seemed so thrilled having me here, either, you know."

"It's not that. It's just…" A wry smile tugs at my mouth. "Different."

Rachael cups my face in her hands. Her skin always smells nice. Lotion-y, but not overdone. It's one of the few simple things about her. She can't leave the house if her shoes don't match her outfit, but she doesn't need a ton of makeup, and she doesn't need to drench herself in perfume. I wish more things about her were this simple. It would make her—*us*—so much easier.

Chance isn't simple. But his complexity is of a whole different sort. Emotionally, mentally, I can keep up with Rachael in ways I can't with Chance.

Why am I thinking about him again? My girlfriend is

getting on a plane for Florida soon. I have no idea when I'll see her again. And all I'm thinking about…

"We should get going," I say, averting my gaze because I can't stand the way she's studying me. She moves off my lap with little prompting, but I know by the stiff way she grabs her carry-on and heads for the door without a word or even a kiss—because I know she won't give me one at the airport in public—she's not happy. I answered everything wrong. I always do. She wants reassurance I haven't hated her being here. I haven't hated it, not *entirely*, but it's been uncomfortable and tense. I've been waiting for her and Chance to go at each other with claws and fangs bared, and if she isn't willing to offer me consolation that she feels her trip wasn't a waste, why should I be expected to? It's always a double standard with Rachael. I'm supposed to extend courtesies and kindnesses she doesn't have to.

Maybe Chance was right. Maybe I'm a crap boyfriend, and that's all there is to it.

Downstairs, Rachael says her good-byes to Dad and Ashlin. Neither of them offers to come with for the drive, and I sort of wish they would so I'm not sitting in the car with her by myself for so long. Even with the radio on, the silence looming between us is stifling, and all I can think is how horrible I am for wanting to get her to the airport sooner rather than later.

The silence lingers until we're twenty minutes from the airport, when Rachael bombshells me with, "You're not planning on going to college with me, are you?"

Given that I'm on the freeway, I can't exactly turn to look at her. A brief glance tells me she's staring straight ahead, hands in her lap. Is now really the time to talk about this?

"Rach…"

"Because if you're not even going to apply, I'd rather you tell me now than continue to put me off with empty promises."

"They weren't empty promises." I can't help the defensiveness creeping into my tone. What would she know about my promises? "I never told you I would for sure. Just that I was *thinking* about it."

"You've had your time to think, Hunter. Months of it. How long do you want me to wait? At this rate, I'll be out of college before you've made up your mind."

I could tell her to stop pushing me, but in reality, she has every right to be unhappy. I'm always asking for *time to think*, and although she's hinted and nagged more times than I care to count, she still gave me that time. I haven't given her anything in return. I never filled out the applications for her college near Miami, yet I looked into places in Maine and other campuses along the East Coast. I even put off having sex with her. For that alone, plenty of guys would tell me I'm out of my mind.

I've put her off like I've put off everything. Like I've avoided looking at any colleges outside of Maine. Outside of Dad's city.

Because I wanted to be…

No, no, no. Don't think it. Don't even…

Honesty. It's now or never.

"I can't promise I'm going to apply to college in Florida. I want to stay with my dad. Go to a community college or something."

Rachael is so still that if I couldn't see her from the corner of my eye, I would think I was alone in the car. She finally says, "This isn't working, is it?" Her voice cracks, so I know she must be crying. I wish I could pull over to the side of the road, but knowing my luck, we'd be late for her flight, and we'd be stuck together for the long drive home—and however long it took them to get her on another plane.

Out of reflex, I want to gather her up and apologize again and again, tell her how sorry I am and to let me think a little bit longer...

I really am the world's shittiest boyfriend. Holding onto something *normal* for the sake of having it, for nothing other than to keep what is familiar and safe close to me because the alternative is so fucking terrifying I can't begin to wrap my head around it. It has nothing to do with it being another guy and everything to do with it being *Chance*, and Chance has the ability to shatter me into the minuscule fragments and base elements of the star I supposedly came from.

Who walks willingly into something like that?

I have no words to make this better. None that I can back up with my actions, at least. The only thing I can say and mean—and I do mean it, every syllable, more than I've meant anything I've ever said to her—is, "I'm sorry."

Rachael stares out the window. "Sorry you're breaking up with me, or sorry you're too much of a coward to admit the real reason why?"

Tension snakes up into my shoulders, coiling around my spine. I keep my mouth shut. Which only earns me a bitter smile from Rachael after a moment.

"And you're too scared to say anything to that, even. God, Hunter. Do you think I'm stupid? This has nothing to do with your dad. You want to stay in Maine because you want to be near Chance."

"Don't bring him into this," I say quietly, drawing the car up to the airport terminal, the only one it has, and lingering there. Not so sure she wants me going inside to walk her to her gate at this point. "It has nothing to do—"

"*Yes*, it *does*!" Rachael whips around in her seat to face me. "I see the way you two look at each other. Like everything you say and do is to get each other's attention. You don't want to do anything that might upset him, and he barely put up with me—not because he liked me, but out of respect for you. I see how *different* you are with him."

"Maybe it's *you* I'm different with. Did you think of that?" Resentment and frustration bubble in the back of my mind, and I fight them off, aware I'm feeling defensive because I know she's right. "It's over and done with. I'm sorry. I'm an ass. Why can't we leave it at that?"

"You're always like that," Rachael huffs. "*It's done, so why are we still talking about it?* We'll talk about it as long as I want to, Hunter Jackson, because *I'm* the one who was wronged here. I've spent my whole trip competing with Chance—"

"You have not!"

"—and I, for one, am relieved I don't have to do it anymore." Rachael shoves open the door and gets out. Groaning, I put the car into park, slipping out and circling around to help get her bags from the trunk. She shoves my arm away and does it herself. At least she lets me close the trunk while she hauls her bags onto the curb.

"Rachael…"

Stopping, Rachael takes a deep breath and finally turns to face me. Much of the anger has ebbed away, but in its place is a resigned sort of hurt, which is far worse. Her dark eyes are red from crying. Now would be a great moment for me to get some sort of grand epiphany about how she's the one I'm meant to be with, and of course I'll go to Florida because I love her.

I do care about her.

But that's all it is. Caring. A sort of affection that isn't all that different from what I've felt for any girl I've ever been friends with. A simple emotion with zero passion behind it. It's a safe and familiar love that has never made me crazy or broken my heart or put it back together again.

There is no grand realization, and when Rachael also comes to the conclusion one isn't coming, she takes a deep breath and brushes at her eyes. "I sincerely hope when you go home today, you put some long, hard thought into what it is you want out of life." She presses a brief kiss to my cheek. "Before you break anyone else's heart."

Ashlin

Still no response from Chance to my texts. Funny, given he's usually pretty quick to text back. I figure he must be busy, or forgot to charge his phone, or went out somewhere with his parents. All things that strike me as extremely un-Chance-like.

Isobel drops by with a bag of fresh produce, and while she's there she unloads the dishwasher and puts on a pot of coffee because Hunter forgot to do it before leaving for the airport. She moves around the kitchen like she lives here, and Dad watches her like he wishes she did.

It makes me smile.

You'd think I'd have issues with Dad being interested in another woman besides my mom. But those sorts of things never mattered to me. Our family situation was a bit weird, but it worked out all right. Dad loves us. He doesn't love our moms. There's nothing wrong with that, and I'd like to see him happy with someone.

Isobel is younger than my mom or Hunter's. She's plainer, a bit on the curvy side, with mousy brown hair but a very sweet smile. She gets the coffee going and gives me one of those smiles. "Did you want breakfast, Ash?"

"Yeah, please." I take a seat at the dining table, content to let myself be catered to for a while. Dad arches an eyebrow.

"She's a guest. Shouldn't you be making *her* breakfast?"

Isobel laughs. "I don't mind it, Lou. Leave her alone."

I stick my tongue out at Dad. He rolls his eyes. "Your brother sure scooted out of here early this morning. Would've thought he'd be dragging things out, taking Rachael back to the airport."

I pretend to be busy doing something on my phone so I don't have to look at him. "Sure. I guess so."

"You guess so?"

"I don't know, Dad." I sigh. "You'd…have to ask Hunter."

Out of my peripheral, I catch him and Isobel exchanging worried looks.

Isobel murmurs, "Trouble in paradise, maybe?"

"Whatever it is," Dad says, "I'm sure they'll be all right."

Yeah, I'd like to hope so. All these dreams and pretty images in my head of Hunt and Rachael getting married, me getting to be a bridesmaid, them living this perfect life… Well, all that's gone down the drain, hasn't it? God, reality sucks.

But then there's Chance, and how sad and tired he'd looked. If things with Rach don't work out, will he and Hunter…?

I'm still not sure I'm ready to think about it.

Hours later, while replying to e-mails from friends back home, I'm still thinking of ways to bring up the subject with Hunter. He is such a *boy* sometimes. If I don't handle it delicately, he'll get all defensive and cranky, and neither of us will leave the conversation feeling any better.

Isobel and Dad have gone out for the afternoon, which leaves me with some coveted alone time in the house. Hunter's entrance is a quiet one. I don't even hear the front door open and close, only his footsteps in the hall, passing by my room. Either he thinks no one is home, or he's trying to go unnoticed, and that is a really bad sign something is wrong.

I close my laptop and wander out into the hall. Hunter's door is ajar, so I take that as an open invitation to push it open and step inside without knocking. "Hunt?"

Except it's Chance standing near Hunter's bedroom window, not Hunter. He startles visibly, straightens up, and turns to face me.

The left side of his face is a mottled patchwork of black and blue.

Bruises line his jaw, creeping onto his cheek and around his eye. It's all I can do to clamp a hand over my mouth to keep from expressing the mixture of shock and horror that has made my blood run cold.

Someone hurt him. Someone hurt our Chance.

"Oh my God… Chance…"

He blinks once, then grins. Standing there looking like someone smacked him with a two-by-four, and he's *grinning*. "What, this?" He gestures to his face. "It's no big deal. I fell."

"You fell," I repeat dubiously, closing the gap between

us and lifting my hand. Not touching, because I can't even imagine how much his face must hurt, but—hell—what do you *do* for something like that? Ice? Heat? Does he need to see a doctor? "How do you fall and get that kind of bruising?"

"My front porch." Chance shies away from my fingers. "Slipped on a patch of ice and went down good and hard. Pretty impressive, isn't it?"

"A pretty impressive lie." Because while it could be true, given Chance's track record, I don't think so.

Chance's expression is unchanging. "I'm not lying."

"You *are*. You're always lying, Chance!" I throw my hands in the air and whirl away, straining for any noises outside that might be Hunter coming home. Feeling like I need to get this situation under control *right now* before he comes back. "Look, just tell me the truth. Your dad, right?"

"Ash—"

"It doesn't need to be like this! I don't know what's going on in that house, but you're eighteen now and you don't have to put up with it. Get the hell out of there. Come stay here. You *know* Dad would let you in a heartbeat!"

"Mr. J would also send his hounds after my folks if he got wind something was going on." Chance's smile tightens but doesn't waver. "And since they haven't done anything wrong, I hardly see the reason to leave home and get them in trouble. I fell. Got it? Nothing more, nothing less. I'm a victim of my own clumsiness."

Chance's bruised face turns blurry in my vision. I want to believe him because it's easier, less painful than thinking anyone could do this to him. Why is he always— Why can't he just— Have Hunt and I proved to be such horrible friends he can't rely on us? Or is he really so deluded into thinking there's nothing wrong? Has he told the same stories for so long he's become a believer of his own lies?

I sink onto the edge of Hunter's mattress, shaking my head, pressing the heels of my hands to my eyes and trying not to sob. A million thoughts are flying through my head. Every bruise I've ever seen on Chance. Every instance where he said he wasn't going swimming or wouldn't take off his shirt. Was it to hide something from us? The summer he broke his arm—he said the same thing he's saying now: *I fell off the front porch.*

How do I pick the truths from the lies? And what do I do once I've sorted it all out?

Chance kneels on the floor in front of me, elbows coming to rest on my knees, and his voice is surprisingly gentle.

"Hey. Hey, come on… Don't do that. I'm totally fine, all right? Don't get all crybaby on me."

"You're an asshole," I manage in a voice choked with sobs. But I pull my hands from my face to look down at him. The sight of the bruises makes me want to cry harder. "Why won't you let us help?"

Chance brushes a few tears from my cheeks. "Because no one will believe anything I say. I'm a high school dropout known for getting in trouble."

"You didn't finish school?"

"What was the point? Dad would never drive me, and getting all the way into town every day on foot for school or work was too much. At any rate, it's my word against theirs. I need evidence. Proof."

A dropout. Something else we didn't know, though I can't say he ever lied about it. He never told us he graduated, we just…assumed. His sudden honesty renders me momentarily speechless. I stare into his eyes and at the smile that looks more sad than anything else. "The proof is on your face, Chance. Literally."

He shrugs. "No. Again, my word against theirs. They'll say I fell."

"Not if you tell Dad's old friends on the force. You *know* they would—"

"I'm not telling anyone anything." He shakes his head then buries it against my stomach with a sigh. "I'm doing what I can. Just…trust me. Nobody ever does."

I do trust him. I do. Maybe not to tell me the truth, but I trust him to always be there if I need him. I trust him with my life. But with everything else? How can I? I don't know what to say, so I rest my hands atop his head and slide my fingers through his messy hair. "Hunter is going to go absolutely postal. I hope you know that."

Chance sighs wearily. "Yeah, I guess he will. Which means I should get out of here."

I bite my lip. "You're not going home again, are you?"

He shrugs. "Don't see why not. Where else would I go? I'm lacking in the friends department."

"Then stay here. In my room if you have to. I'll talk to Hunter first and…" I trail off, because *and what*? What will I tell him? But I think Hunter's reaction to all this comes secondary to Chance's safety.

He gets to his feet, tugging at his hair and turning away.

"No. I need to go. Running away never does any good. One of these days, he's going to catch me. Maybe… Maybe I could get him before he gets me. Anyway, I'm not sure why I came here to begin with."

"Because it's safe," I press. The tears are coming again. I don't want to think about Chance getting into it with his dad. How could he even entertain the thought? Either he's going to hurt someone or he's going to hurt himself. I grab his hand tight, trying to convey to him the fear and worry that is so overwhelming to me, and the confusion that Chance can act like this is no big deal. "Stay. *Please.*"

Chance gives my palm a squeeze, pulling me to standing. His free hand cups the back of my neck, and his mouth, chilled, kisses my forehead. "Everything will be okay, Ash. Trust me."

• • •

Dad calls to tell me he and Isobel are catching dinner and a movie, so Hunt and I are on our own for the evening. Normally, this would be a night where Chance, Hunt, and I pig out on junk food, turn off all the lights, close the shutters, and play hide-and-seek. Which is totally not as uncool as it sounds. Getting older means getting bigger, which means it requires a lot more creativity to find hiding places. Last time we played, Chance crawled on top of the fridge and huddled there. In the darkness, it took us forever to find him.

Now, though… Hunter arrives home an hour after Chance makes his escape, no matter how much I tried to talk him into staying. Tonight will not be a fun night. Tonight, I'll be struggling with my own conscience on what to do, what to say, how much to tell Hunter and whether or not I should take this whole thing to Dad.

A few years ago, we might've been able to do more. Chance was a minor. It would've classified as child abuse. Now that he's eighteen, what does that mean? Dad would know. But I get the impression it's only Chance's dad hurting him. Chance might be staying for his mom, or because he feels too ashamed to come stay with us. I don't know.

I don't know anything.

But...I think I need to talk to someone about it or it's going to drive me crazy. Hunter is the only one I *can* talk to at this point. Although the downtrodden look on his face when he comes into the living room and plops down on the couch next to me is a sign I shouldn't mention anything right now.

"I thought you'd gotten lost," I say. He places a bag of fast food in my lap. Burgers. Yum. "What's wrong?"

Hunter shakes his head, running his hands over his face. "Nothing."

"Liar." I pull a burger out of the bag and dig into it. I skipped out on lunch because sandwiches didn't sound appetizing. Being stranded at home without a car kind of sucks. "Once more, this time with honesty, please."

He grunts, eyes locked onto the gloomy glow of the television. I'm halfway done with my food before he says, "Rachael and I broke up."

I pause mid-chew and process that. Finish chewing. Swallow. Still processing. Nope, not surprised. Sad, disappointed, but not surprised. "What happened?"

"Same old crap. She wants me in Florida. I want to stay

here. Obviously, it wasn't going to work."

"God, you both have such short-term visions." I take a second to polish off my greasy excuse for a burger. "It's not like you'll be in college forever. Plenty of couples go to different colleges and move in together after they graduate."

"I know that. We weren't happy, Ash. That's all there is to it."

The wrapper crinkles as I compact it into a little ball. "Because of Chance."

He stiffens and goes impossibly still.

"Chance told me he kissed you. On New Year's."

Hunter's hands squeeze his knees once, then he stands. "I'm going to bed."

So much for broaching the subject carefully. I throw the wadded-up wrapper at his back. "The world isn't going to implode if you talk about it."

"There's nothing to talk about," he snaps. "I'm not— You *know* I'm not interested—"

"In other guys?"

"In *him*." He turns around, spreading his arms wide. "Why in the hell would I ruin a friendship we've built for more than a decade?"

I lean back, studying the shape of him with the TV serving as a backlight. Not saying a word because I sense he isn't done.

"I can't be with someone who has no plans for his life, or who can't even be honest about something as stupid as what his parents do for a living. Give me a break." He begins pacing, one hand on his hip, the other pushing through his hair. It's rare to see Hunter so distraught over something. Usually, I'm the one flipping out and he's the voice of reason. But this is about Chance. There are no rules where he's concerned.

Hunter continues. "He's irrational and impulsive. And it's fun, sure, doing stupid shit like that. But we're growing up, and it won't get us by in the real world. I have no idea what I'm going to do for a career, or college, or…anything. But I am *not* going to pretend to be a teenager forever, overlooking every lie Chance wants to throw my way."

He's trying to rationalize. Because it's the sort of person Hunter is, and it's how he's gotten through life. He rationalizes that Boyfriend Bob is what helped Carol get over our dad. That it's fine for Carol to keep Hunt so busy with school and sports because it will look good on college applications. Or that it's fine if Bob and Carol drink because they aren't angry, violent drunks. He rationalizes everything. Only with Chance has he ever *let go* and had fun no matter how stupid or reckless it might be.

I don't know if having a *them*—Hunter-and-Chance— would be a terrible idea or a brilliant one, but above all else, I have to point out the exact same thing Chance told me. "I think you're overreacting."

"No, I'm not. You don't understand."

"I understand perfectly," I snap. "Because, surprise! *I feel it, too.*"

He stops pacing and stares at me, arms falling limply at his sides. "What?"

It's more than I meant to say, but maybe it needs saying. I fold my hands in my lap and stare at them to avoid meeting his gaze. When I don't speak, Hunter says, "You and him…?"

"No. There is no me and him. There's what I feel for him, and there's *you* and him."

"Why didn't you ever tell me?"

"Please. You knew. You accuse me all the time of flirting with him."

A guilty frown tugs at his brows. "I just thought…"

"You didn't think, Hunter," I say, and I'm suddenly just… so tired. From all of this. The pair of them is exhausting. "I get it, you know. I do. I get why you're scared and you've got this intense fear about feeling not in control and uncertain of any situation. But all you're doing is listing excuses why you two shouldn't act on whatever the hell it is you're feeling."

"What am I supposed to do?"

"If you honestly aren't entertaining the thought of being with him, why not just say you don't feel the same way about him?" I ask. "Instead of giving all these reasons why you've got some doomed, destined-to-fail romance. Seems like a more logical solution for a logical guy like you."

Hunter is defined by all the words he doesn't say. So the fact he's looking at me like I've winded him with a punch to the stomach, but not saying a word, is enough confirmation for me.

"You can't say it because it's not true. Right? You're in love with him."

His jaw tenses. "I don't know why we're talking about this."

"Because it needs talking about." I point at him. "You get pissed off at Chance for keeping secrets, but you can be just as bad. The difference is Chance makes up stories to fill in the blanks, and you leave it all hanging in the ether, unsaid. Does that really make you better than him?"

"It's different," he mutters.

I tilt my head. "Because he's lying about his parents abusing him and you're not?"

The words drop out of the air and stun us both into silence, because I've just spoken what we've both known and didn't have the courage to directly say. Chance's parents are hurting him. Have been hurting him since we were kids. I shouldn't say anything, but how can I go on about being honest if I'm not being entirely honest myself? Like the fact Chance was here today.

"He stopped by earlier," I reluctantly admit. "With bruises on his face."

Hunter smoothes a hand over his jaw and turns away. I see him breathing in, breathing out, trying to pick apart what I've thrown at him. "How bad?"

I fidget, toying with the hem of my shirt. "He said he fell."

"How bad?"

This is not going to end well. "Pretty bad."

He gives a curt nod, turns, and heads for the front door. I leap to my feet and dash after him. "Hunter!"

"Stay here," he instructs, but he doesn't stop me when I worm out of the room and put myself in front of him, blocking his path.

I brace a hand against his chest. "I don't think so! You're not driving over there to cause problems. Will you stop for a minute and use your head?"

Hunter stops, a muscle ticking in his jaw as he looks

down at me. I don't think I've ever seen him so angry, and if
it were anyone other than my big, teddy bear of a brother, I'd
be scared. Slowly, I reach for his hand, which is clutching the
car keys, and loop my finger through the key ring. He doesn't
relinquish them, but he's listening.

Deep breath. "You don't know what you're walking into.
What if you go over there and cause a scene, and we make
things worse for Chance?" It's brief, but a flicker of doubt and
worry passes over his features.

"I want to get him out of there, Ash."

"I know you do. So do I. But forcing him and confronting
his parents isn't the way to do it."

He lets out a heavy, tired sigh. His anger is slipping away,
and he's thinking again. Good boy. "What if we just go talk to
him? See if we can get him to come home with us?"

I debate this. It's risking Hunter losing his cool again once
we get there. He's had a long couple of weeks. Guess even my
almighty brother is entitled to a breakdown or two.

"I'll go by myself," I say.

"Forget it."

"Then no deal."

Hunter arches an eyebrow, a smile tugging at his mouth.
"You think I can't leave right now if I wanted to?"

"You think I can't kick you where it counts and grab the
keys?" I counter. "Fine. We'll go together, but I'm driving, and
you'll wait in the car when we get there."

He looks doubtful, but, slowly, his fingers loosen and I'm
able to pull the keys from his grasp. Score one for me.

HUNTER

The morning started out pretty clear, but sometime during my trip home from the airport, the snow began coming down in blankets. It's remained steady, even after the sun went down. Driving on the unlit, poorly maintained road to Chance's trailer park is not an easy feat. Ash hunches forward over the steering wheel, squinting into the darkness. It's a picturesque opening scene for a survival-horror game.

One lone light is burning from a window in Chance's house, and the beat-up truck belonging to his parents sits out front. Habit has me going for my seat belt until I remember I promised to wait in the car. Ash swings open her door, letting in a burst of icy air that makes me shiver and hunker down in my seat. I watch as she approaches and ascends the steps, careful of her footing, and raps on the screen door.

She has to knock three times before someone answers. It's hard to see through the snow and the fogged windows, but I can tell by the figure it's Chance's dad. I crank my window down halfway for a better look, ignoring the sting of cold air against my face. All I can make out is the dark outline of him in the lit doorway, looming over Ash like a bear.

"He's not here," Chance's dad is saying. He doesn't sound mean, just…curt. Clipped.

"Do you know when he'll be back?" Ash is keeping a careful distance from him, likely without noticing. I wonder what kind of vibe she gets from the guy, looking into his face now that we know for sure what he's been doing to Chance.

The anger begins to burn hot and vibrant under my skin, and I fight it back. Ash was right. I can't get in this guy's face and cause a scene. It would make things worse. I don't pretend to know how she can remain so calm, though, especially now knowing that her casual flirting and closeness with Chance meant so much more to her than I thought it did.

"Nope. Try back later." Mr. Harvey steps into the trailer, and the door closes. Ash takes a minute to regroup, sighing, before traipsing back down the steps and getting behind the wheel.

"He said—"

"I heard him." I roll up the window. "What do we do now? Text and hope he's not too pissed off at me to answer?"

"Pretty much." Ash gives me a withering smile. "He never stays away for long. Don't stress."

Don't stress. Right. She tells me that like she isn't worried, but I know she is, because Ash isn't capable of not worrying about everything.

...

I wake up repeatedly throughout the next two nights, checking my phone for any sign of Chance. He hasn't called either of us. Hasn't texted. His phone is going straight to voice mail, in fact. So either it's off or it's dead. Either way, not a good sign.

Neither is the fact he's missed two days of work. Whenever he decides to show up again, I doubt he'll have a job anymore. Poor Ash has had to hear about it from her boss. I guess it's a good thing she hadn't recommended him to begin with, or they might be looking twice at her.

In the entire time since we reunited with Chance, we haven't gone more than twenty-four hours without contacting him. It happened now and again when we were little; he'd vanish for a few days, and he would come back saying his parents took him on an impromptu trip to see a family member or on a vacation. Now that we know better, now that we're aware he stayed away so we never saw the bruises he couldn't hide, the distance and not knowing is unbearable.

We're approaching the seventy-something-hour mark.

Even Dad asks at dinner, "Where's Chance been?"

Ash and I exchange glances, and I'm willing to bet she wants to tell him the truth as much as I do, but I don't know if we should. If Dad made a call into his old cop buddies and they arrested Chance's folks, then he denied the charges... what would happen? Chance would be pissed off at us for interfering when he told us not to, and his parents—

There is no right answer.

Ash shrugs around a bite of pot roast. "He's been busy, and the idiot came down with a cold from running around in the snow without his jacket. We warned him."

"Hmm." Dad doesn't look convinced. "Normally he comes over here for you two to baby him when he's sick."

Another shrug from Ash. We have no excuse for that. No reasoning. Nothing we can say that isn't the truth, but the truth is not an option right now. A few seconds tick by, and I can't help but ask, "You've never run into Chance's parents before, have you? Like, met them around town or something?"

Dad pauses mid-sip of his milk and lowers his glass. "Why would you ask me that?"

I slouch in my chair. "It's just a question."

"Can't say that I have. Not knowingly." He's studying me.

"What about his dad's name?" Ash asks. I get why she's pushing. Dad has to know something; he found Chance's address for us, after all. We caught his mother's name. Tabby, which has to be short for Tabitha. If we learned his father's name, maybe we could figure out where he works. Though what we would do with that information, I'm not yet sure. I don't think us showing up to his workplace and asking if Chance is all right would go over very well.

"Jeez, what's with the inquisition here?" He holds up his hands. "What aren't you two telling me?" In joined silence, we only stare at him. Dad finally gives up. "All right, all right. I can take a hint."

After dinner, Ash and I get into the car and head for Chance's house again. We stop halfway down the road because the snow is getting too thick to slog through, and no one has bothered to clear this backwater street that hardly anyone uses. In Dad's truck, we could make it. In this little compact, it'd be risky. We sit, idled by the shoulder, staring ahead into the trees and endless white.

"We could walk it," Ash murmurs. Any other day, I would roll my eyes at the idea. But I have the worst gnawing sensation in my gut, so I swing open the door and crawl out. I haven't seen Chance's bruises, which means I'm envisioning them in my head and wondering what would happen if, one day, Chance's dad decided to just…not let him run away.

The thought leaves me cold down to my bones.

It's a slow, arduous walk, with our hands tucked under our arms and heads bowed against the snow. If we'd been driving, we would've definitely missed the narrow turn-off for the trailer park in all this darkness. Junkers and abandoned vehicles in some yards are halfway buried, and the unoccupied trailers themselves look forgotten by time.

The trailer park feels empty and abandoned. All the lights are off in Chance's house. We knock, wait a few minutes, and knock again. Repeat process. No one answers. There's no point in sticking around in the cold for someone who might or might not show up. Defeated, we start back down the way we came. If no one is home, then I want to get the hell out of this creepy place.

Halfway down the stairs, Ash grabs my arms and says, "Look!"

I jerk around, catching only the tail end of a fluttering curtain in the window beside the front door.

"It was his mom," Ash says. "She's home!"

And not answering the door, it would seem. I stomp back up the steps and knock again, louder. "Mrs. Harvey, please open up!" Still, we're met with resounding silence. What is she doing? What is she hiding from? *"Please,"* I repeat more urgently.

"We're worried about Chance!" Ash peers through the window with her hands cupped around her face, trying to see inside. When Tabitha Harvey still doesn't answer, I open the unlocked screen door, and Ash jerks upright, eyes wide. "What are you doing?"

I go for the doorknob. It doesn't budge. That fact snaps me out of whatever place my mind just went to. What *was* I doing? Planning on marching in there and scaring some poor woman half to death while I demanded to know where her son is? I step back. "Nothing. Let's go."

We linger a few seconds more, searching the windows for some sign of Chance's mom. She doesn't make the mistake of peeking at us again.

During the walk back to the car, neither of us says a word. It's too damned cold. We kick away some of the snow that's piled up around the tires in our absence and get inside to relish the heater. Ash presses her hands against the vent.

"That was productive. Why was she hiding?"

"No idea. Maybe they're tired of us stopping by. There's always the possibility Chance asked her not to tell us anything."

Ash frowns. "He wouldn't do that."

"A week ago, would you have thought he'd fall off the face of the planet?"

"Point taken."

"But my gut feeling tells me he isn't home. And if he isn't home..." I swallow a deep breath. "...then he's out there somewhere."

We sit, letting the heat warm us, while watching the snow fall and the blackness stretching out ahead. Just us and the snowflakes gathering on the windshield. Thinking about Chance hiding somewhere out there in the cold.

• • •

Dad has fallen asleep on the couch. We put our coats away and slip out of our snow-caked shoes, leaving them on the front porch so the snow doesn't melt all over the entryway. Ash vanishes upstairs to get changed because the bottoms of our jeans are a bit on the wet side. I nudge Dad awake and help him to his room before heading upstairs as well.

He didn't ask where we went. He never does. Maybe some tiny part of me subconsciously wishes he would, because if we said we went to Chance's but he hasn't been home, it would spark more questions. More inquiries. Dad's smart; he'd pick up on the fact something was wrong. Maybe he already has and simply hasn't said anything.

I feel lost. All my life, I've had Dad to stand up and take care of all the really hard stuff. This might be the hardest thing yet, and now I'm floundering, at a complete loss for what to do, for what the right answer is.

After changing into sweats and a T-shirt, I pop into Ash's room long enough to tell her good night. She's flipping through photos on her camera. Christmas. New Year's. Chance, with the bow on his head. Grinning. I sit on the bed beside her.

"He borrowed my old camera," she says without looking up. "He swore up and down I'd get it back. So if he's missing and hasn't brought it back, has something happened to him?"

"You're over-thinking," I promise, sliding an arm around her shoulders and kissing the side of her head. "He's all right. Everything's going to be okay."

Ash nods mutely. Nothing I say will convince her of that, and it likely won't make her feel better, but it's all I have to offer when I don't really believe things are all right myself. I stay until she sets her camera aside and crawls into bed, then I flick off her lights and return to my room, figuring sleep is probably the best and only cure for this aching anxiety eating away at my insides.

I clean up a bit. Play around online. Check my e-mail and reply to a message from Rachael. I'd written to make sure she got home all right the day after her plane left Maine. She wrote back to say she was home safe and sound. It was curt and cold, not at all like the e-mails I usually got from her. But it's to be expected. Honestly, I'm lucky she wrote me at all. Situations reversed, I'm not so sure I would've been as kind.

I make a lame attempt at conversation, asking if she's looking forward to classes starting back up after winter break. It's the least I can do. Just because we split up doesn't mean I don't care about her, and it doesn't mean I want to lose her as a friend. I don't exactly have many of them. Not close friends. Ashlin, Chance, and Rachael were the closest I had.

It's entirely possible and, in fact, pretty damned likely that I've lost Rachael as a close friend. But I'll always have Ash. And Chance—

I don't know. I don't know anything.

After an hour of trying to focus on a late-night TV show, I flick off the television and slump back, sighing, staring up at the stars on my ceiling. Chance's stupid stars. I always told myself I never took them down because Dad put so much effort into getting them up there, but in truth, I think it was more because Chance loved them so much and I never had the heart to see his face when he realized they were gone.

I trace the outlines of constellations with my fingertip, pinpointing every one of Chance's favorites and wondering what it is about them that fascinates him so much. Is it a resemblance of freedom? Of being somewhere so very far away from where he's at?

He's an idiot. Not for the stars thing, but for everything else. For every lie he's told and every time he's avoided the help I could have—would have—*gladly* offered. As hard as I try, I can't picture it from his side. If he were in this shitty situation for so long, wouldn't he be *desperate* for an out? Willing to try anything? A few years ago, they would've taken him from his parents and put him in a foster home, but I don't doubt for a second Dad would've prevented that. He would have taken Chance in himself, and the courts probably wouldn't have told him no. Not an upstanding ex-cop like him. And now that Chance is eighteen, what's stopping him from leaving? I can't entertain the thought that he's run away. Not without Ash and me. Not without telling us.

Restless, I kick off the covers and get out of bed. What if something's gone wrong, something unfixable? Like Ash said, if he truly, honestly is *missing*, whose fault will it be? Chance's for not coming to us for help? Or ours for not forcing our help on him when we knew he really needed it? Or am I the one over-thinking all of it?

I pace the length of my room, trying to work out the anxious itch in my legs, rubbing a tension spot from my shoulder. Passing by the window, I come to an abrupt halt and do a double take. I rub at my eyes, convinced I'm hallucinating.

Chance is on my back porch, in the snow, head tipped back as he watches my window.

When he catches my gaze, he lifts a finger to his lips, signaling me to be silent.

There's no easy way to tear through the house without waking everyone, but I manage it. Chance is waiting at the back door, ankle-deep in snow in shoes but no socks, and without his coat. I'm going to throttle him—except it looks like someone else already has. He doesn't say anything. I take his ice-cold hand and lead him to my room, and he goes, docile as I've ever seen him.

"You're freezing." At least for the moment, I'm too overtaken with distress and relief to start yelling about how worried we've been.

I'm not even entirely convinced who I'm staring at isn't a ghost.

Chance releases my hand and sits on the bed, flexing his fingers like they've forgotten how to bend. The remnants of bruising cross one side of his face—they must be the bruises Ash told me about. But there's more of it. Recent work. Bruises that are brand new and still forming along his jaw over the old ones. Bruises in the shape of fingerprints around his throat. The undeniable proof someone has hurt him. There is no way to make excuses for that. If he tries to tell me he fell, I'll be tempted to hit him myself. As it is, Chance isn't saying anything, and I haven't found any words just yet.

I grab a pair of socks and a set of clothes from my dresser. When I crouch down to peel off his half-frozen shoes, I'm expecting a toe or three to come with it. His feet are solid blocks of ice. I shiver just looking at them.

First things first, I try rubbing some warmth back into his skin and get a pair of socks on to do the rest of the work. Then I stand, mumbling instructions for him to get up and change. Chance rises on command, needing my help to get out of his shirt and pants. A task that ought to be a lot stranger than it is, and yet my eyes are too busy scanning over every inch of revealed skin, taking note of the bruises. His ribs. One of his arms. Even a mark on his back when he turns away from me to put on the dry shirt.

A bruise lines one of his shoulder blades, close to but not quite touching the constellation of his dragon. He stills, shirt in his hands, and I realize I'm touching it. Touching him. Tracing a finger down the length of his tattoo because it seems to be the one piece of flesh safe from assault. Chance turns around and asks, "Do you want to know why I got a dragon?"

I open my mouth to ask him what the fuck is wrong with him. He's been missing for days and shows up on my back porch, bruised, barely dressed in the snow, and he wants to tell me about *dragons*? But Chance's eyes are dark and distant, his lips slightly parted. His expression is so still and calm, but I can see his fingers trembling, twitching slightly at his sides.

So I say, "It's your favorite constellation. Always has been."

Chance *hmm*s. "Do you remember what you were wearing the day we met?"

A lifetime ago. How could I possibly? I shake my head. This had better be going somewhere profound.

"A red shirt." He touches a hand to my chest, just above my heart, fingers splayed out. "With a dragon on the front."

Against his palm, my heart beats a notch too quickly. Can he feel it? "What are you—"

"And the first present you got me, do you remember what it was?"

"It was years ago, Chance."

"A green dragon in a snow globe."

Yes, I remember now. It was something silly and small from the dollar store. The green had reminded me of Chance's eyes, and I used my allowance to buy it for him our second summer at Dad's. Chance held it so delicately, as though breathing wrong would cause it to break.

"The notebook the three of us passed back and forth with stupid letters and treasure maps the summer you left had—"

"A dragon," I finish, quiet. There are other things, too. Other things flooding to the forefront of my brain. A trip to the planetarium one year, just so Chance could learn more about the stars, but Draco in particular. The book on dragon mythology he snatched from a garage sale. A plastic lunchbox with a generic star pattern, in which Chance swore he could pick out the dragon's design.

Was it my subconscious or his that did this? That somehow

associated Draco, the stars, dragons, to Chance and me?

"Some Eastern civilizations thought dragons were protectors. Guardians of Earth and fortune and all that." He stares at his fingers against my chest as though mesmerized. His hand has grown warm, leeching the heat from me.

Exasperated, I pull away, putting a few inches between us. He could still reach out to touch me but doesn't try again. "Where the hell is this going?"

His gaze hardens, snapping up to my face. "When I was ten, I brought home that baby bird we found by the creek, remember? The one I thought I could save?"

The temperature in the room plummets.

I want to look at anything other than him, but his faraway, sharp stare has rendered me immobile.

"You asked me the next day what happened to it, and I told you I set it free. Actually, Dad found it in my room and had a fit. He threw it out in the woods and hit me so hard I couldn't go swimming with you guys for weeks." He laughs, short, weak, and turns away, hands in his hair. "It was always stupid shit like that. Because I left something where it didn't belong. Or because I tried bringing home an animal that needed me. It was best if I stayed gone as often as I could and I thought...I'd just hang in there. I thought it would get better. Until—"

I know where this is going. I know. And I don't want him to say it.

"Chance, please..."

He doesn't turn around.

"Fifteen. Where did you and Ash find me that summer?"

I brace myself against the bedpost, resisting the urge to sit down. Near Harper's Beach. The cliffs overlooking the island where Chance stood, too close to the ledge, staring at the water and sky and everything in between.

"I was imagining what it was like to fly," he says dreamily. "I was going to jump. No one would have found me. Even if I managed to fuck it up by surviving the fall, I'd be hurt too badly to climb back up. The tide would've swept me away, and no one ever would have known."

I remember.

I remember Ash and me being late to get here that summer. Riding our bikes the achingly long trip to the beach without telling Dad because it was the only place besides the creek we knew to search for Chance.

And, God, I want to say he's lying again, but the pieces fit too well. Ash spotted Chance off the bike path, catching sight of his bright yellow T-shirt through the trees. We dropped our bikes to the ground and ran to him, calling his name. Chance, who stood on the edge of the cliffs with his arms spread wide, slowly let his hands drop to his sides as he turned to face us.

"You have great timing," he'd said.

I remember the haunted look in his eyes, the way I thought he'd slip right off that ledge if I so much as breathed his name. I think back to New Year's, watching him on the edge of the rooftop and feeling so sick to my stomach because he was *too damn close* and I wanted to pull him back.

Chance is right. He could have jumped, and no one ever would have known unless his body washed up on shore weeks, months later.

"At that point," Chance says, "I was sure I'd be okay as long as I held onto the knowledge you would always come back. You and Ash and Mr. J... You're the only good memories I have, Hunter. Then you were gone for those few years and although I knew in my head why—there was this nagging feeling you had left me and you were never coming back."

I wanted honesty. If this is honesty, though, I'm not sure how much of it I can take. My legs are weak with the weight of it all. I sink onto the bed. "What happened to you?"

Chance holds up one finger with a shake of his head. "I got the dragon because it reminded me of you. A reminder that the guy I loved would always come home to me, and he'd always have my back." He smiles a tired smile and rolls his gaze to the ceiling. To the stars. "How's that for ridiculously sentimental?"

I don't know what to say. I don't know what to think. Except— "You don't love me."

His smile fades. "Sorry. Forgot you know my feelings better than I do."

"No," I say sharply. "You don't, Chance. If you did, there wouldn't be all these secrets. You wouldn't have hidden so much. You wouldn't be avoiding telling me *what happened*."

Chance turns full-circle once, a distressed look pulling at his bruised features. "When I was little, really little, Mom told me she and I would get away from him. She had these hand-me-downs from a relative who died. Barbies. Collector's editions, I guess; they were worth some good money because they were in such great shape.

"For three months, all I thought about was her selling

those stupid dolls and getting us the hell out of there. Then...
for whatever reason, she told my dad. I overheard them talking
about what they would do with the cash. What *they* would do."

Realization dawns. "The day we met you...the dolls you
were playing with..."

He got rid of them. Because he refused to let his dad have
any part of the money that was supposed to rescue him.

Chance crawls onto the bed beside me, his skin cold
now but not as bad as it was. "And it's not like Dad has a
shortage of money. He's a fucking mechanic. But he blows it
all gambling, or on drugs, or whatever else catches his eye.
Because of him, we lost our nice house, we lost our car, and
whenever something goes wrong, he blames Mom and me. It's
why I could never leave. Someone had to be there to protect
her. She's the only family I've got, and I let her down."

I seek out his hand, fingers wrapping around his thin wrist,
one finger at a time. "You haven't let her down. She should've
been protecting *you*, Chance. Not the other way around. She's
as much to blame as he is."

Chance's shoulders sag, like a weight bearing down on
him has been lifted. "I don't know what I'm doing anymore.
I'm so tired, Hunter. I've been so *desperate* for something to
change."

There is so much I can say. So many things I've thought
to say the last few weeks. Comforting words and reassuring
statements...but nothing comes to mind right now. Just, "It'll
be okay. I'll take care of you. Let us help."

He shakes his head with a faint smile. Slowly, his arms slip
around my shoulders, his mouth finds its way right beside my

ear. "Do you love me?"

A shiver courses down my spine. The moment of truth, isn't it? I think back to Rachael on the way to the airport, to the night on the phone when I accidentally told her I loved her when I didn't mean it because all my thoughts, all my attention, were focused on Chance looking so beautiful in the snow. My mouth tingles at the memory of him kissing me, the kisses from Rachael after that, and how I couldn't stop comparing the two.

Chance is so still, but I can feel the slow rise and fall of his chest pressed against me; I can't see his face because we're cheek-to-cheek, and I think that might be a good thing, not being able to see him. I don't know that I could speak otherwise.

Because it's the simplest of questions, really. One I'm over-thinking when there's nothing to think about. It's that I don't like the truth of it, because it's terrifying, because it opens myself up to being the one person in the world who can save Chance Harvey, and what do you do with that kind of pressure? That sort of expectation? How do you open yourself so completely to a person you don't trust?

He isn't asking if it's a good idea, though, or if I want to do anything about it. He's only asking if I *do*, and I owe him that much. Maybe in a way I owe it to Ashlin, too, for encouraging me even when it had to have broken her heart.

"Yes," I whisper, the words splintering in my throat. "I love you."

Chance draws back with eyes wide, lips parted. *Startled*, almost. Like he expected anything but that. I search his gaze, grappling for something to say to make me feel less naked and vulnerable. I don't get the opportunity before Chance leans in and kisses me.

It's no different than last time on New Year's Eve. The simultaneous thrill and fear that snakes through every nerve in my body, kick-starting my adrenaline. Only now there is the absence of guilt over Rachael, just the worry and unease of not having any idea what I'm doing, kissing the boy I've thought about kissing for years.

Chance cups my face in his hands, and my arms go around him, itching to pull him closer. It occurs to me I could be hurting him, triggering every bruise, but if I am, Chance doesn't tell me, so instead I'll focus on kissing him the way he deserves to be kissed. There's a stark contrast between the heat of his mouth and the chill of his lips.

My hands clutch at his hips, adjusting to how different this is. How different it is from kissing someone like Rachael. Different. Better. Because it's *Chance* and why wouldn't it be? I'm aware of everything about him. Every breath he takes. Every beat of his heart, lost somewhere in time with mine. Aware of his mouth and the way it sends heat and light like stars to every nerve in my body.

I don't know what we're doing. If we should be doing it.

If I even care about all that anymore.

All that matters is Chance. The solid, angular feel of his body, the taste of him, the way he sighs against my mouth when we lay back and I lean over him on the mattress. And no matter my level of worry or uncertainty, despite it all, this feels good. Right. Chance-and-me. Two people derived from the same star billions of years ago, searching for each other in a vast universe and only now really finding each other.

"I'll keep you safe," I mumble into his mouth. "I'll protect you. I can. I promise."

Chance's lips curve into a sad smile. His hands smooth up and over my ribs, my shoulders, into my hair. Like he's mapping out every part of me. I'm content to do the same to him—until he winces, and I know I've hit a bruise.

Immediately, I draw back, the rest of the world coming into focus. "Sorry, I'm—"

"Shut up." He chuckles and drags me down to lay beside him, my head against his shoulder. Strange, yes, in the sense we don't fit like some magical puzzle pieces. He doesn't mold to my body like Rachael would have. But it's still perfect, and I won't question it.

Chance stares up at the stars on the ceiling through half-lidded eyes, absently stroking my hair. "Look how bright Draco is," he says.

They're just plastic stars, I think to remind him again. But if it makes him happy, I hardly see a reason to argue with him. I close my eyes, though sleep is the last thing on my mind, and I'm not even sure I'll be able to now with the way my blood is still thrumming with electricity. "You'll stay, right? We'll talk to Dad tomorrow?"

The noise he makes is a noncommittal one. But he says, "Maybe," and that's likely the most I'm going to get out of him. He buries his face in my hair and breathes in deep. "Say it again."

"Say…?"

"That you love me."

I grope blindly around by our legs to drag the blankets up and around us. Going to take some getting used to, hearing things like that. "I do love you."

"No matter what?"

"Yeah, Chance. No matter what."

• • •

Chance is gone in the morning.

His side of the bed is still warm, so it hasn't been long since he left. I roll onto my back with a groan, running my hands over my face, halfway convinced last night was a dream. If so, it was a really vivid one.

Except the clothes Chance borrowed from me are still gone, as are the ones he was wearing when he got here. I swear I must have lost a fourth of all my clothes to him over the years. Now I wonder whether it was out of necessity, because he needed them and never would've asked, or because he liked feeling closer to me. Maybe a little from column A, a little from column B.

I shuffle around in a dazed state between awake and what-the-hell-happened-last-night. And what happens *now*? Maybe that's the more important question. Did Chance go back home? If so, I'll get dressed, go over there, and retrieve him. Once and for all.

Ash is still sleeping. She growls dangerously at me when I ease into her room and say her name, but all it takes is, "Chance stopped by last night," and she's sitting up, trying to make sense of her hair while shoving aside blankets, speaking with all the slurredness of someone pretending she's more awake than she is.

"Why didn't you wake me up?"

"He didn't want anyone to see him." Which is half a lie, because he wanted *me* to see him, obviously. But if he'd wanted Ash woken up, he would've said as much. That's how Chance works. "Come on. We're going over to his place and bringing him back home, even if we have to break down the door."

"That doesn't sound like a lawsuit waiting to happen," she mutters, but she shoves me at the door to leave so she can get dressed.

Ten minutes later, we head downstairs with every intention of skipping breakfast and getting out of there. Halfway down the steps, I make out Dad's voice, and from the living room we see him at the front door, talking to two men in uniform. I vaguely recognize one of them as Roger, an old friend and partner of Dad's from the force. The other guy is several years younger. Well-groomed. Likely a new cop, I'd bet.

They look past Dad and catch sight of us, and their somber expressions tell me this isn't a social visit. Dad twists around, and his expression is tight and worried. Fear clutches at my heart, making every beat a struggle.

"Dad?" Ash says. "What's going on?"

He glances at Roger, who says, "We're looking for Chance Harvey."

I let out a strangled breath. They're looking for him. That's a step above *we found him in a ditch last night*. Not great, but better. I think. Before I can respond, Ash shakes her head.

"We haven't seen him in a bunch of days. We've been trying to get ahold of him. Did something happen? Is he okay?"

She's better at this whole lying thing than I am. I simply stare at the two officers and Dad, unblinking, trying to keep myself calm. Logical. What in the world could have possibly happened?

Dad takes a deep breath. "Chance's mother was murdered."

ASHLIN

The words hit me like a bag of bricks. Immediately, Hunter collapses onto the couch, head bowed, hands running through his hair again and again. I sit slowly beside him and reach for his hand, letting him squeeze mine as tight as he needs to. For my own comfort as well as his.

"His mom," I repeat. "That doesn't…make any sense."

Dad lets the officers farther into the house and shuts the door. He sits on the other side of Hunter, keeping close to us. Roger takes a seat in Dad's armchair while his partner remains standing. No more sitting room.

"Kids," Roger says gently. "Anything you can tell us would really, really help."

Oh, there are plenty of things we could tell him. Now I wonder if we shouldn't have lied about Chance being here last night. Could we have been his alibi? Does he *need* an alibi? "We haven't seen him in a few days," I repeat. "We were sort of… He was… There was some stuff going on at home and we figured he was dealing with it."

"What sort of stuff?"

My brother and I exchange glances. "Is he a suspect?" I ask.

"It's a possibility," the younger officer says. "First things first, we'd like to know if he's all right. Judging by the state of the house, it looked like there was a struggle, and Zeke Harvey is also missing."

Roger shoots his partner a look, like he's said more than Roger wanted him to say, then adds, "Chance needs to come in for questioning. We can't rule anything out."

"Chance wouldn't hurt his mom," Hunter insists. "If he hurt anyone, it would be his dad."

Roger rests his elbows on his knees, hands clasped loosely together. "What makes you say that?"

I close my eyes, knowing Hunter wouldn't have said such a thing if he hadn't planned on going all the way with it. Now, whether Chance wants us to or not, we're letting his secrets spill. Hunter stares at his hands, mouth pulled into a twisted look of uncertainty.

"Because," he says, "his dad is the one who beats the hell out of him."

• • •

It takes two hours for us to give Roger and Allen—his partner— all the information we can think might be helpful. Helpful for

Chance, that is. We're careful not to say anything that might not look good on him. It isn't lying. Not really, right? Withholding information? *We* know Chance didn't do it, but no sense in giving the police more reason to harass him than necessary. I'm still torn; if we tell them now that we lied about Chance being here last night, they might not be inclined to believe anything else we've told them. They don't let us in on much information to the murder. We know it happened yesterday afternoon or evening, when neighbors reported hearing a gunshot. So, it's a safe bet to say she was shot to death.

Only a short time after we left Chance's, too. It's possible that we were the last people to see Tabitha Harvey alive.

By the time they leave, Hunter is frazzled, and Dad has been deathly quiet. As soon as the front door shuts, he gets to his feet and hobbles into the kitchen without a word. Hunter and I follow, lingering in the doorway to watch him.

"Dad?" I say.

His back is to us while he fusses with the coffee maker. There's a heaviness to his movements. After a moment, "I never knew."

"Neither did we," Hunter mumbles.

"You were *kids*. I was the adult. I saw Chance more than his own parents did, and I should've recognized the signs. I always knew he didn't have a happy home life, but this…" He shakes his head. He's beating himself up over it. I hate that. It wasn't his fault. He's also getting frustrated with the coffee maker, so I nudge him gently aside, and he sighs, shuffling to the table to sit down. "I tried mentioning it to him a few times…asking if things were okay. He always brushed me off."

"He did the same thing with us," I say.

Hunter sits across from Dad. "You don't think he did it…
right?"

Dad folds his hands on the tabletop, sighing. "Chance isn't
the only suspect."

That isn't a "no," but it's not a "yes," either. I'll take what
I can get. "His old man."

"Zeke Harvey." Dad gives a solemn nod. "He works as a
mechanic at a shop across town, Roger said. Never one I've
been to, but I've driven by it plenty of times. He's got a bit of
a record, so…"

"It has to be him." Hunter gets back up, clearly too restless
to remain sitting. "It has to be. He's been hurting Chance all
these years, and we've seen his mom—right, Ash? She's this
tiny little cowed thing. I wouldn't doubt he's been abusing her,
too. Chance said he's been trying to talk her into leaving for
years, so maybe she was finally going to and he found out…"

Dad gives him a thoughtful glance. "When did he tell you
that?"

Hunt opens his mouth, barely catching himself from saying
last night. No matter how much Dad wants to protect Chance,
he would totally not be okay with us lying to the police. "I
don't remember. Whenever we saw him last."

"Hmm." Dad nods when I set a cup of steaming coffee in
front of him. He stares down at it like he isn't sure what to do
with it. "Roger will keep me updated on the case. All I need
is for you two to keep an eye out for Chance. You see him or
talk to him, let me know, hear? The best thing we can do for
him right now is to get him to cooperate with the police so

they can clear his name."

Hunter and I exchange looks. Getting Chance to cooperate with the police? Not going to be easy.

• • •

I call in sick to work for the next two days. When I show up on the third day, everyone falls quiet when they see me. It takes twenty minutes into my shift before I realize the cops must've stopped by here, too, looking for Chance, and they would have found out he hasn't been in lately and was fired. Or would have been, if Deb could ever get her hands on him.

Deb pulls me into a back office long enough to say, "I hope whatever's going on with Chance has nothing to do with you and won't affect your work."

I stare at her incredulously. *Really*? Does she think I might've had something to do with all this? "I'm not hiding him in my apron, if that's what you mean," I say tightly. Deb eyes me but lets me go about my business. Great, even my boss is treating me like a leper.

I pull on my apron and decide to handle this by keeping my head down and my eyes on my work. It's best for Chance. Probably best for the safety of my job, too. Let me survive my shift and I can get the hell out of here and resume looking for Chance. Small comfort is in the fact that Hunter is also at work, just as distracted as I am.

I text Chance all day, any time I can find a second to pull out my phone. It's been three days. I don't know why I think he'll magically respond when he hasn't any other time. But the cops haven't found him, and they haven't found Zeke, and it doesn't look so good on either of them.

At lunch, I head to the back of the building and slump down with a sandwich and a granola bar. Sitting in the break room is too much of a headache. Where I used to be able to eat with my coworkers, now I can't even sit down without someone giving me a curious glance. Regardless of how it happened, someone has *died*. I may not have been Mrs. Harvey's biggest fan, and she wouldn't have won any parent of the year awards, but she was still a person. She didn't deserve this. Even so, everyone wants in on the gossip, and I'm not about to indulge them.

Outside by myself it is. I'm working the evening shift, so "lunch" is, technically, at dinnertime. Although it's too cold outside to enjoy eating and I don't have much of an appetite anyway, I nibble at my granola bar, knowing I need to get food in my stomach, while I check my phone yet again for a call or text I'm starting to think I'll never get.

"If you're not going to eat that, can I have it?"

Chance's voice makes my head whip around so quickly I smack it against the brick wall. I grab the back of my skull with a wince, vision blurring with brief tears as he takes a seat next to me.

"Jeez, nice one. Are you okay?"

"Am I okay?" I grind out, rubbing at the knot most definitely forming. "Am *I* okay? You *asshole*. Where have you been? The cops are looking all over for you!"

Chance has on his jacket, hood pulled up and around his face. But it doesn't hide the bruises. I can see why Hunter was so upset. The edges are fading into a sick brown and yellow—

healing, but slowly. He shrugs.

"Here and there. What did they tell you?"

"That your mom was murdered." I twist around, narrowing my gaze. Aside from a subtle flash of pain in his eyes, Chance doesn't react. "You need to go to the police department, Chance. You need to tell them whatever you know. They think you're either dead or a suspect."

"And get arrested?" He makes a face. "I don't think so."

"Why would they arrest you if you didn't do it?"

"Because I'm still a suspect. And I'm willing to bet they'd find a way to hold me."

"Only because you keep running and they'd be worried about you taking off again," I hiss. "If you'd gone to them immediately, it wouldn't be a problem."

Chance sighs, absently twirling a strand of my hair around one of his fingers as though we're talking about something inconsequential, like the weather. The gesture is a familiar and yet sharp reminder of how normal things were just a few days ago. "It's my word against his, you know. We were both there."

All the anger seeps right out, leaving me feeling instantly drained. "You were there...?"

He shrugs, staring off at nothing. He is sitting right next to me, but he looks like he's a million miles away. Bruises aside, his face is drawn and tired, and his eyes are red, like he's been crying recently.

"Chance."

"What?"

I wrap my hands around his bicep, noticing the way he

winces when I do. "You need to talk to me."

"There's really nothing to talk about. Let them catch my old man and toss him behind bars." It's brief, but there's a hitch in his voice at the mention of his father. "It has nothing to do with me."

"You can't just avoid them until they convict your dad. That's not how it works." God, how dense can he be? I know Chance isn't this stupid. "You're scared, and I get that, because I would be, too. Hell, I *am* scared. But running away and ignoring this isn't going to fix it. You lost your mom, and you might have evidence that can help convict the person who did it."

Finally, he looks at me, lips curving into a sad smile. "I do have evidence, just not with me."

I frown. "What evidence?"

Shrug. "Doesn't matter."

I resist the urge to beat him with the remainder of my granola bar. Losing my temper isn't going to accomplish anything. "You have to go to the police."

"And if I don't"—Chance takes my untouched sandwich, puts it in his coat pocket, and stands—"are you going to call and tell them I'm here?"

He looks down at me. I look up at him. He didn't say it like a challenge. It's nothing more than a simple, honest question. *Would you turn me in? Do you think I did it?*

When I don't answer, he continues. "If Dad finds me, he'll kill me. If I'm behind bars, even for a while, he'll take off and they'll never catch him. So long as I'm free and running around, he'll keep looking for me and eventually he'll make a mistake and get caught."

In this moment, I almost hate him for doing this to me. For forcing this decision on me—between doing what is right according to the law and what I think is right for *Chance*. Because he might be right about his dad, but then what? If Chance is locked up until they clear him and Zeke Harvey gets away, will Chance spend weeks, months, years, always looking over his shoulder, wondering when his dad will come back for him? On the flip side, with Chance running around like he is, what if Zeke finds him anyway? He won't have anyone to protect him.

I run my hands over my face, exhausted. What would Hunter do? I have no idea. I don't think he'd know, either. So I say nothing.

"You two should stop coming after me, though," Chance says as he pockets his hands and begins walking off down the back alley. "You'll get yourselves in trouble."

He rounds the corner, and I'm alone again with a missing sandwich, a half-eaten granola bar, and more questions than answers.

HUNTER

Dad would kill me if he knew I was sitting in my car outside the Smooth Running Auto Shop where Zeke Harvey works. He might also kick himself for mentioning it to us. Not that he gave a name, but there aren't many mechanics on this end of town. It confirms what Chance told me last night, about what his dad did for a living. Mechanics do bring home good cash. At this point, I guess there isn't anything left to hide. No reason for him to lie anymore.

I don't know why I'm here other than I'm grasping at straws for wanting to find Chance…or Zeke. Which is stupid. Of all the places either of them could run, Zeke Harvey's workplace would not be one of them. The cops have already checked here, no doubt. They're likely keeping an eye on the place. Told the other mechanics to report anything suspicious.

My wandering in to ask about Zeke's whereabouts? Yeah, that could be reported as suspicious.

So could my sitting here in the parking lot. I should really be heading to pick up Ash from work, but I can't shake the feeling I need to be out doing something. Looking somewhere. That I should know precisely where to go.

I'm so intently focused on the shop and the unfamiliar faces coming in and out that I don't notice Roger's face next to my window until he knocks on it. It startles my heart up into my throat and, groaning inwardly, I crank the window down.

"Roger. Uh, hey."

Out of all Dad's friends on the force, Roger is the first one he'd consider a good friend. They were partners. Roger used to sneak us ice cream and candy when we weren't supposed to have any and always said, "If I can't spoil ya, who can?" Aside from Isobel, he was the person who helped Dad the most through his recovery. Even though we haven't seen him for a few years, I look at him as a sort of distant uncle figure. Which means the way he's frowning makes me sink down in my seat.

"Do I even wanna know what you're doing out here, Hunter?" he asks.

"I was just…" God, I wish I were better at lying. Roger might know if I tried to lie, anyway. Truth it is. "I was worried about Chance."

He strokes his mustache. Some of the irritation eases out of his face. "Hunter…"

"He could be anywhere. What if Mrs. Harvey wasn't the only one hurt?" My throat constricts at the thought, cracking my voice and making it waver. "What if he's dead in the woods somewhere? It's not like him to up and leave Ash and me. If he isn't hurt, then he's hiding somewhere, scared."

Roger listens with quiet patience, folding his arms and bobbing his head in a nod. "I get all that, kid. Really, I do. But you think you'll find him in a place like this? What's your old man gonna say?"

I stare off at the Smooth Running Auto sign, studying its weathered paint like it's the most fascinating thing in the world. "What are *you* doing here? Did you get a lead?"

An amused smile tugs at his face. "'Fraid not. Just checking in with the employees."

"If you had a lead, you wouldn't tell me anyway," I point out. He might tell Dad. Maybe. But he wouldn't tell me.

Roger shakes his head. "Go on and get out of here, Hunter. I'll see you around. Stop trying to play detective." He pats the roof of the car and takes a step back, then waits until I roll up the window and drive away. Halfway down the block, I still see him in the parking lot, watching me go. Making sure I'm heading back to the right part of town, I guess.

I'm twenty minutes late reaching Ash's work, and she's already standing outside, head down, a fresh wash of snow on her shoulders and the crown of her head. Guiltily, I crank the heater up full blast as she crawls into the passenger's seat, shivering.

"I'm sorry. I completely lost track of time."

"No big deal," she mutters. "Not like it's cold or anything."

I get her being grouchy; I would be, too, but it isn't just a me-forgetting-to-pick-her-up thing. She twists her body in a way that clearly says she's not happy. She's also giving off a vibe that, whatever it is, she doesn't want to talk about it, but when we pull onto our street and the house is in sight, I decide I don't feel like abiding by those unspoken rules today.

"Bad day?" I ask.

Ashlin makes an affirmative noise. "Wasn't yours?"

Every day has been a bad one since we found out about Mrs. Harvey. I may not have liked the woman much, considering she did a shit job at keeping her son safe, but it never meant I wanted her dead. More than that, the idea of Chance out there somewhere, dealing with all of this alone, makes me sick to my stomach.

"Work was fine. What happened?"

"That makes your coworkers better than mine." Ash shifts, twisting almost entirely away from me and pressing her forehead to the window.

I grimace. "The police came to question everyone, huh?"

"Everyone knew him, so of course they're all drawing their own conclusions. And trying to get me to talk about it. Or trying to get me to say if I know where he is."

"Sorry." I turn into the driveway next to Dad's truck. "I'm sure he's okay, though. Wherever he's at."

"I know he is. I saw him today." Ash pops open her door and gets out. I sit behind the wheel, stunned into immobility, before I kill the engine and hurry after her.

I catch her in the entryway where she's toeing off her shoes, grab her arm, and keep my voice down so Dad—wherever he is—doesn't overhear. "What do you mean, you *saw him* today?"

"Just what I said." She tugs her arm out of my grasp. "He stopped by the shop while I was on lunch. He said we needed to stop looking for him because he didn't want us to get in trouble."

The rest of what she says hardly sinks in; I'm too busy focusing on the fact that Ash *saw* him. She saw that he was all right, alive, in one piece. Legs suddenly weak, I sink back against the front door and try to remember to breathe.

Ash resumes pulling off her snowy sneakers. "He's not going to the police, Hunt. He thinks he has to wait until Zeke gets caught first. I tried talking sense into him, but, well..."

Well. Yeah. What more can you say? Chance is Chance. Infuriatingly so. "You could've called the cops on him."

"Could have." She hangs up her coat then swivels to look at me. "Would you have?"

I meet her gaze levelly, giving the question due consideration. Which is useless because, "I have no idea."

Ash's smile is a sad one. "Yeah." She heads farther inside and leaves me to get out of my coat and boots so Dad doesn't kill me for leaving wet footprints halfway across the house. He isn't watching TV in the living room, which means he's probably reading in his bed. I follow Ash upstairs, where talking about all of this is safer, away from prying ears. She deposits her purse on her nightstand and flops across her bed with a sigh. I ease the door shut, taking a seat in her computer chair.

"Are you going to tell me what he said or are you going to have me guess?"

"A guessing game might be fun." Ash squints at the ceiling.

"I already told you: the cops won't believe anything he says, it's his word against his dad's, and he wants to stay in hiding. That about sums it up."

Sounds like Chance. Being as fucking cryptic and vague as humanly possible. I could strangle him. "He didn't even tell you what happened?"

"Just that he was there. No details." She drapes an arm across her face.

He was there. He was in the house when his mother was murdered.

I try to imagine being in his shoes. My mom and I have a strained relationship, but I love her. And I know Chance resents his mom, but he also loves her and wants to keep her safe. This was what he meant that night in my room. He thinks he let her down because he couldn't protect her from being murdered. To have witnessed her death and to be out there all alone, feeling like he can't trust even the law to help…

What is it like?

What is going through his head, in this very moment?

What am I supposed to do?

"Whether he thinks it is or not, his eyewitness testimony is evidence," I say.

"He said he has actual evidence, he just doesn't *have* it… whatever the hell that means."

A frown tugs at my brows. "So, like, he has evidence…but it's not on his person at this exact moment in time? Did he lose it?"

A second ticks by, and Ash looks off at nothing in particular as though she's grasping for an answer to that. But she finally says, "I have no idea. Look, I'm totally exhausted. Can we talk about this tomorrow? Do you have to work?"

"Evening shift again," I lament.

"I'm off. Thank God. Sooner this is over with, the sooner people will stop looking at me like I hooked up with Charles Manson." She rolls her eyes and gives a wave of her hand, effectively dismissing me from her room.

I would argue, but I'm tired, too. Work wasn't draining, exactly, but I think Ash, Dad, and I have all felt sucked dry of our energy these last few days. I've heard Dad on the phone with Roger more than once, asking for updates, for any shred of information Roger might be willing to feed him.

Everything will be okay, I tell myself again and again.

There's a reply from Rachael in my inbox again. Her letters still read stilted and distant, but at least she's e-mailing. I haven't told her about what's going on with Chance. I can't bring myself to. Isn't that bad form? Talking to your ex about the person who, technically, was the reason your relationship ended?

Not that Chance and I are together now. Right? Whatever the other night was—

I don't know.

Sometimes, I get a brief glimmer, a flicker of certainty on how all this will end. Zeke will be arrested, Chance will come stay with us, he and I can fumble our way through whatever the hell this is between us, and things will be good.

He will be safe. We will be happy.

Then I remember I have no idea where he even is right now, and whether he's going to end up doing something stupid.

Because Chance is a complicated, wild creature who can be as idiotic as he can be brilliant.

These are all things I can't tell Rachael. Hell, they're things I can't even tell Dad, and Ashlin has enough worries of her own right now than to have to listen to mine. I can't imagine what it was like for her, seeing Chance in person, being unable to help him, unable to get any solid answers out of him.

I can't say I would've had any better luck.

ASHLIN

Sleep doesn't come easy that night. I toss and turn and pace the room repeatedly, mind racing a hundred miles a minute. Plotting. Thinking. Planning.

The camera.

Why didn't I think of it sooner?

Evidence, Chance said. He had evidence, but he didn't *have it*. What sort of evidence could he possibly have that authorities wouldn't have found already at the scene of the murder? Blood samples, clips of carpet, bullet fragments, DNA, fingerprints...they would've found all of it.

But would they have found the camera Chance borrowed? And does it contain something that could clear his name?

The problem being, Chance isn't likely to go anywhere near his house. By this point, the police would be done with it. The yellow tape might still be up to prevent anyone from coming in, but they would've collected anything they were going to collect. Dad hasn't said anything about a camera.

I don't tell Hunter because I'm well aware my idea is seriously out there. We've already lied to the police and Dad, and I didn't report seeing Chance like I should have. How much further are we willing to break the rules for this?

What worries me is that Hunter won't stop. Whether he's aware of it, whether he's told Chance, I think I've come to terms with the fact that my brother is in love with one of my best friends. That sort of devotion and protective instinct isn't easily swayed. I love Chance, too, but in this, I trust my own judgment better than Hunter's.

Isobel is over when I get up in the morning. She's been a quiet presence this last week, trying to be supportive and help out while we're going through a difficult time. She smiles at me when I sit down to breakfast. I could get used to someone cooking for me all the time, to be honest.

"You look like you haven't slept a wink, honey." She places a glass of orange juice beside my plate.

"A lot on my mind." I rub my eyes. How am I the first one here when I was probably the last one to go to sleep?

Isobel pulls up the seat next to me. "Anything you want to talk about?"

Plenty. But I can't trust that whatever I say to her won't go right back to Dad. Even if it didn't, I wouldn't put her in the situation of having to keep my secrets. I shrug and take a sip of my OJ, not feeling very hungry no matter how good the eggs look. "I don't think you'd want to hear it."

"Try me."

I take a deep breath and straighten up, pivoting slightly in my chair to better face her. "Well…okay. Can I ask you a question?"

Her eyes light up in that way that says she's delighted at the idea of me possibly opening up to her about something. Isobel walks this fine line of wanting to be involved with us but never seeming to know how. Which is kind of amusing in a sad way, because Hunter and I both adore her. "Go for it."

I *hmm*, putting serious thought into this very serious question. "How long is it going to be before you and Dad tell us you're officially dating?"

First, all the color drains from Isobel's face, and is then replaced with a bright red flush to her cheeks. "Who said…?"

"No one, but we're not dumb." I prop my elbows on the table, chin in my hands, basking in the flustered look on her face. She's adorable, and I want to give her a hug. "The movie you two went to the other night, it was a romantic comedy, wasn't it?"

"Well, yes."

I pick up my fork and gesture at her with it before taking a bite of food. "Dad makes this big secret out of liking romantic comedies. If he's admitted to you he enjoys them and went out in public with you to see one? That means he really likes you."

Isobel leans back in her chair, fingers against her lips where she's trying not to smile. I see her gaze flick behind me and hear the telltale sounds of Dad shuffling into the kitchen. We both turn to watch him as he walks to the counter to get his coffee.

When he turns around with mug in hand and catches us staring, he pauses. "What did I do?"

"Nothing." Isobel winks at me. "Your daughter wants to know why we haven't told them we're dating."

Dad nearly chokes on his coffee mid-sip. He clears his throat and places the mug on the table. "Is the phone ringing? I think I hear the phone ringing…"

There is no phone ringing. Mainly because we don't have a landline, but I let him off the hook this one time. After he's wandered out of the kitchen, mumbling, Isobel rises to her feet to make herself a plate of food. Before she sits down again, she leans over, kisses the top of my head, and murmurs, "I'm here if you want to talk."

I don't know how to explain to her that I feel a little bit better already without having said a word.

. . .

Hunter heads off for work in the late afternoon, bundled up against the blizzard brewing outside. I taunt him as he walks out the door about how glad I am not to have work today. He flips me off with a grim smile before disappearing out the door.

Now it's a waiting game.

Dad and Isobel are going out tomorrow morning, which means Dad will hit the sack at a decent hour. Hunter works until midnight, which should give me some time if I'm going to pull off this crazy idea of mine. I make an early dinner and, like clockwork, Dad heads to bed around nine. I wait until the light vanishes from beneath his door before flicking off the

TV and creeping upstairs.

I get dressed all in black, as warm as I can manage, tucking my hair beneath a knit cap and pulling on gloves. I shove a flashlight into my pocket—a little one, because the ones we took to the island are in the car and this is all I've got—before heading out. The walk is going to be a long one and really flipping cold, but I remind myself Chance made this same walk for years so there's no reason I can't do it.

The mobile home park looks creepy and desolate under the shade of night and snow. I only see one set of lights on, far in the back, but I scout around to make sure there isn't anyone roaming the premises before approaching Chance's house. All I need is my own *Mission: Impossible* theme.

The yellow police tape trembles in the wind, and it's snapped in more than one place, which suggests the cops haven't been here recently to check on things, or else they would have fixed it.

The front door could be locked and is otherwise too visible to any other homes, so I creep around the back. There is no other door, but I find a window I can reach by standing on a stack of old cinder blocks. It opens with a bit of effort, grinding and protesting every inch of the way.

Once I have it open, I pause. I'm about to enter the lion's den. I don't know what I'll see, what I'll find, if someone will catch me here. I stare into the blackness of the room before me. I don't even know where to look or if I'm doing all this for nothing. I'm so used to having Hunter or Chance at my side whenever I do something that scares me. For the first time, I'm braving something completely alone.

But I have to try. I've come this far.

I haul myself up and through the window, hiking a leg over the pane and feeling around with my foot until I find something—a mattress—beneath it to ease onto.

The trailer is still and silent. It smells musty, closed-in. Like weed and something darker, more metallic. Dried blood, maybe? I can't say I'm familiar with the smell, but whatever it is, it makes my stomach roll, and I can only be grateful for the chill weather because the heat would amplify the odor.

I ease the window shut behind me, figuring I can leave out Chance's bedroom window when I find it. The camera, if it's here, will be somewhere in his room, and where I am now has to be Zeke and Tabitha's room. It's cluttered, and I think maybe the police went through everything. Drawers are open, clothes are on the floor, the bed is unmade.

For a minute, I feel sick. Was this the room she was murdered in? On this very bed? That thought has me scooting off it and to my feet quickly, but a look around with the flashlight doesn't show blood or any sign that someone was shot here.

Deep breaths, self. I'm here for a reason.

Cautious, I creep out the door and into the hall. It's a small mobile home, so finding Chance's room can't be that hard. There's a bathroom to my right, the living room to my left…which is blocked off with more police tape. That must be where it happened. Which means I only need to turn my eyes away as I move past and try not to think too much about it. Totally would *not* be okay for me to throw up when I'm taking care not to leave evidence behind that I was ever here.

Toward the end of the hall, I find an open door and, inside, what must be Chance's room. I don't dare go for the light switch, so my only reliance is on the tiny flashlight, which I use to scan around. If I thought Zeke's room was a bit messy, Chance's is chaotic.

Posters for bands I've never heard of line the walls. His bed has a few threadbare blankets shoved at the foot of it, but there is no sheet on the mattress. His clothing is in a pile in the corner beneath a window, and the floor is littered with magazines, clothes, and seashells. Five feet into the room, I step on, and almost stumble over, a sock with something in it. Upon closer inspection, it's a rock. A sock with a rock inside it. *What the hell?*

There isn't a lot in the way of furniture in here. Small blessing. A quick look through his dresser yields nothing but more clothes and random knick-knacks. A dragon lunchbox that looks vaguely familiar, and inside it a cheap dragon snow globe, and a few photos. Me, Chance, Hunter. All from when we were younger, taken by Dad before he was shot. There are a few of Chance and his mother, mostly from when he was little. The pictures are faded and frayed at the edges, like he's had to fight just to keep them from vanishing altogether. Also inside is a lone Barbie head that makes me flash back to the day we met by the creek. Staring into its expressionless face for too long sends a chill down my spine. I close the box and put it back.

There is no door on the closet. The floor is a mess of shoes that have been there for God knows how long. They're falling apart, some of them, and I spot a pair I recognize. Apple red sneakers, way too small for Chance's feet. But they didn't used to be. He still has shoes from when he was a kid. You could line them all up and see the progression of his growth.

I search through the junk on the floor, feel around under the bed, finding nothing but more clothes and a few *Rolling Stone* magazines. Sighing, I sit back and survey the room again, letting the flashlight roam every inch of space. Then, in the pile of clothes, the light catches off something shiny, and I pause, go over it again, and locate it near the bottom of the pile.

Heart in my throat, I scramble over Chance's bed and make a grab for the camera, which is nestled among a bunch of T-shirts with the lens pointed out. Like he's used it as a hidden security camera. Either the police didn't search his room, or they didn't do a very good job. I press the power button a few times, but nothing happens. The battery is dead.

But I have it. I found it. And given its location, I'd say it's safe to wager there is something on here we can use. I can go home and charge it, and then we'll have our evidence to save Chance.

Across the house, the front door opens.

HUNTER

For some reason, one of the delivery trucks at the store doesn't show tonight. Which is a problem, considering I'm on truck duty and a few hours before my shift is supposed to end, I have nothing left to do. Rather than pay me to sit around for nothing, my boss ushers me out the door. "Go home. Get some rest. Tomorrow's gonna blow for everyone because we'll have that extra truck to unload…"

Fine by me, because I don't work tomorrow. Still, I think she could've found something to keep me busy, but she knows—everyone knows, it seems—that someone I'm close to is a suspect in a murder. Our town isn't big and maybe not everyone knows each other, but when someone is shot to death, it generally makes its way around pretty quickly.

I hop in the car and linger in the parking lot, at a loss

for what to do. Other than check my cell. Again. And try to call Chance. Again. When he doesn't answer, I drop the phone into the empty passenger's seat, close my eyes, and wonder what it would be like if I never got to see Chance again. It was bad enough having no way of contacting him all those years. I tried.

Just as I put the key in the ignition, my phone lights up and rings.

Ash, probably. Or Dad. Though I don't know what either of them would need from me while I'm at work. I get the engine going so the heater can warm me up, then I pull the phone to my ear with a sigh. "Hello?"

"You should really stop calling."

I freeze, heart lurching into my throat. "Chance."

The line is infused with static. He sounds far away, like he's speaking from the end of a tunnel.

"I told Ash…you need to…lling, or you'll get yourselves in—"

"You're cutting out," I interrupt. He keeps talking, and I wonder if he can hear me at all. "Chance, listen, where are you? Let me see you and we'll talk."

For a minute, he's so quiet I worry he hung up on me, and then— "I shouldn't have dragged…this. I've cau…these problems."

"Don't worry about it right now." My throat constricts. I try to breathe. In and out. I try not to yell at him, to say anything that might make him disconnect or get upset. Everything about his voice is tired, heavy, cold. I can hear the waver to his words; he's been sitting in the snow for too long. "Just tell me where you are. I'll come by myself. Just me, all right?"

"No," Chance hums. "No, no, no. This is the last…m calling, Hunt. To say I love you. Promise you won…me anymore."

"Chance!"

"Promise me."

I wet my lips because my mouth is a desert, but before I can say anything further, the line clicks and disconnects.

Dead. Gone.

Swearing, I try to call back. Chance's number goes straight to voice mail.

Damn it. *Damn it.*

"Calm down," I tell my reflection in the rearview mirror. "If you were Chance, where would you go?"

Where, indeed? I stare into my own panicked eyes, struggling to find some sense of inner calm to think this through. Where would Chance feel safe from the police, from Zeke? Where would he hide that would be cold and have horrible reception? The town is only so big, and he wouldn't have gone too far…

Yes.

That's it.

He's not technically in town anymore.

• • •

The wind and snow scream at me on the beach. The rocks are slick and icy under my shoes, and the cold stings my eyes, making it difficult to see. I drag the raft behind me, one step at a time, praying to whatever higher power exists that a rock doesn't snag and tear it because it's my only method of getting to Chance.

That's assuming I'm right. And that I haven't completely lost my mind, because I'm starting to wonder. I tried to call Ash on my way here, and she didn't answer. I don't want to waste time going all the way home to drag her out of bed. By the time we got back, Chance could be gone…or worse.

By moonlight, I struggle to get the raft blown up and into the water. The ocean swirls around my feet, soaking my jeans up to the knees, instantly numbing my toes and making my jaw tense to keep my teeth from chattering. I could be wrong, and this could be useless, but it's my only lead.

My only chance.

Ha.

I tuck my phone into an inside pocket of my coat, hoping it'll stay dry, and shove the raft farther out before crawling in. Manning the oars of a multi-person raft with just me in this weather isn't going to be easy. The tide threatens to throw me right back onto the shore until I manage to paddle out a safe distance.

The island is an inky blob against the dark sky. Wind throws flurries of snow into my face, blinding me, making every stroke of the oar a guess as to whether I'm veering off the right path.

Chance could be out there. Somewhere on that island, alone and scared and freezing to death and why, why, *why*? Why doesn't he ever let me keep him safe?

Finally, by some miracle, by some grace of the stars, the nose of the raft glides onto the island shore, lodging on the rocks and dirt and sand. I clamber out, struggling to pull the raft to safety so the current doesn't sweep it back out to sea. When I drag it behind the shelter of the broken wall we used last time, I spot another raft tucked away there.

A smaller raft. Better fit for one or two people as opposed to many.

Chance's raft? Who else would come out here in this weather? No one is that stupid. He would've had to buy the smallest he could find. I don't know how he did it, or how he got it all the way out here without a car. Then again, I should never underestimate the power of Chance's will when he wants to do something.

I cup my hands to my mouth, screaming his name in a cold-hoarse voice and listening to the silence that answers. The wind whistles eerily through every tree and broken building, crying a hundred phantom voices, playing tricks on my ears until I don't know which way to go.

The island is only so big. I head down the main path between the crumbling structures, searching for something, anything. A source of light, a fire, a voice, a sign of life. I need Chance to be here. I need him to be okay.

I find the building we picnicked at on New Year's and find my way up the stairs to the rooftop for a better look around. I have to approach the edge of the building on my hands and knees, because the footing is slippery and the wind threatens to shove me right off the ledge.

From up here, I have a view of a good portion of the island. The snow is clean and glimmers brightly under the moonlight, and in it, I spot a set of tracks, footprints that aren't my own. The footprints of the one other person who could possibly be here. I do the only thing there is to do; I get off the rooftop and follow the tracks across the island.

Where they lead me is a leaning structure, bent against the wind. The prints circle then vanish at the building's entrance, where the door is a heavy wooden thing barely hanging on by a single hinge. I put my shoulder into it; it scrapes against the aged flooring. Inside, it isn't any warmer. Not really. But minus the chill factor of the wind, it has to be an improvement. Still, no human being could stay out here for long.

"Chance?"

No answer.

I search the first room with nothing more than a glance, flashlight beam swinging from one side to the other. A faint scuffling from a neighboring room alerts me to a door in the corner I almost missed in the darkness. Could be an animal. Could be Chance.

"Chance, it's me." I move across the feeble floorboards to the other room.

Chance doesn't answer me, but I see him. On the floor. In the far corner. Huddled in on himself with his head down, hood pulled up, knees to his chest, arms locked around them. Tiny and still, but here. Alive.

I found him.

The flashlight clatters to the floor. I drop to my knees in front of him, touching his arms, his shoulders, pushing his hood back.

"Chance. *Chance*, look at me."

Slowly, Chance tilts his head, like that little bit of movement takes him so much effort. "Hey," he mumbles, and then, "Hi."

A relieved breath rushes out of me. I cup a hand to his cheek, barely refraining from jerking away. God, he's so *cold*. His eyelids flutter and then close at my touch. I shake his shoulder gently with my other hand.

"No. I need you to stay awake, got it? We're going to get you out of here and someplace warm." I pull back and skim out of my jacket so I can wrap it around him. Immediately, the cold bites through my sweater and the T-shirt beneath, but I try to ignore it. I pull the phone from the jacket pocket and try to dial 911. There's no reception for regular calls, but I remember learning something about emergency calls working via satellite even if you aren't getting service.

I tell the dispatcher where we are and that Chance needs an ambulance immediately. She asks me not to hang up, but I don't have a choice. There's no telling how long it would take them to get out here with something like a helicopter, so I need to at least get us back to the beach.

Chance heaves a sigh as I pull his arm around my shoulders, circle mine on his waist, and drag him to his feet. He only halfway holds his own weight, leaving me to bear the rest of it, and he mumbles, "We going to the beach?"

"Sure." I start out of the room. *Calm, Hunter, calm.* He's conscious, he's talking. Maybe not coherently, but still. "We'll go to the beach if you want. Only if you stay awake and keep talking to me."

Together, we stagger back out into the snow. Chance begins to shiver, as though the flakes dusting his cheeks have reminded his body how unbearably cold it is. I lead him back to the rafts, prodding him with questions that he mumbles nonsensical answers to. Anything to keep him talking and, even if not walking, still moving his legs like he's *trying* to walk.

I don't trust myself to get us back in the big raft. I'm also not sure how to drag it out to the water and get Chance inside at the same time. His little raft is easier to manage while still hanging onto him. I haul Chance unceremoniously into it while shoving it away, and he only lays there and lets out a low, displeased groan. When I clamber inside, I pull him up into my arms, keeping him as close as I can, letting him feed off my body heat for however much or little it helps.

Chance's raft is a flimsy, cheap thing, easily pushed around by the wind even with the weight of two people in it. I row until my arms burn. Until I'm positive we're going in the wrong direction because I row and row and row and eventually, I'll have no strength in me to keep going. Chance and I will float out to sea, just the two of us, and together beneath the stars he loves so much, we will freeze to death.

But then the tide helps push us toward Harper's Beach, though it still isn't close enough. I keep hold of his arm with one hand, and slide over the edge of the raft and into the frigid ocean. I anticipated it being about thigh-high, but the water reaches the center of my chest. The shock of cold renders me unable to move at first as my lungs and limbs seize up. But the shore is *right there*. With every bit of effort I can muster, I dig my feet into the ground and pull until the raft gives a satisfying scrape against the shore.

I haul Chance out, ignoring the abandoned oars and the way the water threatens to carry them away. We won't need it again. Chance drops his head to my shoulder as I stagger up the beach, panting, shivering, muscles aching from carrying almost dead weight. But I make it back to the car, pull Chance into the back along with me, and shut the doors, protecting us from the wind.

Here, I can shove my key in the ignition and get the heater going. For Chance, and for myself before I'm in as bad a state as he is. I tilt my head back against the window, still trying to catch my breath and telling myself everything will be okay now. Chance presses his face into my throat, and I feel his shaky breathing against my skin, warm and labored. He whispers, "Can't see them."

I force my voice into cooperation, rubbing at his arms to warm him. "Can't see what?"

"Stars." His lips move; I can feel them on my neck. So, so cold. "Can't see the stars."

Of course. He would be thinking about something like that at a time like this, wouldn't he? I shift back, until I can look at his face and slide a hand through his hair. "We're made of stars. You said so yourself. So can you just look at me for now?"

Chance's bright green eyes slit open to watch me. I'm pretty sure that's a smile tugging at his mouth. He doesn't try to talk anymore. I let him stare at me while I stare back, touching his face, his hair, pressing the occasional kiss to his forehead.

The paramedics arrive within ten minutes, a blur of whirling lights and deafening sirens. They pull Chance away from me, bundling him up, getting him on a gurney. I want to go with him, but a paramedic puts a hand to my chest.

"He'll be all right, son. Best not to leave your car out here. Just follow us to the hospital, hmm?"

That's true, but I still linger even as they load him into the back of the ambulance and drive away. Guilt, anger, worry all knot in my insides and broil beneath the surface. He's fine. He's going to live.

But is he going to be *okay*?

ASHLIN

I freeze for the five seconds it takes my brain to register what's going on: someone is in the house with me. And unless it's Chance—which I know it's not—that is a Very. Bad. Thing.

Off goes the flashlight. I whip around and try for the window, giving it a good yank, only to realize it's been nailed shut. Chance never would've done such a thing, meaning Zeke did it. He locked Chance inside so he couldn't sneak out.

No way would I have time to slip into the hall and find another hiding place. So under the bed it is. Dust bunnies tickle my nose along with the smell of unwashed laundry, and it's all I can do to make myself as small as possible and pray to every deity I can think of to make me invisible.

The footsteps come into the hall, one slow, cautious step at a time. Not the police, then. Honestly, I'd rather deal with

Roger or one of the other officers busting me for this than come face to face with Zeke Harvey.

Adrenaline pours through me, flushing into every vein, every nerve, making my muscles twitch and tense even as I'm trying to stay still. Maybe he'll walk past. Maybe he'll go to his room—*shit, shit, shit, did I close the window?*—and he'll never come in here.

Except the footfalls travel right past the door…and stop.

My phone is going off.

It's on vibrate, but the buzzing of its movement is a sound in and of itself, and I don't know how loud it is. If it's loud enough for someone to hear it from the hall. It buzzes a few times then goes still again in my back pocket; I exhale as slowly as I can. It could have been Dad. It could have been Hunter. Either way, whoever it was is going to worry that I didn't answer, and—

Chance's door swings open.

I press my hands over my mouth and nose. *Breathe, Ash. Breathe slowly. Easy. Relax. Calm.*

From my position, I can see feet. Dirty, old, tan work boots, laces knotted tightly. The kind of boots that would belong to someone like Zeke Harvey. He strolls through the mess on the floor and stops, just by the foot of the bed. All it would take is for him to lean down and peek underneath and we'd be eye to eye and he'd kill me.

I want to shut my eyes so badly, but if he does look under here, I have to be ready to roll out and make a run for it. Run as fast as I can. Take off out the front door and into the woods where he'll never find me, and I can follow the creek back home.

Escape plan. See? Everything will be okay.

(I have never wanted my brother with me so badly in all my life.)

Zeke starts over toward the pile of laundry beneath the window. I think he's looking outside. When he turns around, he comes across one of the rocks stuffed into a sock and steps on it, startling him to his knees.

"Fuck," he snarls, snatching up the sock and chucking it at the wall. "Bash that boy's head in…"

The rocks weren't Chance's craziness, I realize. They were protection. A deterrent to keep Zeke out of his room. Or at least to give Chance an opportunity to get away. His room is an obstacle course.

Still swearing threats under his breath, Zeke leaves the room. I strain my ears for the sound of him, wondering if maybe, maybe I could risk a phone call to the police to tell them Zeke is in the house. Maybe they could get here in time to arrest him. I'd have to explain myself for breaking in, but who cares? In the grand scheme of things…

No, first things first, I need to get outside. He'll hear me if I call now, and then I won't be of use to anyone.

After a few painful minutes of hearing nothing, Zeke's steps sound in the hall again, this time accompanied by the noise of something being dragged…rolled? A suitcase? Did he come home to get some things so he could take off? What if he doesn't plan on sticking around in town like Chance thought? What if he chalks it up as a loss and decides to get the hell away while he can?

My stomach lurches as the front door opens and closes again. I wait a few seconds longer and then, trembling, biting back tears, I roll out from under the bed and shove the camera into my pocket.

I need to get out of here. Now.

I dart down the hall, back into Zeke's room, not taking any time to try to figure out what he packed and brought with him. The window is shut. I can't remember if I closed it. I slide it back open, swinging my leg over the frame to crawl outside. My feet hit first the cinder blocks, and then the snow. I'm free. Safe.

Then I turn to see Zeke a few feet away, eyes locked onto mine.

His mouth pulls up into a sneer. "You…"

I don't let him finish that sentence. I'm tearing off for the trees as fast as my legs will take me. Zeke roars after me and oh, God, I don't even know which direction to go in the dark. He screams for me to stop. Right. Like I'm about to come to a screeching halt because a rampaging bull tells me I should.

The sound of the creek is a symphony to my ears. I take a left, ducking branches, fumbling for my flashlight. Not realizing Zeke is close. Not until his strong hand wraps on my bicep and spins me around.

Except we're close enough to the creek now, and the ground here slopes drastically. I throw my full weight back, catching him off guard enough that we both lose our footing… and down we go.

For a minute, the world goes black.

But I've stopped rolling. Pain blossoms hotly from my

right shoulder. Snow is melting down the back of my shirt. I grasp for my flashlight—gone. My phone—gone. Only the camera is still in place. Whether in one piece or not, I don't know. Not sticking around long enough to find out.

Nearby, Zeke groans and begins to pick himself up. I roll onto my back and scoot away, scrambling for purchase as he crawls through the snow toward me. A rivet of blood creeps down one side of his face.

"Where is he?" Zeke rasps. "Where is Chance?"

The heel of my shoe catches a rock firmly embedded in the frozen ground; it grants me enough leverage to push to my feet and start up the hill. I don't say anything. I don't look back. I keep going until my lungs are fit to burst and I'm on solid ground again. Only then do I look over my shoulder. Zeke is still at the bottom of the hill, struggling to climb it. I take a few steps back, mourning the loss of my phone.

But I have the camera, and right now that takes priority.

I vanish into the darkness and try to find my way home.

HUNTER

I don't have the luxury of running through every red light like the ambulance, so I figure by the time I get to the hospital lobby, they must have Chance already registered and in there somewhere. The emergency room is surprisingly quiet this time of night. Only a few parents with sniffly children and an old lady with a bad cough. I'm still wet and cold, but I had a change of clothes for work in the trunk, so I take a detour for the bathroom to at least get into something dry.

In the lobby, no one is in line so I go straight to the receptionist. "My friend was brought in just a bit ago," I say. "Last name is Harvey."

The lady, a younger girl with her hair braided and wearing thick glasses, checks her computer. "Hmm... No, I don't see that name."

I know he's here, I start to say, then realize—I never told the paramedics his name. He's a John Doe, for all they know, especially if Chance didn't have an ID on him. "He came in the ambulance, he's about my age. They probably don't know his name." When she only stares at me, I add, "Please. Please, can you just…make a phone call and see?"

She relents, picking up the phone and ringing somewhere else in the building to ask about a teenage boy brought in. I strain to hear whatever is said, but the voice on the other end is too muffled.

The receptionist hangs up and inclines her head. "He's going to be all right. They're treating him for hypothermia, and he's sleeping."

I brace my hands against the counter and exhale. "Can I see him?"

"I'm afraid not. Family only."

"How do you know I'm not family?"

"You said he was your friend." She smiles wanly. "I'm sorry. Though any information you can give us on his identity would be appreciated. They said he had no identification on him. What did you say his last name was? Harvard?"

My eyes narrow. "So I'm not allowed to see him, but I'm allowed to tell you who he is?" I push away from the counter. "No thanks."

She doesn't try to stop me as I stomp off. It's a dramatic gesture, only done out of spite, and maybe I ought to go back and tell her Chance's name, but what good will it do him? What if she inputs his name into the computer and it somehow alerts the police department? Will they come down here and arrest him? I can stand a lot of things, but I'm not so sure I could stand watching them put Chance in handcuffs and shove him in the back of a cruiser.

But I can't just go home. I can't sit around here forever, either, and hope a nurse takes pity on me and lets me in to see Chance. Dad might have the push to get access, but that would mean—

I'd have to tell him. He would need to know I went after Chance on that island, and there's no telling if *he* would call Roger and alert them that Chance is here.

I sink onto a bench outside, exhausted from being in the cold but not wanting to be inside with the people and their flus and sniffly kids and normal, everyday problems while our world is spiraling further and further into the realm of *what the hell is happening.* I try to go through the steps of sorting everything out in my head.

First, most importantly, Chance is going to be okay. Hypothermia can kill you, yeah, but he was conscious and talking so he can't be that bad. Whatever else may happen, Chance is going to live.

Second, even if the cops take him in, even if he's arrested and punished for evading the police, it has to be better than all the running and hiding he's been doing. Better than freezing to death. And certainly better than risking a run-in with Zeke.

Third, Dad will be severely ticked off at me, but he'll also be happy to know Chance is safe. The anger will fade with time (and a lot of lecturing), but if Chance had died…that isn't something that would ever go away.

After I've composed myself enough, I pull out my cell and

call Ash again. Her phone goes straight to voice mail. Weird. Unfortunately, that means I'm stuck calling Dad because there is no landline at the house, and even if there were, I doubt Ash would answer it.

Dad's phone rings a few times before he answers blearily, "H'llo?"

"It's me." Pause. "I found Chance."

Immediately, Dad is awake and alert. "Where is he? For that matter— Jesus, look at the time— Where are you?"

"The hospital." I grimace at the way Dad swears loudly. He doesn't do it often, so when he does... "I'm okay. Chance is okay. He's got hypothermia, but they said he'll be fine. Can you just..."

I pride myself on being a pretty tough guy. Level-headed. I'm not a crier. I'm not a baby. I don't rely on others to help me through things. But I realize right now, in this very instant, in this situation where I feel so lost and fumbling and confused...

I really, really need my dad.

Because he's my dad, he understands without my having to finish that statement. "I'll be there as soon as I can, Hunter. Hang tight."

ASHLIN

Home has never felt so good. My bones ache from the snow, which is turning into a full-force blizzard by now. Dad's light is still out, thank God, so I can crawl up to my room, where I sink to my bed.

And cry.

I press my face into my hands, torn between sobbing and laughing. Because I just broke into someone's house. Because a murderer *chased me through the fucking woods*. Because I can't tell anyone about it, so I need to breathe and remind myself it's okay, I'm okay, and it was worth it. Zeke doesn't know where I live; he can't follow me home. No way. He'll have gotten back into his truck and driven the hell out of here.

A failure on my part that I didn't call the cops and get him caught, but at least if he's away, he can't hurt Chance.

I allow myself a few minutes to cry and laugh and breathe and work the numbness from my fingers. Then I pull the camera out of my pocket, tracing the crack across the screen with my thumb. Great.

But the camera itself isn't important. I slide the memory card out of the side and pop it into my computer while waiting for it to boot up. I glance at the clock. Hunter should've been home already. Unfortunately, my only method of contacting him at the moment is lost, probably broken, somewhere in the woods near Chance's trailer.

On the memory card are a ton of sub-folders. The camera automatically creates one for each day pictures are taken. Maybe I ought to start at the end, but I can't bring myself to. Whatever is in this, I have a feeling, is not going to be pretty. Maybe I should wait for Hunter. Maybe I should...

Suck it up and be a big girl. I came this far on my own. Besides, I have to protect Hunter from what is on here, too; I can handle this better than he can, when it comes to Chance.

I open the first folder.

There are some pictures of no consequence. Some shots of the sky, trees, Chance's room. Like he was testing the camera out, seeing how it worked. I skim through them with growing impatience, wanting to get to the important stuff. I didn't possibly risk my life to see scenery.

Then comes a video. Short. Thirty seconds. It takes some courage for me to hit play.

Chance's face appears, smiling and chipper and unblemished by bruises. From the positioning, I think he has the camera set on the dresser, so he can sit on the edge of his bed and talk.

"Hello! Hi!" he says, waving. "Chance Harvey here. Though if you're watching this, you're probably Ash or Hunter. S'up, guys?"

My heart simultaneously melts and tightens all at once. What a drastic difference this Chance is from the one I saw in the alley after work the other day.

Chance continues. "And, if you've found this, I'm guessing something has happened. Kind of sucks, doesn't it? Well, to help things along, I'm using this camera to do some clue-hunting. Collect some evidence. So whatever happens… hopefully this will help." He grins, lifts his fingers in a wiggling wave, then rises from the bed to turn off the recording.

I was right. Chance used this to document the goings-on in his house. His evidence of what his dad was doing to him — and to his mom. Taking a deep breath to steady my nerves, I resume flicking through photos.

After Chance's video, they take a drastic turn.

Bruises.

A hole in the wall.

A bloody nose.

These must have been during the time he was avoiding us. He didn't want us to see what had been done to him.

A swollen lip, a black eye.

Then another video. This time, the lens is positioned from its hiding spot: Chance's pile of clothes. It's tucked away, recording, and anyone else in the room is oblivious to it. This video is longer; thirty minutes, to be exact. It begins with Chance positioning the camera, making sure the lens isn't covered, but his movements are hurried, frantic, and Zeke is hollering somewhere in the background.

Chance himself says nothing. He hunkers down on his bed, still and silent. Studying his door. There's another voice— Tabitha's, I assume—screaming back. Crying. At the sound of that voice, Chance launches himself off the bed and out the door, and his yelling joins the cacophony of sound.

Glass shatters. Tabitha sobs. Chance and Zeke scream and scuffle.

Something hits the wall and again and again, Zeke threatens—"I'll kill you, you ungrateful little"—and Tabitha begs for them to stop.

There are more pictures after that. Proof of the aftermath of what Zeke did beyond yelling, beyond hollow threats.

And more videos to follow. Some like the first. Nothing more than video of an empty room with shouting matches in the background. There are others, where I catch a glimpse of a fight in the hallway. More still, of Chance barreling into his room, chest heaving, nose bleeding, hands trembling with the adrenaline pumping through his system.

"—should've put you in a bag and drowned you—"

Zeke flings open the door with enough force that the doorknob punctures a hole in the wall. In the bedroom, Chance is safer. He is spry and knows the danger of the floor, so he springs out of the way while Zeke lunges for him and trips over shoes, stubs his toes on sock-concealed rocks, snarling and swearing.

Zeke, storming into the room another time, armed with a hammer and a fistful of nails. Chance rears back, like he expects they're somehow meant for him, but for once Zeke ignores him and heads for the pile of clothes. For the window. The camera is knocked askew, covered with cotton, and even the sound is muffled.

"Let's see you sneak out now."

More footsteps. Silence.

Chance grunting while he tries — I assume — to force open the window.

"Son of a bitch."

His voice, weak and angry and tired.

I stop after that video, rubbing at my eyes. Having to pause because I thought I heard something downstairs. Dad's bedroom door, I think. He's probably just getting up for the bathroom.

I wonder why Hunter isn't home.

I watch video after video of similar yelling and fighting, flip through a dozen photos. One more, I decide, then I'll worry about the fact my brother is out later than he ought to be.

In this video, most of Chance's injuries are healed over, or are at least not visible. I can hear Tabitha's voice: " — talk to you?"

"Come in," Chance says as he drops the camera. By the way he doesn't aim it like he has every other video, I almost wonder whether he realizes it's recording. Chance settles back on his bed. The camera lens is catching him from the neck up. It's the first time in all the videos Tabitha Harvey has stepped into Chance's room, despite the number of times he flew to her defense. She never once tried to get between Chance and his dad. What kind of mother does that? What kind of parent so blatantly ignores the suffering of her kid, especially when it's happening right under her nose?

Tabitha clicks her tongue at the state of the room, but Chance just stares at her as she sits beside him.

"I got the call from the lawyer. All I have to do is go in tomorrow and sign the paperwork, and the money is mine." She sounds so excited, so hopeful.

Is this what happened? Was Tabitha finally going to leave her husband and get out of there? And did Zeke find out, so that it finally sent him over the edge?

"Heard that before," Chance mutters.

"Watch your tone, young man." Tabitha pulls her hands back as though burned. "Don't be ungrateful. Do you want me to leave you here? Is that it? Because I will."

Chance picks at lint on his mattress, eyes glued to his bare feet.

Tabitha prods, "Well?"

"No, ma'am." He doesn't look up, but everything about his demeanor is smaller, softer, afraid of being left behind. Maybe she would. She spent all his life not protecting him; why would she start now?

The video comes to an end. I only have one folder left.

"Ashlin!"

Dad's voice jerks me out of my endless loop of dread-filled questions. I spin in my chair to face the hall. What's he doing up this late? More importantly, what's he doing awake and yelling for me at the top of his lungs?

I roll my chair to the door, head popping out into the

hallway and calling back before Dad tries something stupid like climbing the stairs. "What?"

"Down here, now!"

The back of my neck prickles. Going somewhere, in the middle of the night? Where is Hunter? I look at my computer, worrying my bottom lip. Chance's evidence will need to wait, I guess. For now, I flick off the monitor and head downstairs. Dad is dressed, frazzled, worried lines creasing his brow. He looks me over. "I tried calling your phone—were you still awake?" When I stare at him blankly, he adds, "You're still dressed."

I do my best not to look flustered. "Yeah, uh, what's going on? Is everything okay?"

He clenches his jaw, runs a hand down his face, and turns away. "Get your shoes on."

"Dad?" He's starting to freak me out, like, seriously. I head to the entryway to shove my feet back into my shoes, praying Dad doesn't notice my jeans are wet and my shoes have left a puddle of melted snow on the floor.

If he does, he makes no comment. Only grabs his coat from its hook and swings it on. He's either upset or he's angry or—crap, I can't tell which. I've never really seen Dad seriously angry or worried. He's always been the sort to take everything with a grain of salt, to take a deep breath and reassure everyone around him. I let him float in his bubble of silence until we get out to the truck. Then, with me behind the steering wheel, he seems to realize he *has* to tell me what's going on because I have no flipping clue where he wants me to go.

"The hospital," he finally says, strained. "Hunter found Chance."

My hands clench the wheel so tightly it hurts. But I put the truck into gear and pull out onto the road. I don't trust my voice. This is why he didn't say anything—because I shouldn't drive if I'm upset, and because *he's* upset…

"I think he's all right," Dad offers, but his voice is so distant I can only imagine the things running through his head. He hasn't stopped blaming himself for this. Then again, neither have I. Neither has Hunter.

We've been going on and on about how he's part of our family, and every one of us failed to protect him.

I bob my head into a mute nod but keep any commentary to myself. *All right* is such a vague term. Pretty much anything seems *all right* next to, say, death, doesn't it? *All right* equates to *alive* but not necessarily *and well*. Very big differences.

There is no point in trying to comfort each other. I could promise him everything will turn out okay, that nothing else bad is going to happen, but why? We both know all too well this could end horribly. That the best years of our lives with Chance could be behind us, and everything that lies ahead…

Dread weighs heavily in my stomach.

The last time I stepped foot inside a hospital was when Dad got shot. That night wasn't terribly unlike tonight, either. Hunter and I were home alone while Dad worked. He'd promised to be back in time for dinner and left enough cash for a pizza. Dinner had come and gone, and no Dad. We sat on the couch with a movie on, me nestled against Hunter's side, feeling alone without Dad there and without Chance to lighten the mood.

(Thinking back, that must've been one of the times he vanished for a few days because he'd taken a beating and didn't want us to ask questions.)

Close to eleven that night, Roger came knocking on the door to tell us what had happened. A couple of guys wanted a few counties over for bank robbery...and Dad had been a part of the group who had tried to chase them down when they were spotted here in town. He was also the only one who had been shot and almost died.

We stayed at Roger's that night, sleeping on a guest bed, Hunter and me together. We begged to stay home because how else would Chance know what had happened? But Roger would hear none of it, leaving us alone all night. We didn't call our moms. Not right away. Sure enough, when Dad came to and it was clear he was out of the woods, he scolded us, and the next day Hunter's mom came to get him, and I was on a plane back to California.

They took us away from Dad, who I was determined *needed* us, and then—they took us away from each other. I needed Hunter then as much as I think he needed me...and we both needed Chance.

I'm not sure I've ever forgiven my mom for that. Not sure I've forgiven myself, either, for not fighting harder.

This time will be different.

I reach out and wrap my hand around Dad's. He startles then squeezes back.

I find a parking spot right up front. Is the emergency room always quiet this time of night, or are we lucky? I hop out of the truck, circling around to watch Dad—while pretending not to—get out and pick his way on his cane across the icy parking lot.

"Don't slip," I warn.

He replies with a thin smile, "If I do, at least we're at a hospital."

Inside, the air smells funny. Sterile but not clean, if that makes sense. Like the scents of bleach and disinfectant are masking whatever underlying odor of germs and bacteria is on the waiting room seats, the vending machine buttons, the pens they keep at the front desk.

Among the others in the lobby, I spot Hunter, hunched over with his eyes locked onto the television mounted in the corner. He doesn't seem to be watching it, exactly, just staring because it's something to occupy some part of his brain.

Dad says his name, and he snaps out of his self-induced trance, immediately standing. He opens his arms with the same reflex that I go into them and hug him tightly. He bows his head, mumbling into my hair, "They won't really tell me anything. Because I'm not *family*." He spits this last word like it's full of venom. Like the employees here don't know a thing about what constitutes *family*.

"You didn't tell them who he was, did you?" Dad asks, ushering us to sit. I keep hold of Hunter's hand in my own. He shakes his head.

"No. I got sort of…mad they wouldn't let me in to see him, so I refused to say anything."

Dad sighs. "We need to give them his information. Otherwise, you're going to get busted for helping harbor a fugitive."

Hunter pushes his shoulders back. His spine stiffens. The mere idea of calling the cops doesn't sit well with him. Can't say it sits well with me, either.

"How did you even find him?" I ask. Dad nods. Undoubtedly, he's interested in the answer to this, too.

"He called me." Hunt stares down at our joined hands. His thumb touches each of my knuckles, one after the other, distracting himself. "I found out he was on Hollow Island and I…I had to go get him. If he thought the police were coming, he would've left again. We never would've found him."

With a shake of his head, Dad sighs. But a sigh isn't a reprimand. I'm not sure there is a way he can lecture Hunter for doing something that ultimately saved Chance's life. Instead, he asks, "Are *you* okay?"

Finally, Hunter looks up. Really, he doesn't have to say anything. Dad knows. I know. I rest my head on Hunter's shoulder, and his rests atop mine. Dad folds a hand on Hunter's shoulder.

Here we sit, a family, in a hospital waiting room, all of us knowing what needs to be done and no one wanting to do it. No one knowing how we all could have failed so horrendously. All of us thinking of every little thing we could've done differently. Regretting every little thing we *didn't* do.

Finally, Dad stands. "I'd better go call Roger. You okay here?"

Hunter doesn't respond.

I squeeze his arm tight. "Yeah, we're fine."

Dad fishes his phone out of his pocket and trudges out of

the lobby. Hunter watches him go. "I tried calling you. Your phone went straight to voice mail."

"That would be because my phone is lost somewhere in the woods near Chance's house." When Hunt pulls back to stare at me, I give him a frown. "I don't want to hear it. I didn't go swimming out to an island in a blizzard."

"I didn't *swim*. I took the raft."

"How in the world did Chance get out there?"

"He had a raft, too. Guess he swung into somewhere and bought one rather than risk trying to steal ours."

"Maybe. Or some part of him was hoping you'd realize where he was and run to his rescue." That thought pisses me off as much as it upsets me. He should've never put Hunter in that kind of position or danger. He shouldn't have put *himself* in that position. He had to have *known* we wouldn't rest until we found him.

Hunter grunts in acknowledgment. "What were you doing at Chance's house?"

I know we're alone. As alone as one can be in a lobby, anyway. Still, I glance around to make sure no one is listening in. "Nearly getting caught by Zeke Harvey. I got my camera. Chance recorded things."

Hunter's face pales. He seems torn on whether to question me about what happened with Zeke, or the camera. "Things? Did he—"

"I don't know. I didn't have the opportunity to finish looking through them before Dad told me we were leaving to come here. But if so, we'll have evidence. We'll have proof of what Zeke did, and Chance will be okay."

He nods once, slowly, taking all this in.

I poke a finger at his ribs. "You don't look happy about that. It's a good thing, you realize."

"I know." He doesn't budge. "I want to see him."

"They should let us once he's awake, I think." Unless the cops swarm in and refuse to let him have visitors. How does that sort of thing work?

When Dad returns to our little corner of the waiting room, his expression is unreadable. I don't blame him. What he had to do...it had to have been difficult. Calling the cops on a boy he considers one of his own children.

"They're on their way. I convinced the nurses to let you have a few minutes, if you want to see him."

Hunter's head snaps up. "We can go in? But how—"

Dad smiles thinly. "Did you forget how much time I spent in this hospital? They all know me here. I explained Chance's only other visitors were going to be cops." He inclines his chin toward the double doors. "But you'd better get a move on. The police won't be happy if they find out I encouraged visitors to pop in there."

We don't need to be told twice. Dad stays behind as lookout while Hunt and I both grab a visitor's name tag from the receptionist's desk, get Chance's room number, and slip through the doors.

The image of Dad lying in a hospital bed, barely conscious from medication, has dulled over the years but is still fresh enough to make me a little nauseous at the idea of seeing Chance like that. I can only hope he's awake so we can reassure him everything is going to be okay. Hunter grips my hand so

painfully tight, I almost consider letting him go in by himself
to give them some time alone, but…no. Call me selfish, but I
need to be there, too. I need to let him know about the camera.

Chance's room is a double, but the other bed is unoccupied.
We step inside, easing the door shut. Chance's clothing is
folded neatly on the table next to him. Chance himself is
asleep. Hooked up to machines. Small and vulnerable. Hunter
freezes for half a second before pressing forward to Chance's
side, and I follow along wordlessly.

Staring into Chance's face, I decide this is definitely
better than seeing Dad. Chance looks pretty much normal. As
normal as anyone can look in a hospital gown, under a ton of
itchy blankets, and hooked up to monitors and tubes.

"How does he look?" I ask Hunt. "Compared to before."

Hunt extends a hand. The tips of his fingers brush against
Chance's cheek so achingly soft that it makes my heart break.
"Better. Before, he was so…pale. Cold. I thought he was dead
when I first found him."

"Rude," Chance whispers.

We startle. I ease onto the bed, wrapping my fingers
around Chance's hand. "You're awake."

"You're loud," he says in a voice that sounds like broken
glass. He opens his eyes very slowly, rolling his gaze to Hunter
and saying, simply, "Hi."

"Hi." Hunter all but collapses into a chair, dragging
it closer and leaning his elbows on the bed. He can't stop
touching Chance. His shoulder, his face, his hair, such utter
relief visible in his features. "You scared the hell out of me,
you jackass."

Chance soaks up every bit of attention. His fingers curl against my hand. "Let me guess. The cops are on their way."

Hunt and I exchange glances. "Yeah," I say.

Chance nods and looks at the ceiling.

"What about the camera?" Hunter asks.

This gets Chance's attention again. "Camera?"

"The one you hid in your room," I say. "I snuck in and got it." I force myself to grin. "It's the evidence you needed, right? What you were telling me about?"

Chance looks somewhere between amused and sad. "Lovely. Did you look through it yet?"

"Some of it. Got called away here before I was able to finish. I'll give it to the cops, and they'll release you as a suspect in no time."

"You snuck into my house?" He laughs hoarsely. "And Hunter crossed the ocean in the snow to rescue me from an island. You two never stop surprising me."

"What is family for?" I ask.

"That depends. Your family or mine?"

"You *are* our family," Hunter insists.

Chance makes a noise. Someone knocks on the door, and then a nurse pops her head in.

"Sorry to interrupt… Your father asked me to come get you. He said it's time to go."

He wasn't kidding when he said a few minutes, was he? No time for questions, no time for anything. I slide off the bed after giving Chance's hand one last squeeze. Chance tries to hang on, brows crinkling in distress.

"Why do you have to leave?"

Hunter sighs. "No one was supposed to be let in to see you. But we'll be back as soon as they tell us we can, all right? Just a little longer, and you can come home. To us."

"You know…" A serene smile tilts the corners of Chance's mouth. "I really like the sound of that."

"We'll see you soon." I blow Chance a kiss and head for the door. From the corner of my eye, I spot Hunter lingering, then leaning over and placing a kiss on Chance's mouth.

It's the first time I've seen it. Like, a real kiss. Not the fumbling, playful thing the day Chance kissed us both on the beach. It seems like the most natural thing in the world and brings to mind a lot of questions—like if, when this is all over, the two of them can really sort out what this is between them. If Hunter will introduce Chance as his boyfriend.

It breaks my heart a little in the same way that it makes me smile. We're so close to a happy ending.

HUNTER

When I kiss him, Chance fists a hand in my shirt to hold me right where I am. His lips are dry, but his mouth is warm, and I think…this is how life should be. Chance and me. Kissing him whenever I want. This is how it's going to be when this is over, and I'm going to use that knowledge to get through this. To get *us* through this. I've come too close to losing him, and I won't let it happen again.

Ashlin clears her throat. I pull back, heat rushing to my face, but I don't look at her. She's probably got that *I knew it* smile on her face. Brat.

Chance's eyes don't leave mine. "I love you," he says.

The words only make my face burn more, and I don't trust that the smile I give him isn't a stupid one. I run my hand over his hair. "I love you, too. I'll be back soon. I promise." When his fingers release my shirt, I head after my sister.

In the hallway, Ash takes my hand again and elbows me a bit, grinning. I know that look. "Hunter and Chance, sittin' in a tree…"

I shove her gently. "You're so mature. What about you, though? Are you…okay with this?"

My sister shrugs in that way that suggests she doesn't know but she's trying to be. That's Ashlin for you. She'll be happy for everyone around her, even if she's hurting. "I think…you two need each other. I think this is how it's meant to be. Though I do have to ask, does this mean we can go check out guys together? That'd be kind of awesome."

It takes everything not to roll my eyes. "It's not like that. It's just…" Words fail me. How do I describe it?

"Chance is special," Ash says.

There we have it. Summing up in three words what I couldn't do with a hundred. My lips twitch into a half smile. "Yes. Chance is special."

Dad is waiting in the lobby. No sign of the cops yet, but I'm sure it won't be long. He gets to his feet, glancing between us. "Well?"

I drape an arm around Ash's shoulder, hugging her to my side as she says, "He's okay. He's awake."

The relief in Dad's face is almost tangible. "Good. That's good. The police will be here any minute, so we should get going. Imagine they'll have questions for you tomorrow about finding Chance."

Goody. Just what I wanted. But if something I say can help in any way, if I can reiterate to the police that Chance was only running because he was scared, maybe they'll let him off easy for evading them for so long.

I can hope, can't I?

The drive home is a quiet one. Ash and Dad take the truck so it's just me in the car, and I'm too tired to even bother with the radio. In a few hours, it'll be dawn. I have the day off from work, thankfully, so I plan on going home, getting a couple hours of sleep, then going back to the hospital. Dealing with the police comes somewhere in there.

I wonder if Ash told Dad about the camera. He hasn't mentioned it, so even when we get home and Dad heads back to his room, I don't think to bring it up. If she hasn't said anything, she must have a reason for it. We trek upstairs to Ash's room. Only once inside do I feel I won't jinx myself by saying, "I can't believe I got away without being lectured."

"You saved Chance's life and helped the police. I think he has to let your stupidity go for the time being." She plops down in front of her computer.

"You're one to talk. What would he say if he found out you not only broke into someone's house but ran into a wanted murderer in the process?"

"To be fair, he wasn't *supposed* to be there."

I take a seat on her bed where I have a view of her monitor. "You didn't tell Dad about the camera."

She shrugs, flicking on the screen. "How could I? He'd ask me how I got it, and— Well, the whole Dad-flipping-out thing. It'll be easier if Chance tells the police he gave the camera to me or something. I don't know. I haven't thought up a story yet." She pauses and swivels in her chair to look at me. "Are you sure you feel up to looking at these? They're…I mean. I know you think you've got the stomach for it, but it's *Chance*, and…"

My spine stiffens. "I'm not shying away just because it might *upset* me. Chance didn't have that option."

Seemingly satisfied, Ash nods. "I only had these last few pictures left, and another video or two…"

To tell the truth, I *don't* know if I have the stomach for this any more than I would have the stomach for seeing something happen to Ash, or Dad and Mom. Seeing the people you love the most not only hurting, but *being hurt* by someone else?

But I meant what I said: Chance wasn't given the choice. Ashlin went through all that danger to get these pictures. The least I can do is know what we're handing over to the cops.

She opens the last folder and begins with the first image. This one isn't of Chance at all, but his mom. Tabitha has her back to the camera, so she likely doesn't realize she's being photographed.

"Look." Ash touches the screen, tracing a band of darkness around Tabitha's arm. Bruising, I'd wager. There's another along her lower arm. Her wrist. Like she was hitting something or had her hand slammed into something. Proof that Chance wasn't the only one being hurt, right? Proof that Zeke wouldn't hesitate to beat his son *and* his wife.

"In one of the other videos, she was telling Chance about a lawyer and some money." Ash clicks to the next photo. This one is of a hole in the wall, likely put there by Zeke. Another, of a closet somewhere in the house, where a heat lamp is turned on over a growing pot of weed. "It sounded like she was planning on getting her and Chance out of there. Maybe things were escalating…"

"Then Zeke found out, and it set him off," I finish. Ash nods.

There are, thankfully, no pictures of Chance. Ash gets to the last recording and hesitates. Hell, we could be getting worked up for nothing. Maybe this video doesn't have anything to do with Tabitha's murder. Maybe it's the same as the other videos on here. If so, will this still be enough evidence worthy of giving to the cops? It is proof of the abuse, proof that Chance isn't the one to be looking at. But it doesn't entirely clear his name, either.

"Are we ready for this?" she asks.

"It's now or never."

Ash sets the video to play.

• • •

Chance's room is a mess. Clothes, books, junk scattered on the floor. Chance himself is messing with the camera. He's breathless. Eyes wide.

Footsteps. Someone is rushing down the hallway.

He jerks upright, muscles tense, poised, ready to run. The door flies open and—

It isn't Zeke, but Tabitha.

She bears bruises around her throat like a black-and-blue necklace. She slams the door shut, fumbling with a lock, leaning her shoulder into it.

"He broke the lock already." Chance hops onto his bed as though being higher, above her, somehow helps him lord over the room. Makes him feel less out of control of the situation. He sounds calm. More irritated than anything else. "Get away from there, Mom."

Tabitha doesn't move in time. Zeke shoves the door open with enough force it sends her staggering back and landing on the floor. Intimidating enough in his rage, but added to that is the fact that in his hand is a gun.

Zeke goes for her. Chance—with the reflexes of someone who has done this time and time again—springs off the bed and gives his dad a shove for no reason other than to draw his attention.

"Leave her alone!"

Zeke swivels and cuffs him on the side of the head with the butt of the gun. Chance reels, catching himself against the wall and trying to keep his balance. But it worked. His dad's attention is focused on him now. Tabitha, the weeping, cowering woman on the floor, is unimportant.

"You always gotta get in the way!" Zeke snarls. "You think you're so fuckin' smart…"

Chance stumbles out of the room. Tabitha is only momentarily forgotten while Zeke is screaming after his son. Then he remembers her existence. He grabs her up by the arm while she wails and is dragged from the room.

"You know who you've been protecting, you little shit?" Zeke bellows. Heard, but unseen. The room is still. Uninterrupted while the fight continues elsewhere in the house. There's a scuffle. Bodies hitting walls. Punches being thrown. The camera is witness only to the sounds of it.

Zeke says, winded, "Put it *down*—she was gonna leave us

both! Bet you didn't know that, did you?"

"We were going to get the hell away from *you*," Chance sneers. "We were going to get the money and get as far away from you as possible, and if you tried to follow—"

"Is that why I found her packing her shit? Huh? Didn't see you getting ready to leave."

Silence.

"Tell 'im, Tabby. Tell him. Were you going to bring him along?"

Tabitha whimpers, her mumbled explanations falling on the deaf ears of her husband and son.

Chance's words are laced with disbelief. With pain. Betrayal. "You were really going to leave without me?"

"No... I wasn't... It isn't... I would have come back for you!"

The end. The truth.

Tabitha Harvey finally had enough of her husband and she was truly, really going to leave. And she'd planned on abandoning her son to deal with the disaster left behind.

Chance lets out a low, hollow laugh. "No. You wouldn't have."

Something happens. Someone tries to run or someone tries to gain control of the gun but there is—

So. Much. Shouting.

Glass breaking. Tabitha screaming. Zeke hollering threats at her. Only Chance is silent.

Then a gunshot that shatters the chaos and everything, everyone, goes quiet.

• • •

Chills prickle my back like a thousand tiny spiders making a pilgrimage down my spine.

The video feed continues. There are muffled, heated words. Footsteps. Panicked, frightened. Doors slamming. No one returns to Chance's room. The camera films on.

And on and on.

Until the battery goes dead, and the video blacks out.

My sister and I haven't moved. We haven't spoken. She has her hand over her mouth. Her eyes, when she finally turns her gaze to me, are wide and glassy.

"What just happened?" she whispers.

My mouth is dry and wooly, and my tongue won't cooperate. *I don't know*, is what I want to say. It isn't working.

Before either of us can think or say anything further, my phone rings.

Chance

As soon as Hunt and Ash were gone, I pitched myself out of bed.

I unplugged the machines from the wall before yanking out the IV and unclipping the heart monitor from my finger. Whoever thought hospital gowns—especially ones tied in the back where your ass is hanging out—were a brilliant idea needed to be punched.

My clothes, folded on a table nearby, were filthy. So what else was new? I'd have to ditch them and get some new ones somewhere. Somehow.

I rushed to pull them on. My limbs still weren't cooperating like I wanted them to. They moved at the speed of death. Hypothermia, was it? Whatever it was, my body needed to get over it.

My room was on the first floor. Thank the stars for small favors. I pocketed my phone, yanked on my shoes, and pried open the window. I slung my legs outside and dropped to the brush and grass below. Got the hell out of there before the monitors alerted the nurse's station. Or before the cops showed up.

If they thought I was going to lie around while the police came in and handcuffed me to the bed like a common criminal, they had another thing coming.

They don't know. They don't understand. And how could they?

There is no happy ending after this.

I wish Hunter and Ashlin had believed me when I tried to tell them that. It would've made this a lot easier.

The stars are out. Bright and beautiful.

I wish Hunter were here to see them with me. Draco is the brightest, but he never believes me when I say that. I had an amazing view of the stars from the island. Although I'd only intended to be there for awhile, the longer I sat...the more I thought I could have stayed there and watched the stars through a broken window until the cold overcame me.

Obviously, Hunter had other ideas.

I pick a direction and run. Pretty sure this road will eventually lead me to the freeway. What a nice word. *Freeway.* Go this way, and you shall be free. This is the way of the free. I hope that's true, because freedom sounds pretty nice.

Not as nice as going home to the Jacksons. But what could ever be nicer than that?

It's not that I'm afraid to stick around. It's not like there's anything on that camera they shouldn't see.

You were going to leave me here...

It's not like Hunter wouldn't understand. After everything Dad has done, after everything Mom failed to do—

Put down the gun. Put. It. Down.

It's hard to be sad. Truly, honestly sad. Mom is gone and it is sad, sure. A sad event. Death, as an event, is sad. People matter, and the end of a life is a thing to be mourned. But how do *I*, me, myself, find it in me to feel anything at all?

I wanted to protect.

I wanted to *be* protected.

I just wanted to get the hell away. From him. From that house. I wanted to live with Hunter and Ash, with Mr. J and even Isobel. A big happy family. With them, I could be normal. I could be—better. A good person. I could love and be loved.

There aren't words to explain how fucking amazing that feels.

What have you done? What have you...

Where did that dream go wrong? Or have I sabotaged it myself, subconsciously? Because, let's face the cold hard facts, I'm not worthy to be a part of their lives. Not like that. I was able to orbit the bright warmth of the Jackson family for years.

All dreams must be set aside eventually. Reality sets in.

My reality is this: I can't stay here. Hunter and Ashlin will be okay. Mr. J will take care of them. Hunter might not agree that my leaving is for the better, but it is. I'm only ever going to drag them down. This way, they'll go to college, do something great with their lives. Maybe someday I'll see them on TV or on the cover of a magazine. Maybe they'll mention the boy they knew when they were younger.

After all, I don't want them to look for me, but I don't want to be forgotten, either.

It was dark and the freeway was desolate save for the occasional truck rumbling past. I'd done plenty of hitchhiking around town, but never here. Never farther than a few blocks.

My phone was like lead in my pocket. Could the police track me by it? Who knows. It's possible. But more than that, keeping it on me is a tie to them. Right now, any ties to them are unfair. Selfish.

Hunter answers his phone on the first ring. "Chance?"

"I just called to say good-bye." Which sucks. Good-byes in general are sucky. "Did you finish what was on the camera?"

"I…yeah. We did."

"Good." That makes me smile. He wanted honesty, and what they found on that camera is as honest as it gets.

What the hell did you do? You killed her…

Memories of that night burn vivid, painful, in the back of my mind. I struggle to fend them off.

A truck growls past, prompting Hunter to ask, "Where the hell are you?"

"Don't worry about it." Keep walking. Keep putting distance. Every step makes it easier, right? Right. "It's been fun, but things are going to get messy. You two really should've stopped trying to follow me. So…I'll make it so you can't anymore."

"Don't do this." His voice absolutely wrecks me. How can a guy who comes across as so impervious to life as Hunter does break my heart with such a simple inflection in his tone?

I would do anything for him when he sounds like that. I would do anything…if it meant protecting him.

That is what I'm doing. Protecting.

"I need to go, Hunt. Don't worry about me, yeah? Give those pictures and videos over to the cops. Let them throw his sorry ass behind bars, even if only for a while." And please don't tell me they won't, because I'm relishing the thought of Dad rotting in a cell for ever having touched me.

I start to pull the phone away from my ear.

"Wait! Tell me one thing."

Really, I should hang up or he'll keep me talking for days until he manages to convince me to turn back. And yet, damn him, I pause. "One thing."

Hunter takes a deep breath. I hope he realizes the severity of this. He has one question. One thing I'll answer, and that's it. A line has to be drawn.

He settles on, "Was anything you've told me true?"

Truth.

Ahh, what is truth? Truth is in the eye of the beholder. Aren't lies just variations of the truth? Taking a fact and stretching it out, morphing it until it becomes something else?

Even the stars are lies.

They sparkle so brightly, but their shine takes years to reach us. For all I know, Draco could be dead now and I may never know it. How can I say anything in my entire life was *true*, including the things I've told Hunter and Ashlin?

Oh. Yes. There is one thing.

The one thing I can say with absolute certainty: "I love you. That has been true since the day we met."

Which is why I don't give him a chance to say anything further. I hang up, turn, and throw the phone as far as I can over into the field running parallel to the freeway. Gone.

This is me, severing ties from everything that has ever hurt me.

And from everything that I have ever hurt.

Seeking my freedom for however long I can.

I lift a hand, thumb out, to flag down a truck heading up the road.

Maybe I, too, am a star that has already burned out, and nobody has realized it yet.

ACKNOWLEDGMENTS

Made of Stars has been a ride of a different variety in comparison to other books I've written. For the first time, I had a full synopsis and outline done before stepping into the story. I knew my beginning, my middle, and my ending. I also had the help of my miracle-working editor, Stacy Abrams, to help guide me in a good direction and hammer out all the details early on. She helped make this process run smoothly, and I hope we get to do it again.

Another thanks goes to my critique partners for encouraging me and holding my hand through all my self-doubt. Nyrae Dawn in particular. *Thank you* for always being the first person to see what I type. I know if I can get her to like my characters, I'm golden, because I certainly do not write stories she picks up on her own. Bless her heart, she still sticks with me and gives every one of my ideas a try.

As always, the biggest thank-you will go out to my readers. Thank you for giving my books a chance. Thank you for loving my characters, whether they're quirky or happy or vicious or unbearably broken. I'm all too aware I don't write things that fit in with the mainstream market, and the fact that you choose to pick up my stories amongst all the others never fails to astound me in the best of ways.

This is Chance's story above all else, and he is a larger-than-life character I hope everyone will love despite his enormous flaws. Thank you, readers, for letting me tell his story. You're wonderful. You're beautiful. You are all perfect.

Eighteen-year-old Archer couldn't protect his best friend, Vivian, from what happened when they were kids, so he's never stopped trying to protect her from everything else. It doesn't matter that Vivian only uses him when hopping from one toxic relationship to another. Archer is always there, waiting to be noticed.

Then along comes Evan, the only person who's ever cared about Archer without a single string attached. The harder he falls for Evan, the more Archer sees Vivian for the manipulative hot-mess she really is.

But Viv has her hooks in deep, and when she finds out about the murders Archer's committed and his relationship with Evan, she threatens to turn him in if she doesn't get what she wants...

And what she wants is Evan's death, and for Archer to forfeit his last chance at redemption.

Sunday, August 31st

"I feel that suicide notes lose their zing when they drag on too long." Archer emphasized the statement with a tap of his foot. "Don't you think so? Whatever happened to 'good-bye, cruel world'?"

By that point, Brody Hilton had filled four pages from top to bottom in shaky scrawl. He lingered on the last page, hand trembling. Next to him stood an open bottle of vodka and an armada of pill bottles lined up in a neat little row.

Not for the first time in the last hour, Brody swiveled around in his chair to stare up at Archer, pleading. His bloodshot eyes ruined the effect. "Archer… Don't make me do this, man. You don't understand. I don't—"

"You don't want to die." Archer stepped around him, hiked a hip onto the edge of the table, and waved his gun. Brody's eyes followed the weapon. "That goes without saying.

But honestly? I don't care. You've spent the last twenty-five years screwing over everyone who has ever cared about you. Karma is a cruel mistress."

"I'll change." A drop of sweat slid down his brow, over the line of his blocky jaw, and onto the paper. Archer wrinkled his nose.

"Tell that to your sister. 'Sorry your life sucks because of me, Vivian, but I promise I'll be a good boy now.'" Yelling would've made him feel better. No words were enough to beat into Brody's head the impact of his decisions. "Now, sign your letter."

Brody sobbed like no grown man should, but he did as he was told. It didn't matter that Brody outweighed him by a good forty pounds. While Archer was no pushover, Brody was built like a bull and could have plowed him over if he tried.

Brody was simply too high to realize it.

When he finished, Archer skimmed the letter, which could be summed up: I'm sorry, it's all my fault, everything was true. Yes, yes it was. Too bad it took the threat of impending death for Brody to realize it.

"Good enough. Now, let's see what we have here." He tossed the papers onto the table. Brody watched him blearily from behind the great wall of medication separating them. Archer plucked one of the bottles up with a gloved hand.

"We've got your standard-issue Klonopin, Valium, Norco, Stilnox… You could open your own pharmacy with all this." Meds that weren't even prescribed to Brody. Stuff he'd stolen from friends, from family. What he didn't take for himself, he sold. Archer's jaw tensed. He slammed the bottle onto the table before Brody, pills rattling. "A word of advice: the more you take, the faster it will be over."

Beneath the weight of his stare, Brody, slow and mechanical, began removing lids.

The problem with pills? They took forever. Whoever said overdosing was a quick or painless way to go had never watched somebody try it. It was getting late, and Archer had classes in the morning, but he waited.

Brody chased most of the medicine cabinet down with liquor before staggering to his room, muttering the entire way, "Archie, Archie, please…"

God, he hated that name.

Whether he wanted to or not, Archer forced himself to watch Brody crawl into bed. Watched him slip in and out of consciousness. Watched him toss and turn. What did Brody in before the actual effects of the drugs in his system was the way he vomited and proceeded to choke on it, and Archer forced himself to watch that, too.

He was taking a life. The least he could do was suffer through witnessing it.

Soon Brody was gone, and Archer tried not to feel nauseous.

The apartment was silent. Not the sort of silence when one was home alone, but the smothering silence that followed death. An all-encompassing, heavy feeling. Human instincts, maybe. The little warning bells in the back of his head quietly whispering run away because death meant danger.

But Archer didn't leave. Not until he checked for—and didn't find—a pulse. He could take his time sneaking out of the apartment building. It would be days or weeks before the neighbors complained about the smell and kicked in the door. No one would even mourn his passing. Maybe some would say they saw it coming. Just another suicide. How tragic.

Brody made three down…and three to go.

SUNDAY, SEPTEMBER 7TH

Vivian called in the dead of night to say, "Archer, Brody's dead."

Yeah, he knew. He also knew she would call him the second she found out.

She hiccupped and whimpered. It took a few tries before she managed, "Can you come over?"

Stupid question. Of course he would.

Thirty minutes later he arrived at Vivian's place with two coffees in hand, half asleep. Viv answered the door with her hair a mess, eyes red and puffy. Some girls could look gorgeous when they cried. Vivian was one of them.

Archer slipped inside and set the coffee on a small end table in the living room. "Where's Mickey?"

Vivian bit at her lip, sinking onto the leather couch. Her silence was enough. Mickey, such a loving and concerned boyfriend, was nowhere to be found. That was why she called Archer. He wasn't the prick who always let her down.

"He's working late." She sniffed, staring down at her toes as she wiggled them against the carpet.

Right. Like Mickey could hold a job.

Mickey was a jackass. An unattractive one, at that, unless you liked the pothead look. When people saw him and Vivian walking down the street, they stared only because they were wondering what the hell a gorgeous girl like her was doing with a waste of space like Mick.

She could have done better. Much better. Why not him? The one guy who would never ditch her, never hurt her. God knew he'd waited around long enough for her to notice him. He'd been tempted to add Mickey to his list months ago, but there was a line Mick hadn't crossed to push Archer that far. He was an ass, but he hadn't physically hurt her. Yet.

Archer opened his mouth, thought better of saying anything that might result in an argument, and sat beside her instead. Now wasn't the time. "Going to tell me what happened?" Not that she had to. It was hard to forget holding a gun to a guy's head while forcing him to off himself.

Vivian tore at a tissue between her fingers, eyes welling with a fresh onslaught of tears. "I went over to his place this morning. His car was there, but he didn't answer. I got his landlord to unlock the door…"

His stomach somersaulted into knots. No, no, no, no! That wasn't how it was supposed to go. The cops were supposed to find Brody. Hell, even a neighbor. Not Vivian. Not after everything she'd been through.

He scooted up to her side, slipping his arms around her. She twisted and wound her thin arms around his neck and buried her face against his chest. A familiar position. How many times since grade school had Vivian cried all over him?

Like he always did, he pet her hair and let her cry until the sobs died down to sniffles and whimpers. All the while keeping his eyes locked on the opposite wall at an old family portrait: Vivian, Brody, their parents. Before her dad bailed and her mom, Marissa, got sick. Before Brody started popping pills like candy while letting his buddies feel up his little sister.

The thought made his jaw clench.

"You haven't seen him in months. What made you go over there?"

Viv sniffed. "He snuck a couple hundred bucks out of Mom's account again. She's too sick to deal with him, and I've just…had it, you know?" Her body shuddered. "He killed himself. Left this long letter about how sorry he was that he lied to everyone, about stealing from Mom… Everything was in there. I didn't think he cared about any of that."

He hadn't.

"I'm sorry, Viv."

Just like that, she was gone. Gliding away from him like a ghost, she stopped across the room near the bay windows. After a million years of silence…"Can I tell you a secret?"

"Of course."

She took a deep breath, wiped at her eyes. "The entire way to Brody's place…I kept wishing he were dead. Hoping he, like, got drunk and drove off a bridge."

Archer wished she would turn around so he could see her

face. Her eyes told a lot that her body language didn't. Her guilt, her shame, her happiness.

"It's not your fault, if that's what you're thinking."

"I know it isn't."

She sounded sure of that. Good. Part of the reason he'd put off killing her brother for so long was because he worried how Vivian and her mother would take it. The purpose was to help Viv, not screw her up further. "Then why is it a secret?"

Vivian turned. "Because that's not the bad part. The bad part," she said, and her voice dropped as she leaned against the window and stared at her feet, "is that I don't regret it. I'm glad. He'll never make Mom cry again. He won't use or hurt anyone else. He's dead, and I'm happy. Isn't there something wrong with that? Doesn't that make me the worst person on the planet?"

She was beautiful. Oh, she'd always been beautiful, from the first time he laid eyes on her on the playground. But never more so than that exact moment. With those words. With the moonlight wrapped around her body in gentle blue-white caresses that made her hair shine. She should have exuded self-confidence, but Brody and his friends had ruined that for her. The depth of the scars they left behind had never been more obvious. Her brother was dead, and all she could express was relief. That was what he'd hoped for as he watched Brody die.

Archer was a step closer to freeing her.

He allowed a crooked smile and got up. "No, Vivian. There's nothing wrong with that. Nothing wrong with that at all."

WEDNESDAY, SEPTEMBER 10TH

Archer could've had his pick of other colleges in other cities. But he liked it here, where he felt a little distanced from the outside world. Here, in Candle Bay, California, he knew people. Here, even if he couldn't be comfortable, he could manage.

Besides, who would've taken care of Vivian if he left? She did a poor job of it herself. Which was why Archer was stuck in the cold. Because if he didn't wait to see if she came out of class—Wednesdays were their lunch-date days—she would take it personally and he'd hear about it later.

The last of the students filed out, but no Vivian.

So she'd missed class. Again.

When they started college and Vivian told him she wanted to major in some kind of nursing program, Archer made bets with himself on how long she would stick with it. Not because she would get bored but because, undoubtedly, Mickey would screw it up. If not him, then some other guy. Viv was infamous for letting her boyfriends ruin every good thing she had going for her.

Mick didn't like sharing her attention with anything, even school. Archer was willing to bet he even bitched about her going to Brody's memorial service. Not that he bothered going with her for support or anything. He likely wouldn't attend the actual burial, either, once the coroner had finished with Brody's body.

Archer waited a few more minutes, just to be sure Viv wouldn't show, before hiking his backpack up to his shoulder and slinking across campus. As much as he would seethe the entire way home about being ditched — again — he'd be over it before he talked to Viv next. Staying angry at Vivian? Never one of his strong points.

Walking past brick buildings and barren trees, Archer was almost free from the crowds of people moving from one class to the next, coming and going like the tide, when someone dashed by and, in his hurry, slammed his shoulder into Archer with enough force that Archer stumbled, backpack hitting the ground. And someone — not the jerk who hit him and quickly vanished into the crowd — caught his arm to keep him from toppling over.

He hated being grabbed. But he hated falling on his ass in front of a group of people even more. Fair trade.

"Whoa, are you okay?"

Rescuer-boy was taller than Archer by a few inches, so he had to look up to see his face, his dark eyes, and mousy brown hair. Every inch trim and lean where Archer was slim and willowy. The guy took one look at Archer's tight-lipped expression and let him go, pocketing his hands.

Archer scooped his bag off the ground. "I'm fine. People never watch where they're going."

The guy quirked a smile. There was something about the soft shape of his mouth Archer liked, something that made him stare a moment longer than necessary. "You say that like you're used to being bowled over."

"I guess." He shrugged. Not much different from high school. Anyone who said people became kinder and more tolerant when you stepped into college was full of it. People didn't mature; they found sneakier, more manipulative ways to be assholes. "Anyway, thanks. See you around."

"Hey, uh — What's your name?"

What? No. That should have been it. Archer didn't do small talk, especially with strangers. But he was raised with manners so he stopped, turned, looked at him. Patience. Another thing he wasn't great at.

"Archer. I'm guessing you're new." Not because everyone knew him, but because it was a small campus occupied mostly by people he remembered from high school, and this guy's face wasn't familiar. He was also dressed in a T-shirt and khaki shorts, obviously not prepared for the cold weather.

"I'm Evan." He offered a hand. After staring at it for a second, Archer reluctantly took it. Evan's fingers were warm, making up for Archer's freezing ones. "I came in a bit late, yeah. Everything was pretty full up so my class selection sucked."

"I'll bet." If Evan were better at reading people, maybe

he would've picked up on the don't-talk-to-me vibe Vivian insisted he gave off. But no. He kept talking.

"In fact, I'm trying to find the administration office." Evan's grin turned sheepish. "I have some scheduling stuff to figure out. Think you could show me where it's at?"

Archer could've pointed him in the right direction, but it was on the opposite side of campus and in a nondescript little building that took him forty-five minutes to find his first trip there. Again with the manners. Archer exhaled and gestured for Evan to follow.

Evan kept at his side. Funny, with Evan as a shadow, people actually got out of Archer's way. Probably because this guy was bigger. Or maybe it was the way Evan held his head up when he walked, shoulders squared, while Archer tended to shrink in on himself, willing himself invisible. Untouchable.

Archer stole a glance at him. "How are you not freezing?"

"Oh. Used to the cold, I guess. Grew up with it."

"So have I, and I'm freezing."

Evan came to a halt, catching Archer's elbow in a large, warm hand. "Are you? Here–"

Before Archer could protest, they'd made a detour to one of the two coffee stands on campus. That time of day, there was never a line.

"Order something," Evan said. "My treat."

I can pay for my own drinks, thanks. Except his wallet was in the car. Not much help. "No, I don't—"

"Come on. As a thanks for showing me around."

The girl behind the counter stared at him expectantly, and he really didn't want to argue and draw more attention. He let Evan order him a coffee, and Evan got a hot chocolate for himself. Admittedly, the warm cup did feel good when he wrapped his fingers around it, and he muttered a quiet "Thanks" when they were on their way again.

"Like I said, it's a thank you." Evan sounded pleased with himself. How annoying.

They rounded the back of the campus, and the admin building came into view. Evan lingered by the door, offering him a smile as warm as his coffee.

"Thanks again. I get all turned around in new places."

A woman in office-casual and a tight braid moved past them. "Good to see you again, Mr. Bishop. I have those papers for you," she said to Evan and slipped inside.

Archer stared at him. Evan stared back.

"Never been here before, huh?" Archer asked.

Evan's face reddened all the way to the tips of his ears. "I saw her at—you know…orientation. She must remember me."

"Mm."

He didn't know whether to be annoyed that he'd been lied to, confused as to why, or amused by the look on Evan's face. But whatever. Archer had delivered him to his destination, and his drink would only keep him warm for so long.

Evan stared down into his cup. "So I guess I'll see you around."

Smiling thinly, Archer shook his head and turned to leave without a word. But there was something about the humiliated look in Evan's eyes that made him toss a wave over his shoulder and, as he rounded the corner, "It was nice meeting you, Evan."

*Read on for a sneak peek at
Kate Avelynn's
beautiful and unsettling*
Flawed

Sarah O'Brien is alive because of the pact she and her brother made twelve years ago — James will protect her from their violent father if she promises to never leave him. For years, she's watched James destroy his life to save hers. If all he asks for in return is her affection, she'll give it freely.

Until, with a tiny kiss and a broken mind, he asks for more than she can give.

Sam Donavon has been James' best friend — and the boy Sarah's had a crush on — for as long as she can remember. As their forbidden relationship deepens, Sarah knows she's in trouble. Quiet, serious Sam has decided he's going to save her. Neither of them realize James is far more unstable than her father ever was, or that he's not about to let Sarah forget her half of the pact . . .

one

My first memory of James is what keeps me here, smoothing hair out of a boy's blood-spattered face. The sirens screaming in the distance are too late.

They're always too late.

Forehead pressed to his, I choke on the burnt stench of gunpowder and try to hum the lullaby James used to sing to me.

You are my sunshine, my only sunshine…

James is why I never left.

I should have left.

two

I remember the tiny, white flowers that dotted our neighbor's lawn and how my body sank into the lush grass like it was made of pillows. I remember the way the sun baked my exposed skin and the tiny insects and dandelion seeds danced around me on the soft summer breeze. I remember my white, cotton dress, the only sleeveless, legless item of clothing I'd ever owned.

Mrs. Baxter gave it to me as an Easter present a few days before my seventh birthday, leaving it on the porch, folded and wrapped in a pink ribbon. James snuck it into our room before our father saw, and helped me tie the white sash sewn onto the waist.

I remember sitting on Mrs. Baxter's lawn hoping she'd see me in it because I was too shy to knock on the front door and thank her. I remember wishing I knew how to tie bows as well as James so I could have worn that pretty pink ribbon in my hair.

I remember my father's calloused hand clamping down on my shoulder.

He dragged me inside, out of the sunshine and into the dark dungeon of our house. Two of my dolls were lying in front of the television in the living room. My carelessness normally would've cost me the dolls, but not that day. Not when the sharp bite of beer hung in the air and clung to his rumpled weekend clothes. My hands flew out to break my fall a second too late.

"How many times've I told you not to leave your shit on the floor? Huh, Sarah?"

"I'm sorry!" I scrabbled across the worn carpet, gathered up the dolls, and clutched them to my chest, but it didn't matter. He had already unbuckled his dreaded belt and was pulling it through his belt loops.

"Yeah? You're about to be a whole lot sorrier."

The stinging slap of leather against skin reverberated off the dingy walls. Once, twice, three times. I bit my lip and tried not to cry out because crying out only ever made things worse.

The blows stopped abruptly. "Get your ass back in your room or this is gonna be a whole lot worse!" he bellowed down the hall. "I'm not warning you again!"

A door clicked shut. My mother's door.

The *pound-pound-pound* of my brother barreling into the room filled the void she left behind. From where I lay curled on the floor, my brother looked like an angel.

"Don't touch her!"

This is my first real memory of James. In every memory

before that, he's just a flash of color, a warm body with a blurred face, a comforting voice begging me not to die. When he planted himself between our father and me that day, an eight-year-old with small fists clenched at his sides, I think I fell in love with my brother.

Our father sneered at him. "Do you think I'm scared of you, boy?"

James lifted his chin. "You should be." But even I heard the waver in his voice.

"You little *shit*."

I scrambled back into the dining room, dolls forgotten, mouth open in a silent scream as my brother took what was left of the punishment meant for me. It ended when the back of our father's hand sent him sprawling to the floor. Before James could get to his feet, our father staggered toward the garage and the refrigerator of beer waiting for him.

James crawled over to where I lay curled up beneath the dining room table and dragged me into his arms. There was blood on his lip and one of his eyes had started to swell. "Shh," he murmured. "He's gone. Everything's okay now."

I tried to dab his lip with the torn hem of my dress, but he gently pushed my hand away. "I'm okay," he said. "You're hurt worse than me anyway."

I could feel the welts rising on my back and arms. "You saved me," I sobbed into his sleeve. "You saved me."

"I'm never gonna let anything happen to you, Sarah."

"I won't let anything happen to you, too."

He smiled, all dimples and sparkling blue eyes. "Nah, you're too little. Just don't leave me, okay? Not ever. Promise?"

"I promise."

We stayed huddled together under the table for as long as we dared, James holding me and quietly singing our lullaby, me watching the door that led to the garage.

You are my sunshine, my only sunshine.
You make me happy when skies are gray.
You'll never know, dear, how much I love you.
Please don't take my sunshine away.

James, the savior. That's the image of my brother I clung to.

Still cling to.

three

Eleven years later…

I'm probably the only person in school that dreads the final bell before summer vacation. Summer for me equals ten weeks of wandering around town or hiding in my room with the door locked, hoping against hope my father will work extra hours at the paper mill and James will work less.

From my desk in the back of the room, I watch my classmates swap yearbooks for the last time as they walk out the door, happily chattering about the usual lake parties and summer jobs and hour-long road trips down into California. They don't notice me, the skinny girl with stringy hair and eyes too big for her head. They don't ask me to come along or wonder aloud why I don't have a yearbook for people to sign. I've made it a point to be invisible.

The room clears within seconds. The seniors got out three days ago, so it's like everyone is in a hurry to join them. Even my American Lit teacher, Mr. Carter, seems eager to escape to wherever teachers spend their summers. Maybe I'll stay in my seat until the janitor kicks me out, or maybe I'll move from room to room until he locks all the doors and I have nowhere else to go.

The school is probably peaceful at night.

I can't stay, though. I won't. James gets off work early on Fridays—four instead of four thirty, a whole half an hour before our father—and I don't dare worry James by not being there when he shows up. He already worries too much. Plus, he's always starving when he gets home, and he'll burn the house down if someone's not there to guard the stove.

And then there's our father. He expects dinner ready and waiting.

With a sigh, I heft my backpack onto one shoulder and trudge into the hallway, empty save for open lockers and leftover papers that flutter and scrape across the linoleum on the breeze coming through the open doors. Out in the parking lot, cars honk and engines rev as my classmates spill into the streets. Their freedom tastes sweet on the air. I breathe it in and wish it was mine, too.

Next year it will be. James and I are moving out the second I graduate—three-hundred and-sixty-three days from now—that's the promise he makes every time something bad happens. He's been saving the money he makes at the mill for almost a year now while I write out budgets, and fish the Sunday paper out of the neighbor's plastic recycling bin every week to look for places we can rent. So far, we haven't found anything cheap enough.

I cannot wait until we do.

After glancing at my watch, I decide to take the long way home, the one that winds through the nicer neighborhoods east of school, past the seventeen stores that make up the Granite Falls strip mall, and into the park just outside the paper mill's gates. It's deserted, of course. No one goes there because of the gritty haze that drifts down from the stacks and coats the trees in a layer of silt. Our neighborhood is two blocks past the park, and once I skirt the pond and pass the picnic tables, I can see our street.

It's 3:42. And by the time I get to our driveway, I still have thirteen minutes to get dinner started. Perfect.

It's hard to ignore the peeling beige paint on our house. This isn't a "nice" neighborhood by any stretch of the imagination, but nobody else has a house that flakes paint like dandruff.

The low hum of my mother's television and fresh cigarette smoke greets me when I step into the kitchen. I close the door quietly and hope she doesn't hear the *click*. Some days, when there isn't any smoke and the house is too quiet, I creep down the hall and listen for her breathing. It's a weird feeling coming home from school, wondering if this is the day I'll find my mother's dead body. Part of me is terrified of that happening. The other part—the darker half of my heart I keep smothered for James's sake—wishes she'd just overdose and be done with it.

After tossing my stuff into my bedroom, I head back to the kitchen, grab a pot from the drying rack by the sink, and set about boiling some water for mac 'n cheese.

James remembers the way our mother used to be, back when she still smiled and didn't take pills or smoke cigarettes all day. He hates our father for what he's done to her—what he's *still* doing to her—because of us. Sometimes I think picking up her prescriptions and leaving cartons of cigarettes outside her door is James's way of making up for being born.

My father hasn't always been like this, though. Ask anyone who doesn't live with us and they'll tell you he still isn't. Our house is a shrine to the famous ex-boxer who has it all: a close-knit family, a successful athletic career in a former life, and a solid job at the mill.

It's amazing how much people overlook when you're a local celebrity.

Title belts painted an unconvincing shade of gold adorn our living room walls, faded, red boxing gloves dangle from sheetrock nails, and newspaper clippings yellowing in their cheap, tin frames line the fireplace mantle. In the center of it all is an enormous publicity poster from the Armory, the local boxing arena, featuring a man with a crooked nose and a busted lip. He waves triumphantly at our empty living room from atop the crowd's shoulders.

James "Knockout Jimmy" O'Brien, Granite Fall's very own boxing legend—a title he held until a young groupie poked holes in the condom she made him wear "for protection."

My brother was born nine months later, fists already swinging.

I sink into a chair and stare at the pot of water, willing it to boil. Our father only married our mother because he had a public image to maintain—an image that didn't include an abandoned son that might make him proud someday. Desperate and thinking a second baby would make things better between them, our mother seduced him again, lied about not needing birth control while breastfeeding James, and wound up with me.

Two babies in little more than a year and a half. Knockout Jimmy was forced to give up boxing and take a job in the paper mill.

It broke him, and in turn, he broke us all.

four

A truck door slams out front. Even before the sound registers, I'm out of the chair, my body tense and ready to run. It's only 4:09 p.m. He shouldn't be here. Not yet.

My brother's faint, familiar whistling keeps me from bolting to my room.

The door to the garage swings open and James breezes in, all dimples and smiles like always, holding one of our father's beers in his hand. I must look terrified because his grin fades before it can reach his eyes.

"Hey, Sar-bear," he says softly. "It's just me."

I edge over to the stove to check on our water, which has started to boil. My hands are still shaking when I dump the two boxes of macaroni into the pot. "Do you have to drink that crap?"

He doesn't answer. After a moment, I peek over my shoulder

and see him leaning against the counter, arms folded across his chest, eyes narrowed on me. The beer is nowhere in sight.

When James gets serious like this, he looks exactly like Knockout Jimmy in his prime, right down to the bump on the bridge of his nose. Even with sawdust in his blond hair and paper pulp caked onto his coveralls, my brother is gorgeous. Half a dozen girls throw themselves at him whenever we're in public, but he never dates. I don't get it. If half a dozen boys threw themselves at me, I'd be out every night. Anything to get out of this house.

"What?" I ask him.

"Nothing. Nice jeans, by the way."

I roll my eyes, the panic gripping me successfully diffused. James bought me these jeans two weeks ago, one day after I'd drooled over them at the mall on my way home from school. He always does sweet things like that, even when I beg him not to. "To make up for you having to put up with me," he says, but we both know that's not what he's making up for.

He pushes away from the counter, loops an arm around my shoulders, and plants one of the wet kisses I secretly love on my temple.

"Don't...eww!" Laughing, I sink into his embrace. Wriggling out of his grasp never works. I'm way too light, and he's way too strong for me to make him do anything he doesn't want to do. Unfortunately, he knows it. At least he has the decency to grunt when I elbow him in the gut.

"I'm going to get cleaned up," he says. "Save some of that for me, 'kay?"

"I always do. Now go away." I smack him with the hot

wooden spoon I've been using to stir the macaroni. He yelps and jumps backward. Giving me one last smile, he saunters down the hall.

James is a pain in the ass. I love him more than I love anybody, even when I hear the crack of a beer opening in the bathroom.

As soon as he's gone, I rush around the kitchen, rounding up the milk and butter and pepper. No one showers and dresses faster than James or I. Maybe it's because we've always had to get in and out of the house as quick as possible. Whatever the case, I like having dinner done before he gets out.

Nineteen-year-old boys shouldn't be working long hours doing crap jobs in the mill. Especially not ones smart enough to get into just about any college they want. He does it for me, so I do this for him.

Sure enough, before I've had the chance to strain the macaroni, he's out of the bathroom. Our bedroom door slams—he's *always* loud—and he cranks his music full blast. Godsmack floods the hallway. I dump half the pot of steaming mac 'n cheese onto a plate for my father and leave it on the counter where he'll see it. Maybe he'll take it as a peace offering and leave me alone tonight.

Armed with bowls of food and Tupperware cups full of tap water, I kick our bedroom door with the toe of my black sneaker. "Are you dressed yet?"

Sharing a tiny bedroom with a teenage boy requires planning and patience. I give James his privacy as often as I can and take pride in the fact that I've never walked in on him naked or doing any horrifying boy things. Too bad he isn't nearly as mindful of my privacy. I can't begin to count how many times he's walked in on me changing.

The music shuts off and plunges the house back into a quiet that feels even louder than his music. Canned laughter from whatever sitcom our mother is watching seeps through her closed door down the hall. As soon as he lets me in, I'll turn on the fan that sits on my nightstand to block out the sound.

James throws open the door wearing only a pair of jeans and a wide grin. The fading yellow bruises on his ribs make me want to throw up, and I nearly spill the water trying to shield my eyes with the bowls. "Do you mind?"

"You are seriously messed up," he says as I push past him, but I hear the amusement in his voice. "I've got pants on. Isn't that enough?"

No, it's not. Thankfully, by the time I settle onto my bed with our bowls, he's pulled on a t-shirt. Covering up is also something James does for my benefit, though he teases me mercilessly about my "skin phobia." I blame it on a lifetime of hiding bruises and welts under long sleeves and pants, but not all of it. It's easier to pretend than tell him the real reason I don't like seeing his body, so I play along. "Maybe if your skin wasn't DayGlo white, looking at you wouldn't physically hurt."

He plops down on the edge of his bed and scowls at me in a way that I think is supposed to be chastising. When I laugh, he gives up, grabs his bowl out of my hands, and shovels pasta into his mouth. We're a good pair. Neither of us can stay mad at the other for long.

4:26. Nine minutes to go.

My stomach growls, but I only nibble at my food. One bowl of mac 'n cheese is never enough for James. I want to make sure I have some left to give him when he's done. To distract myself, I focus on the posters plastered all over the walls on his side of our tiny bedroom—all horror movie and rock music-related, of course. Sometimes I wish he were into sports or supermodels or something a little less morbid. Other than a lone, teal Mariners pennant hanging crooked on the back of our door, his choice in decorations does nothing for my nightmares.

"So, Dad'll be home soon," he says through a mouthful of food. My pulse picks up, but then I notice his bowl is empty. Sure enough, he's eyeing mine. "You want to get out of here, or are you cool locking yourself in while I'm gone tonight?"

I take one more bite and hold the rest out to him. He's off his bed to grab it before I can blink. "Can you take me to the mall? I need a haircut."

He looks up from my bowl and frowns. "I think your hair looks fine."

"Really?" I smooth down the limp strands that hang almost to my elbow. "I was thinking maybe I'd get it cut really short this summer. Like, pixie-cut short."

"Huh." He resumes inhaling his food. "You can do whatever you want, I guess. All I'm saying is you look pretty as is."

Heat creeps up my neck and bleeds into my cheeks. Even though he's been saying nice things for as long as I can remember, his compliments always do this to me. It's a confusing balance between feeling good about myself and being uncomfortable with that feeling.

"I'm supposed to meet up with Sam and Alex in a few hours," he continues, as if he has no clue he's embarrassed me. "Think we'll be done by six?"

At the mention of Sam, my cheeks go from warm to scalding. I've been nursing a crush on the tall and mysterious Sam Donavon almost as long as he's been James's best friend, which is pretty much forever. I don't delude myself into thinking it's mutual. It made sense that he ignored me at school when he and my brother were popular upperclassmen, but the few times Sam has been at our house, it's been the same way. His gray eyes look through me like I'm a window in the wall.

All-brawn-and-no-brain Alex Andersen, on the other hand, has been flirting with me for years. When I was in fifth grade and he was in sixth—before I knew about his obsession with all things sexual—he lured me out to the rickety shed in our backyard under the pretense of helping him find something for James. Surrounded by rusty lawnmowers and spare car parts, Alex gave me my first kiss.

While it had been a monumental, albeit disappointing, event for me, I doubt it meant anything to him. Alex dates all the girls my brother blows off, plus the few he manages to snag first. James doesn't talk about the girls themselves much, but he thinks shafting them with Alex is hilarious.

Thinking about Alex and that kiss makes me think about Sam again. After he and James graduated last year, I hardly saw Sam anymore. Now that Alex has graduated, I'll probably see him even less. Imagining his dark eyes staring at me and his lips on mine, hot and insistent, sends happy shivers up and down my body that I'm terrified James might notice.

The alarm clock perched on the top shelf of James's headboard ticks off another minute.

4:29. Time to go.

"If we leave soon, we should be back in plenty of time," I say. Hopefully he'll take me with him tonight. Just in case, I hop off my bed and quickly contemplate my meager selection of shirts in our closet. A stretchy pale pink t-shirt—long-sleeved, of course, and also a present from James—is the most summery thing I own. I grab it and head for the door.

"You don't have to change in the bathroom," James says. When I turn around, startled, I see he's shifted around to face his headboard. "You know I won't peek."

That doesn't stop me from positioning myself in front of the mirrored closet door with my back to him so I can make sure. I shouldn't feel weird about changing in front of James— we've shared a room our whole lives, so it's not like we haven't seen each other before—but I can't help it. I may hate seeing his bruises, but I worry seeing all of his failures etched into my skin would kill my brother.

It only takes me three seconds to peel off my drab school shirt and slip on the pink one. The second the soft material clears my belly button, James is off his bed and out the door, mumbling that he'll be back in a second.

While I wait, I rinse out our cups and bowls in the sink. The low rumble of a car pulling into the driveway stops me cold. I frantically glance at the clock in the hallway.

4:36.

We're too late.

Get tangled up in our Entangled Teen titles

Relic by **Renee Collins**

In Maggie's world, the bones of long-extinct magical creatures such as dragons and sirens are mined and traded for their residual magical elements, and harnessing these relics' powers allows the user to wield fire, turn invisible, or heal even the worst of injuries. Working in a local saloon, Maggie befriends the spirited showgirl Adelaide and falls for the roguish cowboy Landon. But when the mysterious fires reappear in their neighboring towns, Maggie must discover who is channeling relic magic for evil before it's too late.

Out of Play by **Nyrae Dawn and Jolene B. Perry**

Rock star drummer Bishop Riley doesn't have a drug problem. But after downing a few too many pills, Bishop will have to detox while under house arrest in Seldon, Alaska. Hockey player Penny Jones can't imagine a life outside of Seldon. Penny's not interested in dealing with Bishop's crappy attitude, and Bishop's too busy sneaking pills to care. Until he begins to see what he's been missing. If Bishop wants a chance with the fiery girl next door, he'll have to admit he has a problem and kick it.

A Tale of Two Centuries by **Rachel Harris**

Alessandra D'Angeli is in need of an adventure. Tired of her sixteenth-century life in Italy and homesick for her time-traveling cousin, Cat, who visited her for a magical week and dazzled her with tales of the future, Alessandra is lost. One mystical spell later, Alessandra appears on Cat's Beverly Hills doorstep five hundred years in the future. How will she return to the drab life of her past when the future is what holds everything she's come to love?

Get tangled up in our Entangled Teen titles

Origin by Jennifer L. Armentrout

Daemon will do anything to get Katy back. After the successful but disastrous raid on Mount Weather, he's facing the impossible. Katy is gone. Taken. Everything becomes about finding her. Taking out anyone who stands in his way? Done. Burning down the whole world to save her? Gladly. Exposing his alien race to the world? With pleasure. But the most dangerous foe has been there all along, and when the truths are exposed and the lies come crumbling down, which side will Daemon and Katy be standing on? And will they even be together?

Hover by Melissa West

On Earth, Ari Alexander was taught to never peek, but if she hopes to survive life on her new planet, Log, her eyes must never shut. Because Zeus will do anything to save the Ancients from their dying planet, and he has a plan. On Loge, nothing is as it seems...and no one can be trusted.

Everlast by Andria Buchanan

When Allie has the chance to work with her friends and some of the popular kids on an English project, she jumps at the chance to be noticed. And her plan would have worked out just fine... if they hadn't been sucked into a magical realm through a dusty old book of fairy tales in the middle of the library. Now, Allie and her classmates are stuck in Nerissette, a world where karma rules and your social status is determined by what you deserve. Which makes a misfit like Allie the Crown Princess, and her archrival the scullery maid.

Get tangled up in our Entangled Teen titles

Blurred by Tara Fuller

Cash's problems only leave him alone when he's with Anaya, Heaven's beautiful reaper. But Anya's dead, and Cash's soul resides in an expired body, making him a shadow walker, able to move between worlds. As the lines between life and death blur, Anaya and Cash find themselves falling helplessly over the edge...

The Summer I Became a Nerd by Lea Rae Miller

On the outside, seventeen-year-old Madelyne Summers looks like your typical blond cheerleader. But inside, Maddie spends more time agonizing over what will happen in the next issue of her favorite comic book than planning pep rallies. When she slips up and the adorable guy behind the local comic shop's counter uncovers her secret, she's busted. The more she denies who she really is, the deeper her lies become...and the more she risks losing Logan forever.

The Reece Malcolm List by Amy Spalding

Devan knows very little about Reece Malcolm, until the day her father dies and she's shipped off to live with the mother she's never met. L.A. offers a whole new world to Devan—a performing arts school allows her to pursue her passion for show choir and musicals, a new circle of friends helps to draw her out of her shell, and an intriguing boy opens up possibilities for her first love. Now that Devan is so close to having it all, can she handle the possibility of losing everything?